FOXL____ ____

To my dear friend

Brenda

With love

Madalyn

Also by Madalyn Morgan

Foxden Acres

Applause

China Blue

The 9:45 to Bletchley

FOXDEN HOTEL

Madalyn Morgan

Madalyn Morgan

British Library Cataloguing in Publication Data.
A catalogue record for this book is available from the
British Library.

ISBN: 978-1546762843

ACKNOWLEDGMENTS

Formatted by Rebecca Emin
www.rebeccaemin.co.uk

Book Jacket Designed by Cathy Helms
www.avalongraphics.org

Cover photograph of Misterton Hall:
Madalyn Morgan

Thanks to Heather Craven who invited me to Misterton Hall to take photographs of the Hall, the lake, and the grounds.

Thanks also to Dr Roger Wood for an in depth critique, to Tony Thresher and author Debbie Viggiano, my beta readers.

Thanks also to my friends, Jean Martin, Geraldine Tew, Kitty Jacklin, and Lynne Root, author friends, Theresa Le Flem and Jayne Curtis, and everyone at the Leicestershire RNA - The Belmont Belles - for their support and encouragement. To Pauline Barclay at Chill With A Book, Sarah Houldcroft at Authors Uncovered, Gary Walker at Look 4 Books, W.H.Smith, Hunts Independent Bookshop in Rugby, and the Lutterworth and Rugby Libraries.

Foxden Hotel is dedicated to my mother and father,
Ena and Jack Smith.

NEW YEAR'S EVE 1948

YOU ARE INVITED TO A NEW YEAR'S EVE PARTY
TO CELEBRATE THE OPENING OF THE FOXDEN HOTEL

R.S.V.P. MRS BESS DONNELLY
FOXDEN HOTEL
MYSTERTON
LOWARTH

CHAPTER ONE

'Happy New Year, Bess!'

A voice, as hard as granite and terrifyingly similar to one from Bess's past, sent panic searing through her body. She spun round. A camera bulb flashed, temporarily blinding her. She stumbled backwards. Someone grabbed her hand, the lights dimmed, Big Ben began to chime, and the party goers started the countdown to 1949. "Ten! Nine! Eight!--"

'Happy New Year!' Bess's sisters shouted above the chanting, kissing her and then each other.

'What is it, Bess?' Margot was the last of her sisters to greet her. 'You look as if you've seen a ghost.'

'I have. Or rather, I've just heard one.' Bess put on a smile and waved across the room to her husband, Frank, who had been in charge of tuning the wireless for the run-up to midnight. *Happy New Year, darling,* she mouthed. Frank raised his arm to wave, but Bess's two youngest sisters, Claire and Ena, had arrived at his side and were smothering him in kisses.

'Come with me. I want you to look at someone and tell me if you've seen him before.' Taking Margot by the hand, Bess led her around the ballroom searching for the face that she felt sure would match the menacing voice that rasped the New Year message in her ear. 'He isn't here. He must be in the public bar,' she said, dragging Margot across the crowded dance floor.

The public bar, which was open to non-residents as well as guests of the Foxden Hotel, was opposite the ballroom. Bess and Margot made their way across the hotel's elegant marble hall and past the traditional Christmas tree. The hall was bustling with people. Those staying in the hotel were making their way up the sweeping staircase to their rooms, others were putting on coats and hats and preparing to leave, and some were still celebrating - shaking hands and kissing each other.

'Happy New Year, Bess!' someone shouted. And 'A great party, Bess!' called someone else, raising their glass. Unable to find her voice to return the greeting, or even to say thank you, Bess forced herself to smile as she edged her way through the jubilant throng.

'Bess? Margot?' Ena and Claire called, catching up with their older sisters. 'The chap from the Lowarth *Advertiser* wants to take a photograph of the four of us,' Ena said.

Bess stopped dead. Was she mistaken? Could it have been the photographer who wished her a happy New Year? He had taken a photograph of her immediately afterwards, so he was near enough. But the voice? A cold shiver ran down Bess's back. The voice she had heard was not the friendly voice of the young man from the *Advertiser.*

'Bess?' When she didn't reply, Ena turned to Margot. 'What's going on?'

Margot shrugged her shoulders. 'I don't know.'

The door to the public bar stood open. From the entrance, Bess's attention was drawn to two men leaning against the bar, arguing. One of the men, in

2

his mid-thirties with a broad face, cold grey eyes, and blonde greased-back hair, was holding the hand of a pretty girl with fair shoulder-length hair. Observing him nervously with big blue eyes, the girl looked as if she was in her late teens, early twenties. The other man - middle-aged with a square jaw, sharp features and receding grey hair - had a protective arm around the young girl's shoulders.

Bess began to tremble; her legs felt weak. Without taking her eyes off the younger of the two men, she gripped the doorframe with one hand, seizing Margot's hand with the other.

Margot followed Bess's gaze and their sisters followed hers. 'Dave Sutherland!' she gasped. 'His hair is longer and the stupid Hitler-style moustache has gone, but that monster is Dave Sutherland.'

Bess couldn't hear what Sutherland was saying to the older man, but by the slimy way he was fawning over the girl it was obvious that she was the subject of their disagreement. All of a sudden Sutherland stepped forward, pulled the girl away from the older man, and squared up to him.

From behind Bess, Ena beckoned the newspaper photographer. 'Any chance of you taking a picture of those two men?'

The photographer winked. 'It would be my pleasure.' A second later he was standing next to them at the bar.

Distracted by the exploding flash bulb, the two men turned from each other and faced the photographer. Sutherland's nostrils flared with anger. The older man put his hands up in an attempt to hide his face. He was too late.

3

'Sir Gerald? Miss Katherine?' The photographer nodded his thanks.

'Give me that camera,' Sutherland slurred. The photographer stepped back. 'If you know what's good for you, you'll hand it over.' Sutherland took a swing at the photographer, but the photographer reacted quickly and stepped back again. Sutherland overreached, lost his balance, and fell to his knees.

Bess let go of Margot's hand and pushed herself off the doorframe. 'And if *you* know what's good for you,' she said, looking down at Sutherland as he scrambled to his feet, 'you'll leave my hotel.'

Sutherland turned at the sound of Bess's voice, an evil grin on his face. '*Your* hotel, is it? Well, well, well, haven't you done well for yourself,' he smirked, pulling on the sleeves of his jacket and doing his drunken best to regain his composure. 'Do your fancy friends know what you got up to in London, Bess?' Sutherland said loudly, surveying the crowd. 'No? Perhaps I should tell them.'

Bess felt sick. She thought she would die of embarrassment and turned her back on Sutherland, so he couldn't see the distress he was causing her. Fearing the consequences if Sutherland opened his drunken mouth, she turned to the barman. 'Close the bar, Simon.'

Bess's cheeks burned scarlet with shame and anger. 'Ena, would you make sure the back door is locked. Then check that the windows on the ground floor are closed, and secure the kitchen? Tell Chef, if there are any kitchen staff still on the premises they should leave by the hotel's main entrance.'

Bess turned to Claire. 'I'd like you to go

upstairs and make sure the windows at the end of each landing - and in the bathrooms - are closed, especially those on the first floor. But first, telephone the police station at Lowarth. Tell Sergeant McGann there's a Nazi in the hotel, and he's threatening people.'

'A what?'

'Just do it!' Ena fled across the hall to the kitchen, Claire to the reception desk and the telephone.

David Sutherland looked doe-faced at the girl and offered her his hand. 'Come on, honey, let's get out of this place.'

The older man, who the photographer had called Sir Gerald, grabbed Sutherland's arm and forced it down by his side. 'Katherine is coming with me.'

He handed Bess a small white business card. 'What happened tonight was regrettable, for which I can only apologise. My address,' he said, nodding at the card. 'I shall be at home tomorrow if the police wish to speak to me. Now, if you'll excuse me, I would like to take my daughter home.'

Sutherland made a grab for the girl, but Bess stepped forward and pulled her away from him.

'This is none of your business, Bess Dudley,' he said, his eyes sparkling with anger. 'There's something about women who poke their noses into other people's business that makes me so mad.' He clenched his fist and raised his arm, as if he was going to strike Bess.

'Don't you dare!' Margot shouted, running from the door to her sister's side.

5

Sutherland's mouth fell open. 'Well, if it isn't Margot Dudley, the pushy little usherette who jumped into her friend's dancing shoes the first chance she got.'

'I had no choice. You almost killed her, you bastard!'

Sutherland shot an embarrassed look at the older man, before turning his attention back to Margot. 'What are you talking about, you stupid bitch?'

He lunged at Margot, but the older man side-stepped and blocked his way. 'Get out of here. Now!' he bellowed. 'That's an order!'

'Come on, David, Dad's right. You should go home.' Looking up into Sutherland's face, the girl took him by the hand and led him across the room. At the door, Sutherland put his arms around the girl and, lifting her face to his, bent down and kissed her long and hard. Bess turned away from Sutherland's staged display of affection. 'What's the matter, Bess, are you jealous?'

The girl whispered something that neither Bess nor Margot heard, then her father shouted, 'Get out, David, or I shall put you out!' He leaned forward until his face was only an inch from Sutherland's and growled, 'We do not need the police asking questions tonight!' Sutherland put his hands up in a gesture of surrender and Sir Gerald shoved him through the door of the public bar into the hotel's main hall.

Bess and Margot followed. They were met by their sisters, Ena and Claire, and husbands Frank and Bill.

'Good God!' Bill said, 'What the hell is he

doing here?'

'Who?' Frank looked across the hall to the entrance foyer where Sutherland, Sir Gerald and his daughter Katherine, were putting on their coats.

'The younger of those two blokes about to leave is a fascist thug called David Sutherland,' Bill said. 'He almost beat one of Margot's dancer friends to death when she worked at the Prince Albert Theatre in London.'

'Sutherland?' Frank turned to Bess, his face distorted with anger. 'Is that--?'

'Leave him, Frank, please?'

'The police are on their way,' Claire said, 'Let them deal with him.'

Ignoring his wife and sister-in-law, Frank stormed across the hall to the foyer and punched David Sutherland on the nose. Sutherland stumbled backwards, but didn't go down. Frank hit him again. This time Frank's fist skimmed Sutherland's cheekbone, removing the skin, stopping only when his knuckles clashed with the bone of Sutherland's right eye socket. The fascist went sprawling to the ground, landing spread-eagled on his back. 'Stay away from my wife, do you hear? Come near *her*, or this hotel, again, and I'll kill you!'

'Stop it!' Bess shouted, running across the hall to Frank. 'He isn't worth it.'

Sir Gerald and his daughter, on either side of Sutherland, tried to help him up but, angry and red-faced, he shook them off. With his hand over his eye, Sutherland clambered to his feet unaided and, without looking back, bulldozed his way through a huddle of partygoers gathered at the hotel's entrance and disappeared.

Frank started after him. 'I'm going to make sure that animal leaves,' he shouted, shaking out his right hand and flexing his fingers. He looked back at his brother-in-law. 'Come on, Bill, we'll see him off the property.'

'No, Frank!' Bess took hold of her husband's arm and spun him round. 'You can't go after him. If he hits you the way you hit him and damages your good eye, you could end up blind.' As if he hadn't heard her, Frank kept walking. Bess ran past him and stopped. She turned and, looking up at him, slapped the palms of her hands on his chest. 'Stop, Frank! Please!' She was near to tears. 'I'm begging you not to go after him.'

Fuming, Frank stood for some time staring at the door that Sutherland had exited by. 'All right,' he said at last, and when Bess let her hands fall to her sides, he pulled her to him and held her tightly. 'All right,' he said again.

'It's time the celebrations ended,' Bess said, relieved. 'Would you go back to the ballroom and ask the band to play the last waltz?'

She summoned her brother-in-law. 'Bill, find the photographer from the *Advertiser*. I saw him scribbling in his note book when Frank hit Sutherland. Tell him there's as much beer as he can drink, every night for a week, if he'll take some photographs of cheerful party-goers as they leave the hotel. And ask him not to make too much of the fracas between Sutherland and Frank, or Sutherland and that Sir Gerald bloke, when he writes up his story. Oh, and find out if he heard any of the conversation between Sutherland and

Sir Gerald when they were at the bar.'

Bill looked around. 'He's talking to the barman. I'll ask him now.'

'I'm sorry, love,' Frank said.

'What about? Punching Sutherland? I'm not. I wanted to hit him myself. I wish I had now.' Bess lifted her husband's hands and inhaled sharply. The knuckles on his right hand were skinned and bleeding. She looked up into his face. 'If he had hit you back, you could have lost your good eye,' she said, thrusting his hands aside in anger.

'I know. But he didn't hit me.' Frank pulled Bess to him and embraced her. 'It won't be me waking up with a black eye in the morning, but Sutherland will have a bloody shiner,' he laughed. Bess's usually gentle husband bent down and kissed her on the lips, before returning to the ballroom.

'Can you imagine what the headline on the front page of Monday's *Advertiser* will say?' Margot asked, as she and Bess watched Bill approach the reporter.

'Unfortunately I can, which is why we need more photographs of people enjoying themselves. If free beer for a week doesn't persuade the guy to be kind to us when he writes his review, I'll buy a large ad. I'll buy a page if necessary, to show people that the opening of the Foxden Hotel was a success.' Bess waited until her husband was out of sight and turned to her sister. 'Frank's right, Margot.'

'About what?'

'Making sure Sutherland leaves. I don't want him hanging about in the grounds, breaking in through a window, or finding some other way to get into the hotel. Come on.'

'Wait for us!' Ena called, her arms full of coats and hats, gloves and outdoor shoes. 'We've checked everywhere. The hotel is secure.'

'And the police are on their way,' Claire added. 'We're coming with you.'

'No you are not!' Bess looked from Claire to Ena. 'You can't help with this.'

'I've been trained to deal with dangerous people,' Claire said. 'If things get rough--'

'And I can handle myself,' Ena put in.

'I said no!' Tears began to blur Bess's vision. She blinked them back. 'Neither of you can be involved,' she whispered, 'not now the police have been informed. Think about it!'

Claire raised her eyebrows at Ena. 'Bess is right.' Ena nodded and helped Bess into her coat, while Claire helped Margot into hers. 'We'll stay here and see the last of the guests out. But if you want me, us--'

'I know. Thank you.'

'Be careful,' Claire said, hugging Bess and then Margot. Bess nodded. Ena kissed her sisters, wrapped a scarf around each of their necks and echoed Claire's words.

Bess watched her younger siblings go their separate ways, Ena back to the cloakroom and Claire towards the ballroom. 'Come on, Margot,' she said, taking off her high-heels and putting on calf-length sheepskin boots.

'Why is it all right for me to be *involved*, but not them?' Margot asked, pushing her feet into fashionable suede ankle boots with kitten heels and

10

a fur trim.

'Because you're already involved, Margot, and so am I. Ena and Claire aren't, and there's no need for them to be.' Bess picked up their evening shoes and took them to reception. Maeve wasn't on the desk, so she opened the office door and dropped them inside.

'Even so--' Margot said.

'For God's sake, Margot, you know the work they did in the war was top secret. Ena is covered; her war record says she worked in a factory from thirty-nine to forty-five, but Claire was overseas so much her WAAF record has huge gaps in it. So, stop going on about it, and do as I ask!'

The wind blew a dusting of snow from the roof of the portico above the hotel's main entrance as Bess opened the door and led Margot out into the night. Margot put her hand up to shield her face, but Bess, after being in the warm hotel, was pleased to feel the snow on her face and breathed in the cold air. She scanned the gathering on the semi-circular steps leading to and from the hotel, hoping to see Sutherland and the girl.

Sutherland's girlfriend, if that's who she was, had left the hotel wearing only a coat. That she wasn't wearing a scarf or gloves on such a bitterly cold night suggested to Bess that she and Sutherland were near, waiting for Sir Gerald to bring round the car from the carpark at the back of the hotel. Bess hoped the girl's father was driving; Sutherland was in no fit state to get behind the wheel of a motorcar.

Bess scrutinised the faces of a dozen people

who were standing around stamping their feet and holding their coats tightly across their chests. Sutherland and Katherine were not among them. She looked down the tree-lined drive to where two couples had braved the weather and were walking home. One couple was too far away to be Sutherland and the girl. The other couple who were only half way down the drive, Bess could see were not Sutherland and Katherine by their clothes. The woman's coat was dark and she was wearing a hat.

Bess wondered if Sir Gerald had collected his car and already picked up his daughter. She decided there hadn't been time and, tugging Margot's arm, made her way down the steps.

'Looks like Sutherland and his cronies have disappeared into the night,' Margot said, trailing behind Bess, trying to walk in the imprints left in the snow by her sister's footsteps. 'And good riddance.'

Bess cast her gaze wide, taking in the open fields and the parkland on the right, the lake and small wood on the left. 'The girl's wearing a light cream coloured coat, so keep your eyes open. In the snow, she won't be easy to see.'

'No, but Sutherland will. He had on a long black overcoat when he left. What about Sir What's-his-name?'

'He'll have gone to fetch the car, I suppose. He might even be the driver of one of these,' Bess said, turning to see a convoy of four or five motorcars rumble slowly past.

Margot looked at her boots and then at Bess's. 'I wish I was wearing old-fashioned boots like yours. This is my best pair. They'll be ruined in this weather,' she moaned.

'Better your boots get ruined than that young girl's life,' Bess said.

'So, we haven't come out in snow up to our knees--' Bess shot Margot a look of incredulity. 'To our ankles, then!' Margot wiped snow from her face, 'to make sure Sutherland leaves the hotel's grounds, we're out here freezing to death to save that silly girl?'

'Silly or not, do you really want her to suffer the fate I did at Sutherland's hands?'

'No, of course not. Sorry, Bess.'

'Look! I think that's her.'

Margot looked to where Bess was pointing. 'I can't see anything but snow.'

'South of the lake, this side of the small wood.'

Before Bess had time to explain further a silver Bentley sped out of the courtyard and down the drive. A couple of cars stopped to let it pass. Bess pulled Margot out of the speeding Bentley's path and Margot, in a panic, lashed out, knocking Bess off her feet.

'Bloody maniac!' Margot shouted, raising her arm and making a fist at the car as it flew past. Looking back at Bess, and seeing her on her bottom in the snow, Margot pressed her lips together to stop herself from giggling.

'You think shoving me over in the snow's funny, do you?'

'No!' Margot looked suitably indignant. 'Well, a bit,' she said, unable to keep a straight face. She put out her hand and helped her sister up. 'Sorry, but I thought that car was going to hit me.'

'Which is why I pulled you out of its way,' Bess said, brushing a thick crust of snow from the skirt and sleeve of her coat. The Bentley screeched to a halt, reversed ten or twelve yards and stopped. 'What the hell is he doing?'

'I don't know, but look! I can see a girl in the car's headlights,' Margot said, 'and there's a man with her.'

'I can't see them, but it's got to be Sutherland and the girl. And I'd bet my last tanner that the driver of that Bentley is her father.'

'Why is he just sitting there?' No sooner had Margot asked the question than the Bentley pulled away at speed and skidded round the bend into Mysterton Lane. Bess and Margot hurried along the drive in the tracks of the car's tyres and stopped where the car had stopped. 'I can see them now. They are still south of the lake,' Bess said. 'Come on, it looks like Sutherland's dragging her into the woods.'

The two sisters hadn't taken more than a dozen steps across the snow-covered grass leading down to the lake when a black car appeared from the lane, swung onto the drive, and slammed on its brakes. Bess squinted, trying to see who was driving the car, but it had started to snow heavily. Even though the windscreen wipers struggled from right to left to remove the snow, the arcs they made weren't clear for long enough.

'Damn!' she said, looking at the spot where she had seen Sutherland and the girl. 'I glanced away for a second, and now I can't see them.' Bess studied the narrow strip of land between the lake and the wood. They weren't there. 'It's as if they have disappeared into thin air.'

'I've got them!' Margot shouted. 'Two figures. Sutherland in a dark coat and the girl in a light one. It looks like the girl's running away from Sutherland. She is, and she's coming this way!'

Bess, distracted again by the sound of a vehicle's door slamming, looked back at the black car from the lane. A tall man in a belted mackintosh leapt out of the passenger door and started running towards the girl. She must have seen him because she stopped, turned on her heels, and ran back in the direction of the wood. Suddenly lights from a second vehicle were visible through the leafless trees and the girl stopped and turned again.

The wind was whipping up and the snow was heavy. Bess strained to see which way the girl was going to run next. She put her hand up to her mouth and gasped in horror. 'She's running in the direction of the lake. What is she doing? Katherine, stop!' Bess shouted. 'Katherine?' Bess and Margot lumbered across the snow-covered field following in what Bess thought were Sutherland's and the girl's footprints and almost collided with the tall man in the raincoat.

'Mitch? What are you doing here?'

'Bess! Margot!' Where's Claire? Where's my wife?'

'She isn't here, and nor should you be.'

'But that woman--' Mitch shook his head as if he was trying to clear his mind, 'I thought she was Claire.' Bess looked at Margot. She lifted and dropped her shoulders as if to say, I've no idea what he's on about. 'It looked like the guy with her was beating her. There she is!'

Bess caught the sleeve of Mitch's coat, as he made to run to the woman's defence. 'Mitch? That isn't Claire. It's a local girl and she's with a well-known fascist.'

'A Blackshirt,' Margot said.

'You mustn't get involved in this,' Bess shouted into the wind. 'Think about it. You and Claire were in occupied France during the war, and he's a Nazi sympathiser.' His gaze still fixed on the girl, Mitch nodded that Bess was right. 'Go up to the hotel and Claire will fill you in with what's been happening. And tell Frank and Bill that Margot and I won't be long.'

Mitch ambled off reluctantly, and Bess and Margot made their way across the thick carpet of snow to the sparse wood, where they saw the shape of a large light coloured motorcar. Its headlights were at half-beam and its engine was idling. Suddenly, the sound of a door slamming echoed through the trees and the car roared into life. A second later it sped off down Shaft Hill.

'That's it, then!' Bess said, as she and Margot trudged back across the field in a snow storm that was fast turning into a blizzard. 'After all that, she went off with Sutherland.'

'And her father. That was her father's car we saw through the trees, wasn't it?'

Bess nodded. 'I think so. At least it looked like the silver Bentley that stopped on the drive earlier.'

Bess and Margot's friends, Natalie and Anton Goldman were waiting for them when they got back to the hotel. 'Frank and Bill not with you?'

16

Anton asked. He looked concerned.

'No. We haven't seen them,' Margot said.

Bess looked back at the lake and exhaled loudly. 'I specifically asked Frank to stay in the hotel.'

'He and Bill were worried about the two of you,' Anton said.

'They went out to look for you some time ago,' Natalie added.

As the last of the cars taking New Year's revellers home left, a police car arrived.

CHAPTER TWO

Lowarth's Sergeant McGann and Constable Peg were out of their black Wolseley by the time Bess and Margot had walked up the steps to the hotel. Bess elected to wait for them, ushering them through the door and into the foyer ahead of her.

Bill followed Margot into the hotel, but Frank hung back. 'Thank God you're safe,' he said in a hushed voice. 'We couldn't see you anywhere.'

'You shouldn't have been out looking,' Bess whispered. Unable to stay angry with her husband, she added, 'If the police want to know where you've been say nowhere, that you and Bill only came out as far as the steps and waited for us.'

Sergeant McGann asked if there was somewhere private where he could talk to Bess and Margot about the events of the evening; the threatening behaviour towards the young woman and the argument between the two men.

Bess showed the policemen into the office, but before entering herself turned to Claire, who was talking to Mr Potts the night porter in reception. 'Where's Mitch?'

'Upstairs checking on Aimee.'

'Good. There's nothing more you can do tonight, so you might as well call it a day. Find Ena, will you, tell her the same. I'll let you know what action the police intend to take, if any, in the morning.'

Entering the office, Bess hung her coat on a hook behind the door and took off her boots. Replacing them with her shoes, she joined Margot by the fire. Adding two logs to what would have soon been ashes, she knelt down beside her sister and warmed her hands.

Unable to delay the proceedings further, the two sisters stood up and turned to face Sergeant McGann. With their backs to the fire they told the policeman what they had seen and heard earlier that night.

Omitting the personal threats Sutherland had made to her, Bess recounted everything she had heard Sutherland say in the hotel's public bar to the girl called Katherine and her father, Sir Gerald.

'So,' McGann said, reading the notes he'd made, 'Sutherland and Sir Gerald were already arguing when you arrived?' He looked up at Bess. 'Is that correct?' Bess nodded. 'And you don't know who started the argument, or what it was about?'

'No, but our barman, Simon, would know. He was on duty all night. The photographer from the Lowarth *Advertiser* might know something too. I only saw him in the bar when my sister, Mrs Burrell,' Bess nodded at Margot, 'and I were there, but I'd stake my life on him going back later and asking Simon what he'd heard.'

'We'll have a word with them both, if we need to.' Sergeant McGann glanced at his notes, again. 'On the telephone, Mrs Mitchell said the man causing the trouble was a Nazi?'

'I told her to tell you that so you knew the situation was serious. He's a fascist. I should have said, Nazi sympathiser.'

'How did you know the man was a Nazi sympathiser, Mrs Donnelly?'

19

Fearing she would get herself tangled up in the details of Dave Sutherland's fascist beliefs, which might then lead to Sergeant McGann suspecting she had known him in London, Bess shot Margot a sideways look and raised her eyebrows.

'Because I told my sister,' Margot said. 'David Sutherland is ex-BUF. He's an apologist who was sent to prison because his beliefs stopped him from answering the call up.'

The sergeant looked from Bess to Margot. 'So, it is you who knows Mr Sutherland?'

Margot shook her head. 'I don't know him; I knew him.'

'Ah.' McGann sucked thoughtfully on the end of his pen. 'Do you have any proof to back up these accusations?'

'I don't have physical proof, but I knew his girlfriend, Goldie Trick. She was a dancer in the theatre where I worked in London and we became friends. One day she found Sutherland's BUF papers and membership card.'

Sergeant McGann's mouth fell open and for a moment he appeared to be speechless. He cleared his throat. 'Was your friend here tonight?'

'Good Lord, no. She isn't even in the country.'

Margot's account of the relationship between her friend and David Sutherland was halted by a knock at the door. Bess looked at her sister and put her finger to her lips. Margot stopped speaking and Bess crossed to the door and opened it. 'Yes, Maeve?'

The receptionist was holding a large tray. On it was a coffee pot, teapot, milk, sugar, cups and saucers - and a plate of biscuits. 'Sorry to interrupt,

Mrs Donnelly, but I thought you could all do with a hot drink.'

'You're a life saver, Maeve, we certainly could.' Bess took the tray from the receptionist. 'Shouldn't you have gone home by now?' She looked up at the clock. 'Your shift finished an hour ago.'

'I stayed to see in the New Year, then there was so much going on I forgot the time. I'll be off now,' she said, turning to leave.

'Maeve? Before you go, were all the guests accounted for after the party?' The receptionist looked at Bess quizzically. 'Were any room-keys left in the pigeonholes at the time your shift ended?'

'No, not that I remember.'

'Would you do something for me?' Maeve nodded. 'Would you ask Mr Potts if he noticed whether there were any keys in the pigeon holes when he came on duty?'

Maeve left the office, leaving the door ajar. By the time Bess had crossed the room with the tray of hot beverages she was back. 'No, Mrs Donnelly. Except for keys belonging to rooms that were not occupied every key was out or, like Mr and Mrs Burrell's, accounted for. All the guests were in the hotel. Most had gone up to their rooms, Mr Potts said.'

'Thank you, Maeve. Goodnight.'

'Goodnight.' The receptionist nodded to the room in general and left, closing the door quietly behind her.

'Nothing amiss according to the night porter,' Bess said. Putting each cup in a saucer she looked from the sergeant to the constable. 'Tea, or coffee?'

'Tea,' said the sergeant. The constable nodded in agreement.

Bess poured tea for each of the policemen. 'Help yourselves to milk and sugar.' She then poured four cups of coffee, adding milk to hers and Margot's, but leaving Frank and Bill to add their own.

'Sorry about the delay, but it crossed my mind that you might want to know if all the hotel's guests were accounted for.'

'I did. Now, Mrs Burrell,' the sergeant said, adding milk to his tea and waving away the offer of a biscuit that the constable took eagerly, 'where were we?'

'You asked if my friend Goldie was here tonight. She wasn't.' Despite the sadness she felt when she thought about her friend, Margot chuckled. 'Her real name was Doreen, but she hated it, so we called her by her stage name.' Tears welled up in her eyes. 'Goldie was lovely. She was pretty and full of life. She was always laughing. She was generous too.' Margot wiped a tear from her cheek with the flat of her hand. 'No! She wasn't here tonight. She wouldn't dare come back to England while that *Nazi's* around,' Margot spat.

'David Sutherland beat Goldie up and dumped her like a piece of rubbish, in an alley.' Remembering that terrible day, Margot bit her bottom lip to stop herself from crying out and looked to the heavens. 'She couldn't stand when I found her, let alone walk,' she said at last. 'I don't know how I did it, but somehow I managed to get her to the theatre.

'It was obvious she wouldn't be able to perform that night, her face looked like a piece of raw meat. One of her eyes was so swollen she couldn't see out of it, and her ribs hurt every time she moved. Sutherland had beaten her so badly she almost died.' Margot took in a breath and blew it out slowly. 'We looked after her; hid her until she was well enough to travel, then we got her out of London.'

'You and your sister did this?' The sergeant looked again from Margot to Bess.

'No, Bess wasn't in London then. It was Goldie's friends, the other dancers in the show, Mr and Mrs Goldman - the owners of the theatre - and me. Mr and Mrs Goldman bought Goldie a ticket to… I'm afraid I don't know where.' Margot did know, but she and her friends had sworn never to disclose Goldie's whereabouts to anyone. 'She never went back to her small flat. The Goldmans packed her belongings, paid her rent up to date and gave her enough money to start a new life.

'I took Goldie's place on stage. We were the same height and dress size. I wore her costumes and wigs, and for a while I managed to fool Sutherland into believing Goldie was still in the show, and therefore still in London. When he realised it was me he'd been watching every night, and not Goldie, he sent me a bouquet of funeral lilies and a card with R.I.P. on it.'

Margot shook her head. 'He used to stand in the shadows opposite the stage door, and when I came out after a show, he'd strike a match and light his cigarette. He did it to let me know he was watching me. He followed me too. I'd suddenly see him in a crowd on Regent Street, or in Oxford Circus underground station.' Margot closed her eyes and exhaled loudly. 'One night, after blitzing the East End, the Luftwaffe dropped incendiary bombs on Fleet Street. Several buildings were on fire, so to keep the roads clear for the fire engines and ambulances the ARP cordoned off the roads around Covent Garden and the Aldwych. There weren't any buses going west, or north west, and there were long queues of people outside the hotels waiting for taxis, so I started to walk.

'It was late and I was tired. And, because of the blackout and the streets being thick with smoke, I took a wrong turn. I hadn't got a clue where I was. I heard footsteps behind me and stopped - and so did they. As I said, it was late and there weren't many people about, so when I started walking again and I heard the footsteps again, I panicked. I've never been so frightened in my life. I ended up hiding in a bombed-out builder's yard.' Margot glanced at Bill and smiled. 'Fortunately, when I didn't arrive home at the usual time, Bill came looking for me on his motorbike. He rode along the bus route, couldn't find me, so he started looking down side streets. Thank God he got to me before Sutherland did.

'After that night, none of the dancers were allowed to go out of the theatre on their own. We went out in twos, even in the daytime. It was fine by me. After receiving those lilies, I was terrified to walk in the street in daylight, let alone at night in the blackout, until he was put in prison.'

'Mr and Mrs Goldman, the owners of the

theatre, were they here tonight?' Sergeant McGann directed the question at Bess.

'Yes,' Bess said, 'but I don't think Sutherland would have seen them. They were in the ballroom, he was in the public bar.' Unless he saw them when he came into the ballroom to terrorise me, Bess thought, but she wasn't going to tell McGann that.

'Then I don't think I'll need to speak to them. If I do, how long are they staying?'

'They're going back to London tomorrow.'

Sergeant McGann's head wobbled from side to side. 'They're not important,' he said, and dismissed them by closing his notebook. 'Sir Gerald, the man with this Sutherland character is a wealthy land owner by the name of Hawksley. The girl, Katherine, is indeed his daughter. Apart from owning a riding stables and several hundred acres of land, we don't know much about Sir Gerald. He keeps himself very much to himself.'

'Some dubious characters visit that big house of his by all accounts,' Constable Peg said. 'Come and go at all hours, they do. My in-laws live at Kirby Marlow, where he lives, and--'

'Rumours and speculation, Constable!' McGann got to his feet and pulled himself up to his full height - which was on the short side of police requirements and several inches shorter than Frank and Bill - and puffed out his chest. 'We're dealing with facts tonight, lad, not village tittle-tattle.'

After putting on his helmet, the sergeant shook Bess's hand and nodded to Margot, Frank and Bill. 'We'll speak to Sir Gerald and Mr Sutherland as soon as possible. 'Do you want to press charges for any damage Mr Sutherland caused?'

Bess's heart began to thump in her chest. She didn't want her shameful secret to come out and if she pressed charges, David Sutherland was bound to make sure it did. She wanted to forget about Sutherland, what happened in London, and what happened tonight. She took a nervous breath and swallowed. In a voice, as normal as she was able, Bess looked across the room. 'We don't, do we, Frank?'

Her husband shook his head. 'No, love.' He moved to Bess and put a protective arm around her.

'Then we'll be on our way. Constable?' McGann barked. The constable jumped up and followed his superior officer to the door. 'I'll let you know of any developments.'

Bess grabbed her coat, pushed her arms down the sleeves, and followed the policemen out.

It had stopped snowing, but was the colder for it. She watched the two men descend the semi-circle of stone steps leading down to the police car, and shivered. The constable took his place behind the steering wheel and the sergeant lifted his hand in a half-salute, half-wave, before opening the passenger door of the car and lowering himself onto the seat. A second later the constable gunned the powerful engine of the black Wolseley into life, pulled away from the verge, and cruised down the drive. The police car was soon out of sight.

Relieved that the police had left, Bess inhaled deeply. The freezing air nipped the back of her nose and throat and she coughed. She pulled her coat around her, holding it tightly across her chest, and took in the view. The ploughed fields of the war years had reverted to pastures and meadows. With an army of Land Girls, she had been responsible for turning the Foxden Estate into arable land during the war. The women she worked with, the farmers, and the staff at Foxden Hall had been like family to her. She thought of her late father who had recently died from injuries incurred during an accident at the foundry. She wondered if her mother would ever get over losing him. Bess knew that she and her sisters never would.

Beneath a layer of snow, Foxden looked much the same as it had done ten years earlier, on New Year's Eve, 1938. Bess hadn't thought about that night for a long time. She smiled remembering how she had fallen asleep in the library while studying for her teaching certificate, and how, sneaking out of the Hall during Lord and Lady Foxden's party, she had literally fallen into the arms of their son, James. He didn't recognise her at first. When he did, it was as his childhood chum Tom's little sister.

Bess could smile about it now, but at the time she had been so embarrassed that she'd fled down the steps. When she stopped running and looked back at the Hall, the French windows were open and she could hear the orchestra playing a waltz. She hummed the tune, "The Blue Danube." She had fallen in love with James Foxden that night and he had fallen in love with her, though at the time he didn't know it. Then David Sutherland came into her life and she was duty-bound to turn

27

her back on James, and on happiness.

Another New Year's Eve, two years later, Bess and James had sipped brandy by the library fire and talked into the early hours. That night they declared their love for one another, made love, and made plans for their future. But fate had something different in store for James. For Bess too.

Bess lifted her right hand and looked at James's ring, the ring that his parents had given him on his twenty-first birthday, which James had given to Bess when he asked her to marry him. A chill rippled down her spine and she cuffed a frozen tear from her cheek.

So much had happened since that night - some of it sad, but much of it happy. Hitler was finally defeated and many loved ones had survived and returned home, including her brother Tom and his old friend, Frank Donnelly. Frank had lost his left eye in Africa and Bess had helped to nurse him back to health. Frank was kind and considerate, and when he asked Bess to marry him, his proposal was followed with, "When you are ready."

Bess didn't think she would ever be ready. She worried that knowing about her first love, James Foxden, Frank would feel he wasn't enough for her. But he was enough - Frank was everything she wanted in a husband.

Bess heard the hotel door open and Frank's distinctive step. She waited for him to join her. When he did, he wrapped his strong arms around her and looked over her shoulder. Leaning back, Bess rested against her husband's chest, her chin tilted upwards. The air sparkled with tiny particles of ice. There wasn't a cloud in the blue-black sky.

She could see every star.

'It's late, darling,' Frank whispered. 'And it's too cold to be standing out here. I'm going up, are you coming?'

Bess turned, and, still in her husband's arms, stood on tiptoe and looked up into his handsome face. 'What would I do without you?'

Frank laughed. 'You would manage, Bess, I have no doubt about that. But for my sake,' he said, burying his face in her hair and kissing her neck, 'I hope you never find out.'

'Post come yet, Maeve?'

'Ten minutes ago. Mr Donnelly has taken it through to the office.'

'Thank you. And thank you for staying late on New Year's Eve. It was kind of you. Make sure Frank pays you for the overtime. Tell him I said it's double-time after midnight on New Year's Eve,' Bess whispered, laughing.

'Thank you, Mrs Donnelly.' Bess picked up three of the four copies of the Lowarth *Advertiser* from the reception desk and turned to go into the office. 'Are you expecting the police to come back today?' Maeve asked, reaching for the hotel's reservations diary.

'No, not today. Sergeant McGann said he was going to see Sir Gerald Hawksley, but he didn't say when. He's going to interview the hotel staff too, but again he didn't say when that would be. I know he intends to ask Simon if he heard any of the conversation between Sir Gerald and Sutherland. But all he said when he left was, "I'll be in touch." I expect he'll telephone first, in which case you'll know before I do.'

'I hope Sir Gerald Hawksley doesn't blame anyone here at the hotel for the trouble that man Sutherland caused.'

Bess glanced across the marble hall to the door of the public bar and pondered the thought. 'No, Sir Gerald was furious at the way Sutherland treated his daughter. He won't blame us, but I wouldn't put it past Sutherland to try. That reminds me, Sir Gerald gave me his card. I can't remember where I put it.'

'I found it on the floor when they'd gone.' Maeve took the small white card from the top drawer of the reception desk and gave it to Bess.

Bess laughed. 'How did your last employers ever let you go?' She turned the card over in her hand before giving it back to Maeve. 'I don't want it, but we'd better keep it in case we need it in the future.'

Instead of taking a newspaper up to the library and one to the smoking lounge, Bess took all three into the office. Frank had come down ten minutes earlier and was waiting with a breakfast tray.

Bess sat in the cottage armchair by the fire with the newspapers on her lap, while Frank poured two cups of tea. He left his cup on his desk and took Bess's tea and toast to her on the tray, setting it down on a small occasional table at the side of the fireplace. 'I'll open the post,' he said, going back to his desk.

'There's a lovely photograph of the hotel in the *Advertiser.*' Bess took a bite of her toast. 'There aren't any cars about and the lawns are blanketed in snow.' She lifted the paper so she could see the picture more clearly. 'He must have taken this when he was leaving. I'll ask him for a copy, and see if I can get it enlarged,' she said, taking another bite of toast. 'I'll get it framed. It would look lovely in the marble hall.' Bess took a sip of her tea. 'Mmmm, thank you, darling,'

Frank looked up from the letter he was reading. 'Don't thank me, thank Maeve. She brought it in five minutes after I came down.'

'I don't know what we've done to deserve that woman. Oh, it's a good headline too,' Bess said, putting her cup down to give the newspaper her full attention. '"The opening of the Foxden Hotel on New Year's Eve went with a bang!"' She sighed, worried that "went with a bang" was a journalistic teaser before a graphic description of the fracas between Sutherland and Hawksley. Or worse still, between Sutherland and Frank. She glanced at her husband. He was reading a letter, his eyebrows knitted together in a frown of concentration.

Bess finished the slice of toast, washed it down with the last of her tea and sat back in the chair to read the review. She read the piece through, and then read it again. 'Not a single mention of Sutherland, Sir Gerald Hawksley, or his daughter,' she said, bemused. 'Ah! Cont. Page 3.'

Bess turned to page three. There was no mention of Sir Gerald Hawksley or Sutherland on that page either. 'Something isn't right here, Frank. You'd think a Nazi and a Knight almost coming to blows over a young girl in a public place would be newsworthy, but there isn't a single word about it in the *Advertiser*?'

'You sound disappointed,' Frank said, laughing.

'I'm not. I'm pleased the trouble that monster caused hasn't been reported. Being associated with a Blackshirt, however remotely, could have been the death knell for the hotel. It's odd, though, that there's no mention of Sir Gerald, or his daughter. His name and title might have been an endorsement,' Bess said, as much to herself as to her husband. 'There's some really good photographs. One of a group of people with their glasses raised in a toast. A smasher of our Margot posing by the Christmas tree, and one of a middle-aged couple in mid flow on the dance floor in the ballroom.' Bess skimmed the rest of the paper. There was no other news.

'I'll take a copy up to the library and the smoking lounge, and leave this one here for you.' Bess folded the newspaper and dropped it on Frank's desk. 'Anything in the post?'

'Nothing that can't wait.'

'That's good. I'll take the tray back to the kitchen as well, if you've finished?' Frank drained his cup and put it on the tray next to Bess's cup and plate. Papers in one hand and tray in the other, Bess bent down, kissed Frank on the cheek, and left.

Frank waited until Bess had closed the door before taking the envelope he hadn't wanted her to see from beneath his leather ink blotter. It was addressed to him but there was no title. The writing was familiar, but there was something different about it; there was no postage stamp. Apart from that, the envelope looked the same as any other envelope. Frank took out the letter and read it again. There was no salutation, just the initial, D. *One last payment. £50. Today. Usual place. 12 o'clock. And you won't hear from me again. Tell the police or don't pay up, and I shall tell the local newspaper about your sordid affair in London. DS.*

'Where the hell does the bloody man think I'm going to get £50 by twelve o'clock today?' Frank got up and paced the floor. He had no money left of his own, Sutherland had blackmailed him out of every penny; only the hotel's bank account was in funds - and that was for emergencies. Frank ran his fingers through his hair. This *was* an emergency.

Barclays bank in Lowarth opened at ten. There was time to get there and back by midday. But even if he went to the bank, the bank manager would no more let him take money out of the hotel's account without Bess's signature, than he would Bess, without his signature.

As he saw it, Frank had two options. He could say he was going into Lowarth for… He'd think of something… and although it was earlier in the week than planned, he would offer to deposit the takings from New Year at Barclays while he was there. If he did that, he could take £50 out for Sutherland and bank what was left. He shook his head. That would mean lying to Bess and stealing from the business. He couldn't do it.

The other option was to tell Bess the truth. Tell her that Sutherland had been blackmailing him and if he paid him one last payment, the man would be out of their lives forever. Frank exhaled loudly. It would break her heart and he was not going to do that, he loved her too much. Besides if this payment was the last, he may never have to tell her. He reached across his desk, picked up the letter, folded it and put it back in the envelope.

Slipping the blackmail letter into the breast pocket of his jacket, Frank turned back to his desk and caught his breath. For some minutes he stared at the black cast iron safe with gold lettering in the corner of the room. There was another option, one that he hadn't thought of until now. He could *borr*ow the money. Take £50 from the safe and put an I.O.U in its place. That would give him time to put the money back before banking the takings on Friday. And if he wasn't able to put the money back, it would at least give him time to think up a decent reason for borrowing it.

Frank went to the door and put his ear to the wood. He could hear voices, but none were Bess's. No one except his wife walked into the office without knocking. Even his sisters-in-law knocked before entering. They didn't always wait to be asked to come in, but they always knocked. Frank looked at his watch. Bess was dropping their breakfast tray off in the kitchen before going up to the library and the smoking lounge with copies of the *Advertiser*. Even if she changed her mind and called into the office before going upstairs, she would be at least five minutes. Time enough to take £50 and scribble a note.

Frank moved quickly to the safe. Opening it, he took out four five-pound notes and thirty one-pound notes from the blue hessian bag that Barclays provided. He then wrote the note saying that he had borrowed £50 and would replace it tomorrow. He added his signature to the note, but not the date. Tomorrow would be the day after whichever day it was that his wife noticed the money was missing.

Closing the safe, Frank put the wad of notes in an envelope, slipped it into his pocket next to the blackmail letter, and went out to reception. 'There was a letter addressed to me personally in the post this morning, Maeve.'

The receptionist looked up at her boss. 'Yes, Mr Donnelly.'

'It didn't have a stamp on it and I was wondering if it had been delivered by hand. And if it had, perhaps you saw who brought it.'

'No. No one has delivered a letter while I've been here.' Maeve looked into the mid-distance, thoughtfully. 'There wasn't anything on the desk when I got here this morning. If there had been,' she explained, 'I'd have thought it strange and would have remembered. And it was only a few minutes after the post arrived that you came down, picked it up, and took it through to the office.'

'And you've been on reception all the time?' Frank asked. 'You didn't leave at all, not even to powder your nose?'

Maeve took a sharp breath. 'Yes. I did leave the desk.' She put her hands up to her mouth. 'I'm sorry, Mr Donnelly, I forgot. I went to the toilet and when I got back the post was here. I wasn't away for more than a couple of minutes, but I suppose it was long enough for someone to nip in and put a letter among the pile the postman had delivered. I can't think who would do such a thing, or why. I think it's more likely that the stamp just came off.'

'Thank you, Maeve.'

'I hope I haven't caused you a problem by not being here when the post came?'

'No, dear, not at all. I was just curious as to how an envelope without a stamp got past the postmen in the sorting office,' Frank said, 'and, if it did, why the postman hadn't waited and asked you to pay the postage cost.'

'He did once before, when there wasn't a stamp.'

'Well, there's nothing we can do about it now,' Frank said, with a smile. 'I think I'll go for a walk; get a breath of fresh air. If my wife comes looking for me, tell her I won't be long.'

CHAPTER THREE

Bess pulled back the bedroom curtains, pushed up the sash window and revelled in the fresh air. After three days of showers the sky was blue with wispy clouds that were being dispersed by the warm sun as soon as they wafted into view. She sat on the window ledge and looked out over the grounds. Daffodils dwarfed the snowdrops in the park, and forget-me-nots and crocuses peeped from beneath the hedgerows. Spring had finally arrived.

This time last year Bess had wondered whether she and Frank had taken on too much by agreeing to oversee the building work and refurbishment of Foxden Hall. It had seemed that for every step forward the builders took, turning the Hall into a hotel, they took two steps back. At the end of the summer Bess had serious doubts about the hotel opening at all, let alone on New Year's Eve.

They had taken a huge risk. Not only had Frank given up his job at the aerodrome, which would have been a job for life, to take charge of the interior maintenance, they had gone into partnership with Lord Foxden, and they had taken out a loan from the bank to pay for more workmen. Even then it was a gamble as to whether the work would be finished on time.

Ena came up from London at the beginning of the autumn to help Bess with the refurbishment. They measured the bedrooms for carpets and curtains and decided where furniture would be best placed to maximise space.

In 1940, when Ena was still working at Silcott's

Engineering, she had helped Bess turn Foxden Hall into a convalescent home for local servicemen coming home from Dunkirk. Then they had cleared the rooms in the west wing for hospital beds and medical apparatus, and had stored the furniture. Now they were bringing the furniture out of storage, cleaning and polishing it, and putting it in newly decorated bedrooms. Anything else they needed after Bess and Ena had refurbished the rooms, they had to buy second-hand from Kimpton Smith's in Lowarth.

Bess stood up, pulled down the window and left the room. The gamble had paid off. Foxden Hotel had opened as planned on New Year's Eve. Dave Sutherland turning up was a blot on the celebrations, but thankfully he hadn't shown his face since.

Bess took two of the four copies of the *Advertiser* from the reception desk and ran upstairs, depositing one in the library and the other in the smoking lounge. Returning with a bounce in her step, she left reception's copy on the desk and took the remaining copy into the office.

'As we'd hoped,' Frank said, greeting Bess with a smile. 'Bookings are up on February. The rest of March is looking good and Easter weekend is almost full.'

Bess dropped the paper on the chair by the fire and walked round Frank's desk. She looked over his shoulder and read the figures he was working on. She exhaled with relief and gave Frank's shoulders a squeeze.

A loud knock at the door took Bess's attention.

Maeve entered without waiting to be asked. 'Excuse me, one of the anglers is asking to see you. He says it's urgent.'

'Thank you, Maeve. Show him in, will you?'

Frank groaned. 'What now? The last day of the fishing season and someone's complaining.'

There was a huffing and a puffing outside the door and a second later Harry Shaw, a local man from the village of Woodcote who had fished the lake since he was a boy, blustered into the room. He was as white as the hotel's bed linen. 'There's a b-b-body,' he stuttered, 'in the lake.'

Bess and Frank stood up simultaneously. Bess shot Frank a stunned look, then quickly edged her way from behind the desk to assist the old gentleman. She pulled out the chair from under Frank's desk. 'Sit down, Mr Shaw.' Bess waited while the old man shuffled to the front of the chair, her arms outstretched ready to catch him if he fell. He lowered himself onto the seat. 'I'll get someone to bring you a cup of tea,' she said, going back to the door and poking her head out.

'Maeve? Would you get one of the kitchen staff to make a pot of tea for three, please? As quickly as you can.'

'You're certain it was a body, Mr Shaw?' Bess asked, when she returned to her seat. 'It couldn't have been a log, or--?'

'What I saw weren't no log, Mrs Donnelly. My legs might be going a bit, but there's nowt wrong with my eyes. It were a body all right! It were floating sideways. Like a whale, it was.' Harry looked from Bess to Frank.

Frank glanced at the clock. It wasn't quite

seven. 'With a bit of luck the other anglers won't be here yet. You're early, aren't you, Mr Shaw?'

'I'm down there sometimes as soon as it's light, so as I get the same spot. Up near the hotel can be noisy with the holiday folk coming and going, and the east side's too open. I like plenty of cover, where it's a bit overgrown, as you might say. Serves to keep the March wind off.'

Bess looked at Frank. She knew the answer to the question she was about to ask. She asked it anyway. 'And where exactly is it that you fish, Mr Shaw?'

'South of the lake. This side, where there's long reeds. The fish get caught in them, and you can sometimes net 'em. I like it down there with Shaft Hill spinney behind me. Gives a bit of shelter see.'

Frank laid his hand on Bess's arm and she looked up at him. His pale face and lined forehead mirrored what she imagined her own face to look like. 'I'd better telephone the police station and tell Sergeant McGann what Mr Shaw has told us. I'll do it from reception, and then go down to the lake, stop any other fishermen setting up near the body.'

'Sergeant McGann might not want any part of the lake fishing today,' Bess said. 'At least, not until he's seen the body and had it taken away. Even then I expect he'll have policemen searching the grounds. Tell the anglers that there's been an accident and ask them to come back tomorrow.'

'If it is a body, McGann won't want anyone near the lake until his men have done poking about. I'll tell them to come back on Monday. The police should be finished by then.'

'Poor blighter. Drowning's a terrible way to

go,' Harry Shaw said. 'I saw a lot of men die that way in the Royal Navy.' He sat upright and stuck out his chin. 'The Great War!' he said, with pride. 'Watched one of my mates drown in the North Sea.' He shook his head slowly. 'That was the coldest and the cruellest stretch of water... He froze to death in seconds, well afore he drowned.' Tears filled the old man's eyes. He took a large grey handkerchief from the pocket of his sou'wester and mopped his face.

Frank got to his feet. 'I'd better get down there. We don't want anyone else seeing the body.' He kissed Bess on the cheek, and as he passed the old man patted him on the shoulder.

'I'll see where your tea has got to, Mr Shaw. I won't be a minute.' Bess followed her husband out to reception. 'Maeve, I'll look after things here. Would you pop to the kitchen and ask how long the tea will be? Mr Shaw's had a terrible shock.'

Maeve left reception straightaway and Frank picked up the telephone. 'Do you think it's him?' Bess whispered. 'Sutherland?'

'Why would it be him? If there is a body--?'

'Of course there's a body!' Bess cut in. 'Mr Shaw saw it.'

'What the old man saw is more likely to be an animal than a human. But if it is a man's body, we won't know who it is until he's been identified.'

'I know it's him, Frank. Don't ask me how, but I've got this horrible, excited, feeling in my stomach. Anyway, who else could it be?' He was probably killed by one of his fascist cronies and dumped in our lake to take the attention away from Sir Gerald Hawksley.'

'Or to make it look as if one of us had killed him.'

'What if Katherine Hawksley killed him on New Year's Eve? Good on her if she did,' Bess said, a congratulatory tone to her voice.

'No one killed him on New Year's Eve--' Frank stopped short of telling Bess why. Instead he said, 'There were too many people about after the New Year party, someone would have seen something.' He looked up at the clock. 'You call McGann. I'd better get down to the lake before more anglers arrive.'

Bess picked up the telephone. Her stomach churned with distasteful curiosity.

As he walked down the drive, Frank came to a decision. If it was Sutherland's body in the lake, he wouldn't tell the police Sutherland was alive on January 2nd. If he did, they'd want to know how he knew. And if he told them Sutherland had been blackmailing him, and that the last letter he received was on the second, they would see that as a motive for killing him.

Frank took a deep breath as he neared the place where the old angler said he'd seen the body, and decided that, as he'd got away without telling Bess for almost three months, he wasn't going to tell her now.

Holding onto the trunk of a silver birch sapling, Frank inched his way down the slippery bank. It was a man's body, sure enough, but he couldn't tell whether it was Sutherland or not. His head was turned sideways and Frank could only see the left side of the man's face. He was unrecognisable. His features looked grotesque with bloating.

Revulsion formed a hard lump in Frank's stomach. It rose to the back of his throat. He thought he would be sick and turned his gaze away. At that moment, something at the water's edge, white, and tangled in the roots of a clump of reeds, caught his eye. It was the man's right hand, and on it was a signet ring. Bringing to mind the black and red crest on the thick gold band when he hit Sutherland on New Year's Eve, Frank sighed heavily. His worst fears were confirmed. The man floating in the lake was David Sutherland.

The sound of a car in the distance broke into Frank's thoughts. He looked up. 'Bess?' he gasped, 'what are you doing here?' Frank scrambled up the bank to his wife who, as if in a dream, stood on the top of the slope staring at Sutherland's prostrate body. 'Bess?' Frank took her arm and tried to walk her away from the horrific scene, but she stood firm.

'I was right, Frank, it is Sutherland,' she said, her expression blank, her voice emotionless.

'Yes, love,' Frank whispered. He looked towards Mysterton Lane. Sergeant McGann's black Wolseley was rounding the bend to the drive. 'Come on, sweetheart. The police are here. Let me take you back to the hotel.' Holding Bess's arm with one hand, Frank waved down the police car with the other. 'If you keep looking at his body it will only upset you, Bess. Come on, love.'

As the Wolseley pulled up, Bess yanked her arm free of her husband's grip. 'I want to look at him. I want to be sure that monster will never hurt anyone again,' she cried, and slumped to her knees.

'He won't, my darling. He'll never hurt anyone again.' Seeing Sergeant McGann and the constable approaching, Frank lifted Bess's chin and leant forward until his eyes were level with hers. 'The police are here, Bess. We must get out of their way, so they can do their job.'

Bess nodded. 'Let's go home.' Frank helped her to her feet and without a backward glance husband and wife, arms around each other, walked back to the hotel.

'Mr Shaw is in the smoking lounge,' Maeve told them as soon as they were through the door. 'I got one of the waitresses to take him another cup of tea and a slice of Battenberg. When she left he was reading the newspaper.'

'That's good. Thank you, Maeve. When you have time, would you find the names and addresses of people who stayed here from New Year's Eve to--?'

'Don't worry about that now, Bess,' Frank said. 'You look all in. Why don't you go up and have a lie down?'

'I don't want to lie down. Besides, I need to be here. The police are bound to want to talk to us. So,' she said, with more than a little exasperation in her voice, 'would you do as I ask, Maeve? Find the names and addresses, and telephone numbers if they have them, of all the guests who have stayed here since we opened and bring them to me in the office?' She looked at Frank. 'I want to be prepared.' Turning back to Maeve: 'I hope the police will have taken the body away by the time today's guests arrive. How many are booked in, and what time are we expecting them?'

'Six. Two double rooms and two singles. Four are booked in for tea and dinner, two for just dinner - both parties arriving this afternoon.'

'Let's hope it's later rather than earlier this afternoon,' Bess said, going into the office.

'I'll go back down there,' Frank said. 'I'll try and find out how long the police will be here.'

'Where's my husband?' Bess asked, as Sergeant McGann strolled into the office.

'At the lake with Constable Peg,' he replied. 'If it's all right with you, I'd like to ask you some questions?' Bess nodded. 'As far as I could see the dead man wasn't carrying identification. However, your husband said he recognised the man's ring and his name is David Sutherland, the man you called us out to on New Year's Eve. The man who was with Sir Gerald Hawksley and his daughter Katherine.'

'That's right,' Bess said.

'You were at the lake when I arrived today, Mrs Donnelly. Did you recognise the man?'

'No, his face was too swollen and distorted. Though I thought his coat looked similar to the one Sutherland wore on New Year's Eve.'

'New Year's Eve...' the sergeant repeated, thoughtfully. 'Would you tell me about that night again? Tell me the sequence of events in more detail?'

'I'm not sure I can. It's almost three months ago, and it all happened so quickly.'

'What did?'

'Seeing him. I mean, hearing David

Sutherland's voice in the ballroom.'

'So you didn't actually see Mr Sutherland in the ballroom?'

'No. I didn't see him. I turned the instant I heard his voice, but the reporter from the *Advertiser* took a photograph, the camera flashed, and I was temporarily blinded. Sutherland must have left quickly, because when I was able to see again, the chap from the *Advertiser* was standing where I expected Sutherland to be.'

'So you decided to seek David Sutherland out, because you thought it was his voice that you'd heard in the ballroom?'

'I didn't *think* it was his voice, I knew it was!' Bess was getting exasperated. She needed to calm down and get her facts straight - and get the timing in order. 'It was a few seconds before midnight when Sutherland hissed "Happy New Year, Bess" in my ear.'

'And you are certain that it was Mr Sutherland who wished you a happy New Year?'

'He didn't *wish* me a happy New Year, Sergeant, he snarled it, menacingly.' Bess sighed. Not because she had any doubts that the voice she'd heard was David Sutherland's, but because McGann was talking about the man - who Bess had said on New Year's Eve was a Nazi sympathiser, and who Margot had said almost killed her friend - with respect.

Bess threw her hands up in despair. 'To answer your question, yes! I am a hundred percent certain that the voice I heard was David Sutherland's!'

'I'm confused, Mrs Donnelly. If you didn't see Mr Sutherland how can you be certain the voice you heard was his?' McGann began tapping his pen on the table. 'Mrs Donnelly, did you know Mr Sutherland before New Year's Eve?' Bess swallowed hard. For ten years she had feared, dreaded, that she would one day be asked if she knew David Sutherland. 'Perhaps he had been one of your circle of friends in London?'

Bess shot McGann a scorching look. 'I did meet Sutherland in London, but he was no friend of mine, and he was definitely not part of my *circle*, as you call it. He was a brute and a bully. He was a nasty piece of work then, and by the threatening way he said my name on New Year's Eve, he hadn't changed.'

Bess looked straight into McGann's eyes, tears threatening to tumble from her own. 'I have already told you that I turned to face Sutherland, the reporter from the Lowarth *Advertiser* took a photograph, the flash temporarily blinded me and by the time I could see again, Sutherland had disappeared in the crowd.' She felt weary having to repeat what happened again. 'Big Ben was ringing in the New Year, and someone pulled me into a circle of people singing "Auld Lang Syne."'

It had been almost three months since the New Year's Eve party and although his was the face she saw in her nightmares, Bess had forced herself not to think about David Sutherland while she was awake. She took her handkerchief from her jacket pocket, dabbed at the tears she could no longer stop from falling, and took an exhausted breath.

'So, to recap. You didn't see the man who wished you a happy New Year,' the sergeant said, almost as if he was speaking to himself, 'and the

47

room was crowded with people singing "Auld Lang Syne?"' His head wobbled unnaturally on his shoulders, as if he was weighing one thing Bess had said against another. 'Hmmm! So, in a crowded room above the noise of dozens of people singing, you are sure that it was Mr Sutherland who--?'

'Yes! I'm sure!' Bess snapped.

'Then why did you need Mrs Burrell to confirm it was him?'

'Because I couldn't believe that after ten years that fascist David Sutherland was still walking the streets!' Bess screamed. 'Of Germany, possibly, but not here, not the streets of Mysterton or Lowarth.'

'What the hell is going on?' Frank shouted, crashing through the door of the office. Sergeant McGann jumped up. His face was red, his mouth turned down at the corners in a sneer. Bess sat behind the desk with her head in her hands.

'I think you'd better leave, McGann.'

'I was only asking Mrs Donnelly--'

'You were not *asking* my wife anything, you were interrogating her.' Frank went over to Bess, stood protectively behind her, and put his hands on her shoulders. 'Good God man, hasn't she been through enough today? Now!' Frank shouted, 'I have asked you to leave once, I shall not ask you again!'

The police sergeant put his notebook in the breast pocket of his tunic and slowly walked across the room. He put his hand on the doorknob, but instead of opening the door, he turned and eyeballed Frank. 'A body has been found in your lake, Mr Donnelly. Does that not concern you at all?'

'Of course it concerns me. It concerns us both a great deal. An accident on our property, causing the loss of a life, is of the utmost concern. But however tragic it is, it has nothing to do with my wife, or myself - or anyone else at the Foxden Hotel. So, unless you can prove otherwise, I'm asking you for the last time to leave!'

Bess parked Frank's old Ford in a side street off the Market Square in Kirby Marlow and wound her way through the market stalls to St Peter's church. Entering by a gate at the rear of the churchyard, she stopped to look at a newly dug grave surrounded by old graves that were so overgrown with brambles and nettles they couldn't have been tended for decades. The oblong hole nudged up to a wire fence that separated Kirby Marlow's departed from the bombed-out buildings of the old railway station, derelict sheds and twisted tracks.

Bess followed the narrow path to the front of the church, arriving at the moment the funeral director began his slow walk into the building, followed by six men bearing a coffin that contained the earthly remains of David Sutherland.

Bess wasn't surprised to see there were no mourners. Traditionally, if the deceased had family or close friends, they followed the coffin into the church out of respect. It didn't look as if Sutherland had any family and he certainly didn't deserve any respect. Bess had no intention of sitting through the church service and praying for

Sutherland's soul. When she heard the door to the vestibule close, she sat down on a stone bench that ran the length of the small porch and waited.

The last funeral she'd attended was her father's. He had been the foundation of the Dudley family. Neither Bess nor her sisters thought they would be able to cope without him, but they did. They didn't fare as well as their mother who, devastated at the time, found an inner strength, which she had probably always had but never needed while her husband was alive. She joined the Women's Institute and busied herself making cakes and jam for various events. She knitted hats, scarves and mittens for war orphans and, although she was a widow herself, was on the Lowarth War Widows Committee and spent three mornings a week visiting young women whose husbands had been killed in the 1939-45 war.

Bess felt a sudden pang of sadness. Thinking about the war always reminded her of James. She smiled at his memory. Her father always said, you never get over losing someone you love, but you do eventually accept it. And that's what Bess had done. Thanks to her father and her husband Frank, she had accepted James's death. What would she do without Frank? He was her strength.

Bess took a sharp involuntary breath. What would Frank do if he knew she had come to Kirby Marlow to see Dave Sutherland put in the ground? She shivered, buttoned up her coat, and looked out of the arched entrance. The sky, no longer pale blue, had turned the colour of tarnished lead and the fluffy white clouds, now black and bulbous, looked as if they were ready to burst. After a week of light winds and warm sunshine, with only the occasional shower, spring appeared to have reverted to winter.

Leaning against the stone arch, looking out into the darkening day, Bess watched the rain begin to fall. Light at first, it soon turned into a heavy downpour. The noise it made on the porch roof drowned out all other sounds. Bess turned back to the door of the church. Even before it started to rain she hadn't heard the muffled voice of the vicar for some time. Crossing to the heavy oak door, she put her ear against it. She couldn't hear anything. The rain was getting heavier and louder. Then, making her jump, she heard the iron latch clunk off its arm, and slowly the door began to open.

Bess grabbed her handbag from the bench and ran. Outside she walked swiftly down the path towards the back gate. Half way along she looked over her shoulder. The funeral procession was in sight. If Bess could see them, they would soon see her. Leaving the path, she ducked behind a hedge. Unless she wanted to be seen there was only one way she could go. So, crouching down, she made her way to the back of the graveyard.

Luckily there was a clump of trees, which would not only give her shelter from the rain, but, standing behind them, she would be able to see the committal without Sutherland's pallbearers seeing her. Her heart was beating fast and her legs were trembling as she watched the small procession leave the narrow path and make their way through the long grass. They took up their positions around the open grave, and through breaks in the wind, Bess caught the words, "Earth to earth, ashes to ashes... in sure and certain hope of the resurrection." She turned away as the coffin was lowered into the ground and began to cry. What on earth had possessed her to come to David Sutherland's funeral?

Bess retreated through the trees and overgrown bushes to the front of the church. The door was open. An elderly woman stood by the baptismal font holding two vases of flowers.

'Come in, dear. Don't mind me. We've got a christening tomorrow,' she said, taking half-a-dozen arum lilies out of two vases and putting the remaining flowers into one. 'What with the price of flowers today, and these chrysies still fresh, it would be a sin to throw them away,' she said, placing the arrangement of chrysanthemums against the pedestal of the font.

Bess stepped into the nave and sat in the nearest pew. No more than a few minutes had passed when she heard the door of the church quietly close. The woman had gone.

A few minutes later the heavy wooden door burst open. Someone, a girl by the sound of her sobs, ran past her down the aisle. Bess lowered her head, pretending to pray.

'Katherine?' a man called from the door. He called the name again, and Bess recognised the voice as Sir Gerald Hawksley's. She heard his heavy footfall as he lumbered down the aisle after his daughter.

Without lifting her head higher than necessary, Bess looked in the direction of Katherine Hawksley's cries and her father's gentle consoling. With her head still bent, as if she was still praying,

Bess slipped out of the pew and crept silently to the door. She looked back at father and daughter. They seemed unaware that anyone else was in the church, or they didn't care - and Bess left unnoticed.

CHAPTER FOUR

'Henry?' Bess flew from behind the reception desk, ran across the hall to the foyer and threw her arms around the neck of her brother-in-law, and old friend, Henry Green. 'What are you doing here?' Leaning to the right, she looked round him at the door. 'Ena not with you?'

'No, she'll be up at the weekend.'

'I've missed her so much since she went back to London after New Year.' Bess shook her head. 'I don't know what I'd have done without her in the months leading up to the opening of the hotel, you know. Well,' Bess said, without taking a breath, 'it wouldn't have opened.' With her arm linked through Henry's, Bess walked him over to reception. 'I'll find someone to take over here and we'll go through to the dining room. Are you hungry? I'm sure Chef will rustle something up for you. George?' Bess called, waving to a young porter who, having seen Henry with a case, had started down the stairs. 'Would you take Mr Green's case up to room...' She turned the page in the hotel's reservations diary. 'You haven't booked in.'

'That's because I'm staying in Lowarth, at the Denbigh Arms.'

'The Denbigh? Why? We've got several vacant rooms. I know room seven is free. A lovely couple and their two daughters were here for a week and they left this morning.' Bess took the bedroom plan from the drawer, opened it and spread it out across the desk, smoothing the creases where it had been folded with the palm of her hand. 'Thirteen is available too, although it doesn't have a view of the lake, which everyone wants-- Oh,' Bess said, folding the bedroom plan and dropping it in the drawer. 'Is that why you're here? Did Frank ask you come up, after--?' Bess looked around to see if any guests were within hearing distance. They weren't, so she continued: 'David Sutherland's body was found in the lake?'

'Frank didn't ask me to come up.' He glanced at George who, hearing Henry say he was staying at the Denbigh, had moved to the bottom of the stairs awaiting instruction. 'But I am here on Military Intelligence business,' he said, quietly.

'Which is why you can't stay here?'

'Something like that. Look, Bess, I don't think we should discuss it here. Is there someone who can stand in for you, so we can talk privately?'

'Yes, Maeve, the receptionist. She's in the staff room tidying her hair. She'll be back any second. Like me she was caught in that awful storm this morning. She went to the dentist in Market Harborough and got soaked waiting for the bus back. Talk about rain! It was torrential. And cold? I got caught in it in Lowarth.' Bess shook her shoulders in an exaggerated shiver. 'Go through the office and make yourself at home. And put a log on the fire, will you? I'm still cold after getting drenched earlier.'

Maeve returned as Henry closed the door to Bess and Frank's office. 'Ena's husband has just arrived. He wants a private word. Are you all right to take over?'

'Yes, of course. Sorry I took so long at the

dentist - and now having to--'

Bess waved the apology away. 'If Frank gets back from the wholesalers before Henry leaves, ask him to pop in.' Maeve put her thumb up and leant forward to answer the ringing telephone.

'What's this about, Henry?' Bess asked, entering the office.

'David Sutherland.'

The bitter sweet taste of bile rose in Bess's stomach and she swallowed hard. 'Damn the man! He has been dead for goodness knows how long and he's still causing grief.' She shivered, for real this time. 'I think I'm coming down with something.' She opened the cupboard in the ornate mahogany sideboard and took out a bottle of brandy. 'Want one?'

'I didn't think you drank the hard stuff, Bess!'

'I don't, very often. I never drink in the daytime, except in extreme circumstances, or for medicinal purposes.' She poured a good measure into two tumblers and gave one to Henry.

'So what's today? An extreme circumstance or a medicinal purpose?'

'Both!' Bess said, and took a swig of her drink. Henry laughed. 'Mm, that hit the spot.' She shivered again. 'Or perhaps not. I still feel chilled to the bone. I got caught in one hell of a downpour earlier. Well, I told you, didn't I? Even my shoes were sodden.'

'That's what happens when you stand for a long time in torrential rain. Especially in an overgrown churchyard on a hill, where the wind cuts across an open space, like a derelict railway yard. That'll chill you to the bone, all right.'

56

Bess lifted her glass to her lips and downed its contents. 'How did you know?'

'What? That you were at Sutherland's funeral?' Bess nodded. 'Because I was there.' Bess put her hand to her mouth. 'Don't worry, no one else saw you.'

'How can you be sure? If you saw me--?'

'Because it's my job to see people but not be seen. I was there to see if any new faces from the fascist movement showed up, or any known ones for that matter. Anyone connected to Sutherland and Hawksley is of interest.'

'And?'

'No one there who shouldn't have been, unfortunately. There were a couple of women in the church who didn't go to the graveside, but there was nothing suspicious about them.'

'I can't think what possessed me to go to his funeral. I expect you know I didn't go to the church service.'

'But you went into the church afterwards.' Bess gave Henry a look of astonishment, closed her eyes and hung her head. 'Did Hawksley or his daughter recognise you?'

'No! I'm certain they didn't. I'm not sure they were aware that anyone else was in the church. I had my head down the entire time I was in there. I would have looked like someone who had come into the building to get out of the rain, and had stayed to pray. That is, if they'd noticed me at all which, as I said, I'm sure they didn't.'

Bess got up and poured herself a single shot of the warming spirit. 'Would you like another?' Henry lifted his glass to show that he still had

57

some left and shook his head. 'I didn't tell Frank I was going to Kirby Marlow and I haven't seen him since I got back, but I will tell him, eventually. He's been so worried about me lately that I think it best not to say anything today.'

Henry took a sip of his drink. 'He won't hear about it from me, as long as you promise you won't do anything that stupid again.' Bess sat up and frowned, pretending to be hurt by her old friend's rebuke. 'I'm serious, Bess. Gerald Hawksley is not the kind of man you want to mess with. He is dangerous.'

'I promise.'

Before Bess had time to ask Henry more about Hawksley the office door flew open and Frank came in. 'Maeve said you were here, Henry.' He took off his hat and coat, hung them on the back of the door, and strode across the room with his hand outstretched. 'It's good to see you. It's been too long,' he said, shaking Henry's hand. He turned and looked around the room. 'Ena not with you?'

Bess laughed. 'That's the first thing I asked.'

Frank turned and kissed Bess. Noticing her glass, he said, 'I don't suppose there's a drop of brandy left for me, darling? As if today wasn't cold enough, I've been standing around in the abattoir at Lowarth for the last hour waiting to see the butcher. I'm frozen.'

Bess grimaced at the thought of the local slaughterhouse and poured her husband a drink.

With one arm draped loosely across Bess's shoulders, Frank lifted his glass to Henry. 'Good health my friend,' Frank took a drink and licked his lips appreciatively. 'Now! Why have you come all this way to see us without your wife? And I want the truth,' he said, walking back to the door and closing it.

'I don't have to remind you that anything I tell you stays within these walls?'

'Of course,' Bess said.

'Understood,' Frank added.

'Military Intelligence has had Sir Gerald Hawksley under the microscope for some years.' Bess gave Frank a knowing look that said, I thought as much. 'When he moved out of London and came up here to live, they weren't too worried. For the first couple of years he played the part of a local landowner and loving father - buying the stables in Kirby Marlow for his daughter Katherine. Except that no one knows exactly how he makes his money, Hawksley appears to be an ordinary but very successful businessman. So while he was minding his own business and leading a quiet life, the security services let him get on with it.'

'I don't think he is an ordinary business man. And having had David Sutherland as a house guest is not leading a quiet life,' Bess said. 'When Constable Peg was here, after the ruckus Sutherland caused on New Year's Eve, he said there were people coming and going from Hawksley's house in Kirby Marlow at all hours of the day and night.'

'McGann shut him up,' Frank put in, 'saying it was only rumour and speculation. Tittle-tattle, he called it, and said the police only deal with facts.'

'But it was obvious that the constable thought something untoward was going on,' Bess said.

'And there is. The men your constable was referring to are fascists, ex-BUF, like Sutherland. Since the end of the war, when the fascists were released from jail, they've been coming to Kirby Marlow on a regular basis. MI5 think - or rather they know - that Gerald Hawksley puts them up for the amount of time it takes him to get them suited-and-booted and procure each of them a new birth certificate and passport. He then gives them enough money to get them started elsewhere, before sending them on their way.'

'If you know all this, why hasn't he been stopped?' Bess asked.

'He will be, eventually. The problem is, Gerald Hawksley is only one person in a network of hundreds of people.'

'Fascists!' Bess spat.

Henry nodded. 'As far as we can tell the network covers the Midlands, the North, parts of Scotland and Northern Ireland. God knows how many people there are living in places like Hawksley's, off the beaten track in the British countryside, or in country houses tucked away in quaint villages. In the early days, when the fascists were first released from prison, there were dozens of wealthy men and women like Hawksley who helped them get set up with new identities and new lives. There aren't as many now, but there are enough. And we think Hawksley is the head of the organisation.'

'If Gerald Hawksley was setting Dave Sutherland up with a new identity, does that mean he's only recently been released from prison?'

'No. Some fascists were released as early as

1943 - Oswald Mosley, for one. Sutherland was released in 1945. The SS organised two main escape routes out of Germany at the end of the war. They were called ratlines, used mostly by escaping German military and spies. But some British fascists "piggy-backed" to get out of England. One ratline went through Spain, and one through Italy. Both ended up in South America, Bolivia, or Switzerland. A few Nazis went on to North America, but it's more likely that Sutherland had been enjoying the good-life in Argentina, or Paraguay.'

'If Sutherland had been having such a wonderful life abroad, why did he want to come back to England?'

Henry looked up to the heavens, as if the answer lie there, and exhaled loudly. 'I can only think of one reason. He must have got himself into serious trouble with some bad people. If he hadn't died, he would most certainly be leaving England for a different country far away, where the government turns a blind eye to Nazis with enough money to buy a small beach bar on the coast. Probably somewhere like Brazil.'

'Could that be why he ended up in the lake? If he was in serious trouble overseas, isn't it possible that someone followed him to England and when the opportunity presented itself, shoved him into the lake? Better still, drowned him somewhere else, and dumped his body in our lake,' Frank said.

Icy fingers gripped Bess's spine and she rolled her shoulders. Having stood inches from the spot where Sutherland's body was found, the police might think she and Margot had something to do with his death. 'Well, no one killed him on New Year's Eve, because Margot and I were right next to the place where his body was found. If there'd been any strangers about we would have seen them.'

'Not necessarily,' Henry said. 'If he was killed - and the police have found nothing so far to suggest he was - it's likely that he met his end at the hands of one of Gerald Hawksley's men. In which case, you wouldn't have seen him, Bess. The *mercenaries* in Hawksley's employ are professionals; they are never seen.'

Henry's brow creased in thought. 'But something has spooked Hawksley. Since the beginning of the year he has sold two houses in London and one on the south coast - and we don't know where the money from any of the sales is. Nor do we know what he plans to do with it. So, until we know exactly what he's up to, MI5 is keeping a low profile.'

Henry looked at Bess. 'My advice to you is do the same. And stay away from Sir Gerald Hawksley and his daughter Katherine.

'And there's something else,' Henry said. 'I told you Hawksley bought stables for his daughter last year. Well, he also accepted a seat on the board of governors at Lowarth's Grammar School.' Bess's eyes widened and she looked at her brother-in-law in disbelief. 'It's true,' Henry nodded. 'It's to get in with the local worthies, integrate with business people. He says he's putting down roots because he wants stability for his daughter. We think he's doing the opposite and one day he'll disappear.

'He has even joined the Lowarth lodge of Freemasons - which,' Henry said with a sardonic smile, 'is the lodge your Sergeant McGann goes to. Hawksley's putting up one hell of a smoke screen.'

Bess laughed. 'Poor old McGann. He won't be so cocky when his fellow Masons find out his pal, Sir Gerald Hawksley, who you can guarantee McGann has been cosying up to, is a Nazi sympathiser.'

'Nor when he finds out the Metropolitan Police are sending up a detective inspector to take over the Sutherland case.'

'What?' Bess and Frank said at the same time.

'Yes. I don't have the details - they're still with the Leicestershire Coroner - but because of Sutherland's connection to Hawksley and the fascist movement there's a possibility that on the night he drowned there was foul play. Detective Inspector Masters will inform Sergeant McGann tomorrow. Masters is six months away from retiring on a good pension and, according to my boss, was content to sit behind a desk and shuffle papers until he left. But when he heard someone from his division was needed to take charge of an enquiry into David Sutherland's death, he volunteered for the job.

'He's ex-Army, won medals for bravery, and has at least one medal for Gallantry from the Met. He's got a reputation for being a bit of a bulldog. He's a good copper and gets results. If he hadn't joined up in 1940, he'd probably be a Chief Superintendent now.'

'Fancy volunteering to put himself in danger, when he could spend the rest of his time on the force taking it easy.'

'My boss at MI5 reckons he has an agenda, which is another reason I'm here.'

Frank laughed. 'McGann won't like working with a detective inspector from London. The arrogant little bugger thinks he knows it all.'

'Detective Inspector Masters will have the pleasure of informing Sergeant McGann of many things that he won't like when he takes over the case.'

'I'll drink to McGann having his nose put out of joint.' Frank drained his glass. 'And what about you, Henry?'

'DI Masters knows I work for MI5, but as far as McGann's concerned I'm attached to Military Intelligence. If he asks me why the military is involved, I'll say we had a tip-off that a couple of men have been seen in the grounds of one of the old top-secret communications facilities in the area, and I've been sent up here to check it out. I'll have to tell him I have clearance to assist with police enquiries, or he might try to stop me.

'And, to ensure McGann doesn't tell Hawksley during a trouser lifting at a Free Mason's meeting, I'll tell him it's all very hush-hush and in no circumstances should he talk about the case, or my part in it, to anyone. Whether he swallows it or not, I don't really care. But I'm as big a fish in my field as Masters is in his, so if he thinks he knows something the DI doesn't know, he might just be conceited enough to keep shtum. I expect he'll delight in getting one over on a high-ranking officer, and at the same time think he's in my good books. We'll see.'

That night, having left the sleeping hotel in the capable hands of Mr Potts, the night porter, Frank followed Bess up to their small suite of rooms. 'What did Henry mean today, when he said stay away from Hawksley and his daughter?' Frank asked, climbing into bed.

Bess, having already settled down for the night, turned over and pushed herself up on her elbows. She looked at her husband and felt her cheeks flush. 'I did something stupid today, Frank.' She bit her bottom lip. 'I went to David Sutherland's funeral.'

'I know.'

'You know? But how?' Bess demanded. 'Did Henry tell you?'

'No. I followed you.' Bess shot Frank a look of disbelief. She was about to ask him why he had done such an untrusting thing, but he answered her before she could formulate the words. 'To make sure you didn't get into trouble.'

'But the abattoir?' Mimicking Bess, Frank pretended to be shy and bit his lip the way Bess had done. 'You didn't go to the abattoir, did you? You are as bad as me, Frank Donnelly!'

Bess leaned into her husband and kissed him. 'I do love you, Frank,' she said, wriggling down in the bed and wrapping her arms around him.

'And I love you, Bess,' her husband said, lifting her body to his.

CHAPTER FIVE

Lowarth police station, the police house where McGann and his family lived, and the Magistrates' Court, had been built in an oddly shaped triangular block. Surrounding a courtyard, the narrow building looked as if it had been squeezcd in between the Leicester Road and the Gilmorton Road. It consisted of the main door to the police station - with a window on either side - that faced down Market Street, the police house that looked onto Lower Leicester Road - and the public entrance to the Magistrates Court on Gilmorton Road. Bess suspected there were cells there too. Not to imprison criminals long term, but holding cells to keep prisoners in until they came up before the Bench.

Lowarth Magistrates' Court was held on Thursdays. According to Elsie Bramley, Foxden Hotel's housekeeper who was in charge of the domestic staff, the public gallery was always full. She knew this because her day off was Thursday and she was a regular attendee.

Bess and Margot sat in the narrow corridor outside Sergeant McGann's office waiting for him to return from the railway station where, according to Constable Peg, he had been ordered to collect a detective inspector from the Metropolitan Police in London. 'And he is not best pleased,' the constable said.

'How do you feel about working with a policeman from London, Constable?' Bess asked.

'I'm looking forward to it. I don't want to work

66

in Lowarth all my life, like Sergeant McGann. Nothing against Lowarth, like, but if I stay here I won't get promotion until the sergeant retires - or dies.' The constable's face coloured. 'I didn't mean…'

'We know what you meant,' Bess said, smiling at him reassuringly. 'And what does Sergeant McGann think about a detective inspector coming up from London?'

The constable shrugged his shoulders. 'I bet he's seething,' Margot said. 'Go on, you can tell us. We won't say anything, will we Bess?'

'Ignore my sister, Constable Peg, she's being nosey.'

'Mrs Burrell's right.' The young policeman looked nervously over his shoulder at the door. 'He's fuming,' he whispered, conspiratorially. 'When the Metropolitan Police telephoned to say they were sending someone up to take over the Sutherland case, Sergeant McGann straight-way rang the Chief Constable. He told the chief that sending someone up from London was as good as telling the people of Lowarth that his superiors had no confidence in him. He said it sounded as if they didn't think he was capable of dealing with a drowning.'

'I don't like the man, but I can imagine how he feels,' Bess said.

'And military intelligence is sending someone up too. The sergeant called him a pen-pusher, a bloody conchie, who most likely sat in an office while our brave boys fought for their country.'

'Which of the armed forces did Sergeant McGann serve in?' Bess asked.

'He didn't. How he tells it, he was too young to fight in the first war, and too old to fight in the last one.'

Margot looked at Bess, her face like thunder. Bess moved her head slightly from left to right, to warn her sister not to react. Margot smiled through gritted teeth. 'Between them, the policeman from London and the man from the military might bring your boss down a peg or two. The arrogant B,' she said under her breath.

'How much longer are we going to have to wait? If neither Sergeant McGann, or the DI from London are here, it's pointless us being here.'

'Shouldn't be long now, Miss.' The bell on the counter in the police station dinged and the constable left, gesturing that he'd be back.

'Fancy McGann calling Henry a conchie. Ignorant bugger.'

'I'd like to be a fly on the wall when McGann finds out the military man is Henry Green, the local butcher's son, born and bred in Lowarth.' Bess looked at Margot and they both burst out laughing.

'Quiet! I can hear voices,' Margot said. The door at the end of the corridor opened and a man in his mid-fifties, about six feet tall and well-built, with fair, greying hair, breezed in smiling. Behind him, looking as if he had stood in something unpleasant, was Lowarth's sour-faced Sergeant McGann.

The Detective Inspector introduced himself to Bess and Margot, thanked them for waiting and asked if they would bear with him a little longer. He looked at Sergeant McGann who, breathing

68

through flared nostrils, led the inspector into his office.

Margot began to giggle and Bess elbowed her in the ribs. 'Shush, they'll hear you.' Margot mouthed sorry and did her best to keep a straight face. But when Bess made a show of reading notices on the Police Public Information board, she burst into laughter. Bess, seeing the funny side, laughed with her.

'Haven't seen you do that for a long time,' Margot said, when she had stopped giggling.

'What?'

'Laugh.'

'No, well there hasn't been much to laugh about recently. But after today, things should start getting back to normal. Ena's coming up at the weekend, which will be nice. And the hotel's full at Easter.'

'Bill and me are looking forward to coming to Foxden at Easter. I wish we could come over more often, but with the school...'

'I know. I don't expect you to run the dancing school, look after Bill, and--' Margot started to laugh again. 'What now?' Bess asked.

'You, saying I look after Bill. It's him who looks after me.'

'Of course he does, what with you being a princess an' all.'

'Miss Dudley?' the Detective Inspector called, taking Margot and Bess by surprise. They both stood up as he approached.

'Sorry,' Bess said, 'we are - were - both Dudley before we were married.' She put out her hand. 'I'm Bess Donnelly now and this is my sister,

Margot Burrell.'

Detective Inspector Masters gave the sisters a sparkling smile. 'Pleased to meet you both. Thank you for coming in at short notice. Now,' he said, looking at Margot, 'I believe it was you, Mrs Burrell, who had the most to do with David Sutherland in London?'

'Yes. I worked with his girlfriend at the Prince Albert Theatre.'

'Then perhaps if you wouldn't mind, Mrs Donnelly, I'll interview Mrs Burrell first?'

'My sister and I both spoke to David Sutherland at the hotel on New Year's Eve, Inspector, and we were interviewed together by Sergeant McGann.' Margot looked nervously at Bess.

'Don't worry, Margot, I'll be here if you need me,' Bess said, and sat down. Margot wrinkled her nose and followed the inspector into Sergeant McGann's office.

Detective Inspector Masters pulled out a chair from beneath Sergeant McGann's desk. 'Take a seat, Miss Dudley.'

'Thank you.'

Margot sat down and the Inspector walked round to the other side of the desk. Before sitting down in Sergeant McGann's chair, the London policeman heaped together an assortment of papers that were spread over McGann's desk, stacked them into a rough pile, and put them on the window ledge. When the desk was clear, he took several large brown envelopes from his briefcase. 'Sergeant McGann's notes,' he said and, smiling, lined them up side by side across the width of the desk.

There was something familiar about the London policeman. Perhaps it was his accent. Margot returned his smile. He was friendly and courteous where Sergeant McGann was remote and self-important. The inspector opened the first of the envelopes, took out a handful of photographs and smiled again. Something McGann never did.

'These photographs were taken on New Year's Eve by a local newspaper man. Would you look at them and tell me if you recognise anyone from the time you lived and worked in London?'

London? It had been four years since she was last in London for any length of time. 'Do you mean from the time I knew David Sutherland?'

'Yes. Anyone who might have been around when Sutherland was walking out with Miss Trick?'

Desperate to find someone, to save Bess from being questioned, Margot scrutinised each photograph. 'Sorry, there's no one from those days other than myself and Sutherland.'

'How about someone who hadn't been invited to the New Year's Eve party? A stranger perhaps, or someone who is somewhere that they shouldn't be?'

Margot shook her head. 'I don't know who had an invitation, who had called in because it was the opening of the hotel, or who were guests staying there. Sorry not to be of more help.'

'That's fine, Miss Dudley. I mean, Mrs Burrell. Thank you. It isn't often the police are lucky enough to have a photographic record of the events leading up to a crime. It was a long shot, but worth asking.' The inspector took a notebook from the second envelope. 'You and your sister gave statements to Sergeant McGann about the disagreement between David Sutherland and Sir Gerald Hawksley on New Year's Eve - and the events afterwards,' Margot nodded. 'Do you have anything to add? Has anything come to mind since that night that could help us with our enquiry?' Margot shook her head. 'The smallest thing, something that you might think is insignificant, could be very important.'

'No. Nothing,' Margot said.

'Then thank you for your time, Mrs Burrell.' The inspector stood up, took a card from his pocket and gave it to Margot. 'If you remember anything, anything at all, that you think could help us find David Sutherland's killer, would you telephone me?'

Killer? Sutherland was killed? Margot got to her feet, but was too shocked to move. She watched the inspector walk across the room to the door and open it. She heard him ask Bess to come in and take a seat. His voice sounded distant and it echoed, as if he was speaking in a tunnel.

'Mrs Burrell?' The inspector calling her name brought Margot out of her daze. She began to walk to the door, but halted half way across the room. She needed to warn her sister, tell her the shocking news that Sutherland's death had not been an accident. She started to walk again. Although she had found her feet, she hadn't found her voice.

At the door, Margot looked back. Bess was already seated. 'See you in Mrs Crabbe's café,' Bess said. Margot nodded, but didn't answer, and with a pleasant but professional smile that said both thank you and goodbye, the inspector closed the door.

'Sorry to have kept you waiting, Mrs Donnelly.'

Bess smiled nervously. 'I told Sergeant McGann everything I knew about David Sutherland on New Year's Eve. I'm not sure I can add anything that would be of help.'

'Perhaps not. However, due to recent developments, I'd like to show you some photographs that were taken that night. Would you to tell me if you recognise anyone from your time in London.'

Bess looked through the photographs carefully and shook her head. 'It's been ten years since I lived in London. I came back to Foxden in October 1939. I honestly don't think I would recognise anyone that I didn't know really well from that time,' she said, laying down the photographs.

'Thank you.' The inspector flicked through the photographs, taking some out. 'Your sister said there were local people in the public bar who were nothing to do with the New Year's Eve party.' Bess nodded. 'I don't expect you to know everyone who visited the hotel that night, but is there anyone in these photographs who looked out of place, seemed odd to you, or was acting suspiciously?' Bess shook her head. The inspector handed her the rest of the photographs. 'If you don't mind looking through them again? Does anyone strike you as being in the wrong place - an invited guest, or a member of the staff? Someone who is somewhere they shouldn't be...?'

73

'Except for David Sutherland you mean?' The inspector gave her a lopsided grin. 'No,' Bess said, 'everyone's where they should be, where I remember them being at the time.' There was something not quite right, but Bess couldn't put her finger on it. She stacked the photographs and placed them on top of the envelope. 'I'm sorry.'

'I have your statement here.' The policeman laid his hand on Sergeant McGann's notes from New Year's Eve. 'It is often the case that witnesses remember things at a later date, or when they are on their own, that they hadn't thought of when they were interviewed with someone else. Witnesses to the same thing at the same time sometimes rely on each other. I'm sure that isn't the case with you and your sister. Nevertheless, if there is anything you'd like to add to your original statement?'

'No, I'm sorry.' Bess wrung her hands beneath the desk. 'I'm afraid there isn't.'

'Thank you. If you think of anything…'

'I shall be sure to let you know.'

'If I need to speak to you again, Mrs Donnelly, would it be all right if I came to the hotel?'

'Yes of course, Inspector. I'm always there. Some days are busier than others and some times of the day are busier, but if you let me know before you come, give me a couple of hours' notice, I'll arrange for cover.'

As he had done with Margot, the inspector walked Bess to the door and opened it.

'You're going to a lot of trouble for a Nazi sympathiser who drowned,' Bess said.

'David Sutherland didn't drown, Mrs Donnelly,

he was murdered.' Bess's pulse quickened, but she felt neither concern, nor surprise. 'The coroner thinks it was as long ago as New Year's Eve.' Unmoved by the news, Bess showed no emotion. 'That doesn't worry you?'

'What? That Sutherland was murdered? Or that it was on New Year's Eve?'

'That he was murdered in the grounds of your hotel, after an argument with you.'

'Not at all. Since it wasn't me who murdered him, why would it? Besides, I wasn't the only person Sutherland argued with. Sir Gerald Hawksley had more reason to kill Sutherland than I did.' The inspector raised his eyebrows. 'My father had a saying, which I'm sure you've heard many times. If you live by the sword, be prepared to die by the sword. David Sutherland was an evil man who lived very much by the sword. Perhaps he got what he deserved.'

Walking along the corridor, Bess could feel the inspector's eyes on her back. Her legs felt as if they were made of cotton wool, but she walked with an even footfall, her pace steady, and her back straight. Once she was outside she slumped against the wall and shook uncontrollably. Sutherland murdered? Her head was spinning. That was what Henry meant when he said foul play. She thought she was going to faint and bent over. With her hands on her knees, to keep her balance, Bess began to breath slowly and deeply until she felt less lightheaded.

When she had regained her self-control, Bess walked from the police station to Mrs Crabbe's Café on Market Street.

Margot jumped up as she entered. 'Did he tell you that Sutherland was killed, murdered?'

'Yes.' Bess put her hands around the tea pot. It was still warm. She poured herself a cup and offered the rest to Margot.

She shook her head. 'You have it. The thought of it makes me feel sick. My tummy's like a coiled spring.' Bess topped up her cup and added milk. 'I wonder who it was,' Margot said.

Bess's brow puckered. It took her a minute to grasp what her sister was referring to. 'I don't know. McGann suspects me,' Bess said. 'I think this London copper does too.'

'Why would that nice inspector suspect you? He doesn't know about you and Sutherland does he?'

'No. I told him less than I told Sergeant McGann at New Year. You didn't say anything, did you?'

'No! How could you even think I would?'

'I'm sorry, Margot. Of course you wouldn't. I don't know why I even asked.' Bess swallowed the last of the tepid tea and pulled a face. 'I'm just sick and tired of hearing that damn man's name. Frank and I worked so hard to make sure everything was perfect for the opening of the hotel on New Year's Eve, and then Sutherland turned up and did his best to ruin it. Because he didn't show his face again I thought we'd seen the last of him.'

'Well you have now.'

'Thanks for reminding me. We'll probably see cancellations for Easter too, once the newspapers get hold of the story.' Bess shook her head. 'Frank will be devastated.'

'I think he likes the hotel business as much as you do,' Margot said.

'He does.' In spite of feeling angry, Bess laughed. 'He's in his element when we have children staying. He loves taking them to see the animals, leading them round the paddock on the pony, and letting them collect the eggs in the mornings.' Emotion rose like a lump in Bess's throat and she looked down and swallowed.

'It's so damn unfair. You'd have made a wonderful mother.'

'It's worse for Frank.' Tears began to fall and Bess didn't hold them back. 'I came to terms with not having children a long time ago. Frank says he's okay with it, but I know he'd love to be a father.'

'He probably would. But he adores you, Bess. As long as he has you, he's happy.'

'That's what he says, but it must be hard for him. He's the one who would make a wonderful parent. He's so patient with children, so understanding,' Bess wiped her tears and put on a smile. 'Right!' She looked at her wristwatch. 'It's time we left. Your bus will be here soon.'

Margot leant across the table and put her hand on Bess's hand, to stop her from getting up. 'There's no rush. Let's talk. I'll catch a later bus.'

'We'll have plenty of time to talk on Sunday, when you and Bill come to the hotel for lunch. We'll find a quiet corner after church.' Bess moved her hand from under Margot's and looked at her watch again. 'Good Lord, I've been out all morning; Frank will wonder where I've got to.'

Margot looked up at Bess, her eyes glossy with

tears. 'What is it, sweetheart?' Bess asked. 'What on earth's the matter?'

Smiling through her tears, Margot said, 'I'm pregnant.'

'But that's wonderful, Margot.' Bess leapt out of her chair. 'Come here,' she said, pulling her sister to her feet and hugging her. 'I'm so pleased for you, darling.'

'Thank you, Bess. You're the first person I've told.'

'I hope you've told Bill,' Bess joked.

Margot made an effort to laugh. 'I have. And he's walking around like the cat that got the cream. But,' Margot said, sitting down, 'I haven't told Mam, Ena or Claire. So don't say anything if you see them. I'll call in and tell Mam on Sunday morning. And I'll tell the girls after church. I wanted to tell you first, because I didn't want it to be a shock. I know how much you'd have loved a child.' Margot's eyes filled again.

'Shush! This is supposed to be one of the happiest times in your life. Don't spoil it worrying about me. I shall just have to be the best aunt in the world.'

Margot laughed again. 'I'm sure you will be. Sorry, I'm feeling emotional - or even more emotional.' Bess squeezed Margot's hand. 'The doctor said it's natural when you're having a baby. Like morning sickness. He says that's natural for the first three months.'

'So, when can I expect to have a new niece, or nephew?' Bess asked, counting the months on her fingers.

'We think the end of September.' Margot bit

her bottom lip and blushed scarlet. 'They say sleeping in a strange bed can do it.'

'What? Did you conceive on New Year's Eve?'

Margot giggled. 'I know it wasn't a romantic night, with everything that happened, but when I got to our room I was cold, and…'

'I get the picture. There's no need to go into detail,' Bess said, laughing.

Bess paid Mrs Crabbe and followed Margot out of the café and round the corner into Church Street. 'I'll see you on Sunday,' Margot said, kissing Bess goodbye as the bus came into view. 'Give my love to Ena, but--' Margot put her forefinger to her lips.

Bess shook her head. 'Not a word, I promise.'

'You can tell Frank, but you must swear him to secrecy.' Bess nodded. 'I don't want him to be shocked when I tell the family on Sunday, bless him. But don't tell anyone else,' Margot repeated, excitedly. The bus pulled up in front of the two sisters. 'Tell our Ena I'll be at the hotel early, so the four of us - I hope Claire can make it - can have a proper natter.'

'It's Easter, don't forget, so we'll be going to church,' Bess reminded Margot, above the noise of the bus's idling engine.

'Oh, and Bess,' Margot shouted as she boarded, 'make sure you and Frank get someone to cover you. It would be lovely if we could all sit down together for once, and have a proper Sunday dinner.'

'I'll ask Maeve to come in.'

'That would be great!' Margot waved out of the window as the bus pulled away from the kerb.

'Congratulate Bill for me,' Bess shouted. Margot put her thumbs up, and then blew her sister a kiss.

Bess had twenty minutes to wait for the bus that stopped at Foxden and Woodcote, and several other villages en route to Market Harborough. She decided to do a little browsing in Kimpton Smith's. Kimp's - as it was known locally - began life as a draper and haberdasher. Now, although there was still rationing, it stocked everything from ladies clothes and lingerie - to household goods. Mrs Kimpton Smith also owned the second-hand furniture shop on the left of the main shop, and the gentlemen's outfitters on the right. Together, the three outlets were the nearest thing the small market town of Lowarth had to a city department store.

During the last year Bess had spent very little money on herself. She needed a summer nightgown, but having to spend so much money on the hotel, she'd put it off and off until it was winter. Now the nights were warmer she could wait no longer and strode into Kimpton Smith's with determination.

Once inside, instead of going up the grand stairway in the centre of the foyer to women's wear, Bess followed the sign for the children's department. She had no intention of buying anything for Margot and Bill's baby today - it was much too soon - but her eyes were drawn to a stand displaying little dresses in pink and cream with smocking on the bodices. Next to the dresses were summer coats. Bess's eyes settled on a pink coat with a Little Bo-Peep style hat. She moved on. More practical for an autumn baby were the vests and socks, bootees and mittens - and winceyette nightdresses. Bess picked one up and held it to her cheek. It was very soft, and very pretty.

'Are you looking for anything in particular, Bess?' Mrs Kimpton Smith asked, with her head in an inquisitive tilt and a knowing glint in her eyes.

'Not really. I've just had news that a friend of mine in London is having a baby. I thought I'd buy something that was suitable for a girl or a boy, and post it to her.'

'I have just the thing.' Mrs Kimpton Smith bobbed down behind the counter. 'These have just come in,' she said, springing up and putting a white box with a silver stencil of a sleeping baby on the glass counter top. 'They're not cheap,' she warned, lifting the lid, 'but then you can't put a price on quality, can you?'

Bess caught her breath. 'No,' she said, 'you can't.'

The shop owner laid three shawls on white tissue paper. One was pastel pink, one powder blue, and the third was a delicate shade of pale yellow. Bess picked up the yellow shawl. 'I'll take this one, please,' she said, forcing herself not to show the emotion that was bubbling up inside her.

'A wise choice,' Mrs Kimpton Smith said, and summoned a shop assistant to take over from her. 'Wrap this shawl for Mrs Donnelly. It's a gift, which has to go in the post, so use the sturdiest brown paper,' she said. 'Is there anything else I can do for you, Bess?'

'Not today, but the mother-to-be is a very good

friend, so I'll be in again.'

'I look forward to seeing you soon, then.' And with that Mrs Kimpton Smith left the children's department.

The assistant waited for the owner to leave the floor and turned to Bess. 'Would you like it wrapped in tissue paper first? I'll tie a bow round it too. It'll look much prettier. I'll wrap it in the strong paper afterwards, so it'll be safe to post.'

'Thank you, that would be lovely.' Bess watched the girl fold the shawl carefully and wrap it in white tissue paper, before laying it in its box. She then took several sheets of tissue paper and some ribbon, wrapped the box, and tied a bow around it.

'I'd like to show my husband before I send it, so I'll parcel it up for posting when I get home.'

The shop assistant cut off a length of thick brown paper, folded it, and put it in a bag with the box containing the shawl. Bess thanked her, paid, and left the shop, all thoughts of a summer nightdress for herself forgotten.

Delighted for Margot and Bill, and pleased with the shawl, Bess skipped down High Street to the bus stop. 'Miss Hawksley?'

'Mrs Donnelly?' Katherine Hawksley looked as shocked to see Bess, as Bess was to see her.

Henry had advised Bess to stay away from Katherine and Sir Gerald Hawksley, but he hadn't taken into account that Lowarth was a small place and the bus that went to Foxden went to Kirby Marlow - and beyond - where Katherine Hawksley lived.

Katherine's face was deathly white and she

looked as if she had lost half her body weight since New Year's Eve. 'How are you, Miss Hawksley?' Bess ask, expecting the girl to say she was suffering from some dreadful illness.

'Fine, thank you,' she said, in a voice that was no more than a whisper.

'You don't look fine, dear. Would you like me to take you home in a taxi? It won't take me a minute to--'

'No!' Katherine Hawksley spat out the word so quickly that Bess stepped back, startled. She put up her hands to signal that she understood and was careful not to move. The girl lowered her head and began to tremble. 'Thank you, but-- I--'

'What is it?' Bess asked.

Katherine looked up, her eyes darting left and right. 'I'm sorry,' she cried, backing away from Bess. 'I really am so, so, sorry.'

'You have nothing to be sorry for.' Bess put down her bags and caught hold of Katherine's arm to stop her from falling off the kerb onto the busy main road. 'If it's New Year's Eve you're referring to, none of what happened was your fault.'

'It was, 'she said, nodding frantically. 'Everything was my fault. If it hadn't been for me, Daddy--' The girl looked like a frightened animal. 'I have to go.' All of a sudden, as if it was the first time she had seen Bess, she said, haughtily, 'Sergeant McGann has warned me about you. He said I was not to speak to you, Mrs Donnelly!'

Katherine looked up and down High Street, as if she was waiting for a break in the traffic before crossing. Instead she ran in front of an oncoming car. The car swerved to miss her, as she zigzagged across the busy thoroughfare, mounted the pavement and almost hit Bess. The driver of the car made a fist at Katherine, then turned to Bess and mouthed, I'm sorry. When the car drove off, Katherine Hawksley had vanished.

CHAPTER SIX

Bess boarded the bus shaking. She was still wobbly on her legs when she left the bus at Foxden. Walking down the lane a thought stopped her in her tracks. Had Katherine Hawksley run in front of the car on Lowarth High Street on purpose? If she had, was it her intention to kill herself, or was it a cry for help? Bess felt a shudder go through her and forced her legs to jog the rest of the way to the hotel.

In her haste to get home, impatient to tell Frank that she had seen Katherine Hawksley, how ill she looked, and that she had almost got herself killed, Bess had hurried past her mother's cottage. It wasn't until she was at the top of the drive that she remembered she'd promised Margot she would call and ask her mother to come up to the hotel for a family lunch on Sunday. 'Damn,' she said aloud. 'I'll have to go back later.'

Seeing Katherine Hawksley in such a state had taken the joy out of buying the shawl. But Bess was determined not to let it dampen the exciting news that her sister was going to have a baby. 'Hello Maeve,' she called, entering the hotel.

The receptionist gave Bess a welcoming smile. 'Mrs Green's in your office.'

'Oh good. Is Frank back?'

'Yes, he's feeding the animals. He said he was going to clean out the stable. We have two families booked in for the Easter Holiday and Mr Donnelly said if the weather is good the children will want to ride the pony.'

Bess laughed. 'He'll have them out there with the animals whatever the weather. I don't suppose he's had anything to eat?' Maeve shook her head. 'He forgets to eat himself, but he never forgets to feed the pony.' Bess got as far as the door to the office and stopped. 'Oh, I almost forgot. Would you put this box somewhere out of sight?' She whispered, handing Maeve the parcel containing the shawl. 'It's a surprise for Frank, but I don't want him to see it yet.' Bess felt an embarrassed flush creep up her neck. She wasn't a good liar, even when she was telling a white one.

'I'll put it in the bottom drawer.' Maeve opened the deep drawer on the right-hand side of the desk and laid the parcel in it. 'Jack's coming in early; just tell him where it is when you want it.' She looked at her wristwatch. 'I'll be leaving shortly, if it's still all right?'

'Of course,' Bess said, looking puzzled. Maeve didn't usually take time off without giving her plenty of warning.

'Inspector Masters wants to interview me,' she said. 'He wanted to come here, but I thought it would be better for the guests if I went into the police station.'

Bess felt her cheeks colour. Maeve's interview had gone clean out of her mind. 'Thanks for reminding me. I'd forget my head if it wasn't screwed on. If Jack hasn't arrived to take over from you by the time you need to leave, give me a shout and I'll cover until he gets here. If I don't see you before you go, good luck.' Bess opened the door to the office, but before she went in she looked back at Maeve. 'Thank you for being so considerate.'

'Who's considerate?' Ena asked, jumping up from the seat under the window and throwing her arms around her sister.

'Maeve,' Bess said, hugging Ena. 'She's…'

'What? You're looking all mysterious. What did she do that's considerate?'

They walked across the room together, Ena sat down in the window seat and Bess walked over to the table where the electric kettle was kept.

'Well?' Ena said.

'It's nothing really.' Bess picked up the kettle and gave it a shake. It was full, so she switched it on. 'It's just that the inspector from London wanted to interview her here, but Maeve said no because of the guests. That's what I meant by considerate. It's uncanny, but she thinks like me. I mean, about things to do with the hotel. She considers the guests in the same way that I do. Guests come first, kind of thing.' Bess laughed. 'She could run this place with her eyes closed. I'm not sure I like that,' she said, putting on a frown and pretending to be worried. 'Seriously though, she's very efficient. I don't know what I'd do without her. If she ever leaves I'll have a hard job finding a replacement.'

'I don't think she will, not in the foreseeable future anyway. She was telling me earlier that she loves her job. She was stationed near Kirby Marlow in the war and became friends with the vicar and his wife at St Peter's. She said on the occasions she visited them after the war, it was like coming home. She's staying with them now, but she wants somewhere permanent so she's looking for a place to rent.'

'That's odd.'

'What is? That she's looking to rent, or that she wants to live here permanently?'

'Both. Her job here is permanent. I mean, she can give a week's notice anytime she likes, but if she loves it, why would she? And if she wanted, she could live in. I gave her the choice when I offered her the post of receptionist. I wonder where she's from,' Bess mused. 'Being stationed somewhere didn't mean you came from the place. Look at Claire. She was stationed in Lancashire, until she went overseas.'

Bess made the tea and took a cup over to Ena. 'Are you staying here tonight, or at the Denbigh with Henry?'

'Here if you'll have me. Perhaps I had better ask Maeve?'

Bess laughed. 'I'd be careful if I was you while I'm drinking hot tea. I'd hate to spill it on you.'

Ena brought Bess up to date with what Henry was doing. 'The main reason he's here is to find out as much as he can about Sir Gerald Hawksley.'

'That reminds me. I ran into Katherine Hawksley at the bus stop in Lowarth earlier,' Bess cut in. 'She looked ill. She was thin, her face was as white as a sheet and she was a bag of nerves. She was twitching like a frightened animal and wringing her hands. And she kept saying she was sorry.'

'About what?' Ena asked.

'No idea. I asked her if she meant she was sorry about what happened on New Year's Eve, but she just said again that she was sorry. Thinking about it,' Bess said, 'it felt as if she was saying sorry to me personally.'

'She didn't cause the trouble at New Year, so why would she apologise for it? It doesn't make sense,' Ena said.

'No, it doesn't, but I'm sure it was personal. She might have meant she was sorry about the things Sutherland said to me on New Year's Eve.' Bess lifted her shoulders. 'Who knows? Oh, and she said, "If it hadn't been for me, Daddy--" Then she said she had to go. She said Sergeant McGann had warned her about me, told her not to speak to me.'

'I don't think you should speak to her either,' Ena said, 'not with Gerald Hawksley being a big shot in the British Patriots.'

'If the poor girl's been exposed to fascists and the like, it's no wonder she was nervous. And there's something else. Katherine started to look up and down the road. I didn't think anything of it at first; she'd been jittery and on edge since we first spoke, but when the road was at its busiest she ran into the traffic. It was as if she did it on purpose. Thank the Lord the driver of the first car slammed on his breaks. He swerved one way and the car behind him swerved the other. I don't know how they did it, but they both managed to miss her.'

'Good Lord!' Ena exclaimed. 'The silly girl could have been killed.'

'So could I. To miss Katherine Hawksley the driver of the first car had to turn the wheel sharply. If the kerb in front of the bus stop hadn't been so high, the car would have mounted the pavement and mowed me down.'

'What? Are you all right?'

'I'm fine. I was shaken up at the time, I don't mind telling you, but I'm all right now.'

'What happened to Katherine? Where did she go?'

'No idea. She must have weaved her way through the traffic to the other side of High Street. I couldn't follow her at the time and there was no point me going after her later. By the time the road was safe to cross she could have been anywhere.'

As arranged, the sisters and their mother met in the foyer after breakfast on Easter Sunday morning. The plan was to walk to church together, as they always did whenever they were all at Foxden.

'Right. Are we ready?'

'No, Margot isn't here. She'll be titivating her hair I expect,' Claire said.

Lily Dudley looked worried. 'She might be feeling poorly.'

Bess knew her mother was right. Margot was more than likely being sick, not fussing with her hair, but she didn't want her mother to give the game away and spoil the surprise Margot had planned for her sisters. 'She's fine, Mam,' Bess said pointedly, nudging her mother as she passed. 'Go and round up the men, Ena. I need a hankie. I'll knock on Margot's door on the way to my room and chivvy her along.'

'Are you nearly ready, Margot? Bess asked, tapping the door. 'It's time we left for church if we don't want to be late.'

Margot opened the door and heaved in Bess's

direction. Bess jumped back and Margot burst into laughter.

'That wasn't funny,' Bess said.

'Sorry, but that's what I feel like all the time. Morning sickness is supposed to get better as the time goes on. Most people don't have it after three months. Talk about pregnant women blooming? I feel bloomin' worse every day.'

'You'd have to be different, Margot.' Bess looked closely at her sister's face. 'You do look peaky. Put some rouge on, or rub a bit of lipstick into your cheeks.' Margot sauntered back to the dressing table and peered into the mirror. 'But be quick, or we'll miss the beginning of the service.' Margot dabbed at her face with the rouge pad and stood back to admire herself. 'There's no time for preening, lady, come on.' Bess led her sister out of the room.

Claire and Ena were waiting at the foot of the stairs, already in their Sunday hats and spring coats. Claire, always the sharpest, spotted Margot's high colour. 'You look flushed, Margot, you're not coming down with something, are you?'

Bess pressed her lips together to stop herself from laughing. 'She's fine, aren't you? She's just overdone the rouge. It's the light in that room. I'll get Frank to put a higher watt bulb in it,' she said, rubbing Margot's cheeks with her handkerchief. 'There, perfect!'

'Well, what are you waiting for, Claire? Ena?' Bess said, winking at Margot.

'Cheek!' Claire cried, and grabbing Bess's hand pretended to drag her out of the hotel. Margot and Bill, and Ena and Henry, followed with Frank and

Mitch on either side of their mother-in-law.

The sisters and their husbands walked into the ancient Cotswold stone Church of St. Leonard, Mysterton, and down the aisle behind the matriarch of the family, Lily Dudley. Rays of dappled sunshine radiated through the stained glass windows, bathing the congregation in pale pink and soft golden light. Arrangements of daffodils, tulips, hyacinths and azaleas filled boat-shaped vases on the window ledges. Long-stemmed arums skirted the altar like a floral petticoat and the familiar sweet fragrance of lavender polish and vanilla candles filled the air.

The Crucifix stood opposite the pulpit and was decorated with dark blue Sea Holly thistle, and Milk and Scotch Cotton thistle. The thorny bunches were held in place by coloured raffia wound around the Cross's simple plain oak plinth. At the foot of the Cross was a basket of eggs, which had been painted in bright colours by the children of St. Leonard's Sunday School.

The sisters took their seats. There were no rules as to where anyone in the congregation sat for Sunday, or any other service at Mysterton Church, but the Dudley family had been worshiping there - and sitting in the same seats - for so many years that the front pew was unofficially reserved for them.

The Church was full. It always was at Christmas and Easter. Mysterton Church was where Lily and Tom Dudley were married, the Dudley siblings were christened, where Margot and Bill and Bess and Frank were married, and where their father Tom Dudley's funeral service was held. That was a year ago, but it felt like yesterday, Bess thought. She still missed her father, all her sisters did. He had been a calming influence and the voice of reason to the sisters.

When the service had finished, Bess walked down the footpath, leaving Frank talking to the Vicar. 'Always willing to give,' Bess heard Frank say, 'but I can't stop now, I need to get back to the hotel, I'm on duty shortly. Call in one morning and have a cup of tea with us, and we'll sort something out.'

'By the look on the Vicar's face he's after money again,' Bess said, when Frank caught her up.

'Does he ever want anything else?' Bess put her arm through Frank's and together they stepped up their pace.

Back at the hotel, Bess's sisters and brothers-in-law went to the bar where the men drank pints of beer and the women coffee. The family had sandwiches while the guests dined. Later, when they had the dining room to themselves, Margot stood up and, looking every bit as radiant as the bonniest of expectant mothers, said, 'Bill and I have some news. We're having a baby.'

Claire and Ena congratulated their sister, kissing her and then kissing their brother-in-law. Mitch and Henry left their seats and, after kissing Margot, shook Bill's hand.

When Margot's sisters had finished asking questions - How far along are you? When is the baby due? Do you want a girl or a boy? - and had returned to their seats, Bess waved to Sylvie, the waitress who had been attending them. Sylvie left the dining room immediately, returned a couple of minutes later, and waited in the corridor with the door open.

When Bess saw her, she jumped up. 'Margot? Bill? Close your eyes and don't open them until I tell you to.' Bess motioned to Frank to close the curtains and turn out the lights, and then called Sylvie in. As the waitress began her slow walk from the door to the dining table, Bess said, 'You can open them now.'

'Oh my goodness.' Margot cried, as Sylvie put an iced cake on the table in front of her and Bill. Written on top in lemon icing were the words *Congratulations Margot and Bill*. And In the middle of the cake were two lighted candles - one pink and one blue.

'Blow the candles out,' Claire shouted.

'Make a wish,' added Ena.'

'Which shall I do first?' Margot asked, taking a deep breath.

'Blow and wish at the same time,' Bess said, and Margot blew until both candles were extinguished. "Hooray!" her sisters shouted, cheering and applauding.

Bess looked along the table at Claire and Mitch, and Ena and Henry, they had stopped cheering and were staring at the door. She followed their gaze. Sergeant McGann and Constable Peg were standing in the doorway. McGann flicked on the lights.

Frank looked over his shoulder and, seeing the two policemen, stood up immediately, followed by Bill and then Mitch. 'We're in the middle of a family celebration, Sergeant McGann, this had better be important.'

'Oh, it is, Mr Donnelly.'

'Then tell us what it is you want, so we get back to enjoying ourselves?'

'You're what I want, Mr Donnelly. I want you to come to the station for an interview.'

'What? I'm afraid you're going to have to wait until tomorrow. Now if you don't mind, it is Sunday afternoon and this is a private party.'

'In that case,' Sergeant McGann said, 'Frank Donnelly, I am arresting you on suspicion of murder.'

CHAPTER SEVEN

'Murder?' Bess leapt out of her chair. 'That's ridiculous!' Her sisters left their seats and joined Bess, standing behind her in a protective semi-circle.

'Frank wouldn't hurt a fly,' Margot said.

'He's a gentle giant,' added Ena.

'Where's your proof?' Claire asked.

'Yes!' Bess said. 'Don't you need proof before you can cart an innocent man away?'

Looking at Bess with a bored expression, Sergeant McGann puffed out his chest and ignored their protests.

'The sergeant is obviously talking about the murder of David Sutherland,' Bess said to her sisters, taking in her brothers-in-law. 'But, Sergeant,' she said, looking daggers at McGann, 'you are right off the mark accusing my husband of killing that pathetic excuse for a man, because he didn't leave the hotel on New Year's Eve. And there are twenty or more people who will swear to that.'

'Six of them are here in this room,' Bill said.

Bess looked at Henry, her eyes pleading for him to say something to help Frank, but he shook his head and lowered his gaze.

'Even if I did go out,' Frank said, putting an arm around Bess, 'I have physical proof that David Sutherland was not killed on New Year's Eve.' Bess steeled herself not to look up at Frank, for fear her face would show the shock she was feeling, while McGann shot him a look that was somewhere between disbelief and anger.

'I have a letter that Sutherland wrote to me on the second of January.' Bess realised she'd been holding her breath and exhaled. 'I'll explain everything later, darling,' he said, turning to Bess and holding her in his arms. 'Don't worry, love, I'll sort this nonsense out in no time.' To Sylvie, the young waitress who was about to leave when the police barged in, Frank said, 'Would you serve coffee, please?'

McGann gave Constable Peg a sharp nod and the young constable took a pair of handcuffs from his tunic pocket.

'If you cuff me I won't be able to get the proof I need.' Frank said, staring McGann down. The sergeant nodded again, and the constable put the cuffs away. 'Thank you. Now, if you will allow me to go to my office?'

'Go with him, Constable,' McGann waved his hand in the direction of the office, while looking at Bess with a smug grin on his face.

'I'm coming with you, Frank.'

'Afraid that won't be possible Mrs Donnelly,' McGann said. Bess glared at him. She wanted to slap him, wipe the satisfied, self-righteous smirk off his face. 'Not when it's a murder enquiry.'

Constable Peg poked his head round the door. 'Mr Donnelly has the documents he needs, Sergeant.'

Bess began to follow McGann out of the dining room, but Henry, suddenly on his feet, caught her by the hand.

'What are you doing?' Bess snapped. 'If you won't help Frank, I will!'

'It's police procedure, Bess.' Before letting go of Bess's hand, Henry gave it a squeeze. She looked up at her old friend and saw the trace of a smile on his face. She had got him wrong. There was a reason he hadn't defended Frank earlier. Bess nodded that she understood.

'I'll accompany Mr Donnelly,' Henry said, giving McGann a fierce look that said *You can't stop me*. 'Sergeant McGann is right,' Henry said, turning back to Bess. 'If he is taking Frank in on a suspected murder charge, it isn't possible for you to go with him.' Bess nodded, her eyes brimming with tears.

'Besides,' Henry added, 'I'm sure Frank would rather you stay here with your mother and sisters.' Bess nodded again. Resigned not to be with her husband during what she knew would be an arduous time at the hands of Sergeant McGann, she flopped down on her chair.

'Look after him, Henry?' Ena said, following her husband to the door.

'I will. And you look after Bess.'

'Of course,' Ena said, looking over his shoulder at her sister.

Henry kissed Ena and left.

On her way back to her seat at the dining table Ena leant over Bess's shoulder and whispered, 'Would you like Claire and me to take Mam home, or are you going to carry on with the party?'

'If I can't go with Frank, we'll carry on with the party. I'm damned if I'm going to let that little Hitler, McGann, spoil Margot and Bill's celebration.'

Claire laughed. 'Atta girl.'

Bess took the cake knife from the middle of the table. 'Will you cut the cake, Margot, or shall I?'

Margot leaned back in her chair and blew out her cheeks. 'You do it.'

'Right! Who's for cake?' Bess called. Several hands went up including Bill's, but Margot, looking pale, declined.

Sylvie returned and after clearing the table of dirty dishes, laid it with crockery for cake and coffee.

McGann taking Frank away had put a damper on the party, but Bess, Ena and Claire, did their best to keep the gathering jolly. Making the most of what was left of the afternoon, the family ate fruit cake, drank coffee, and chatted animatedly, as they always did when they were together.

It was Bess's mother who broke up the party. 'I think it's time I made a move. Be a dear and get my coat, Bill, while I have a word with our Bess.'

Bill got up and made for the door, stopping for a moment at the side of his wife. 'Are you ready to go, Margot?' Margot said she was and that she and Bill would drop their mother off on their way home.

'Thank you for the meal, love.' Lily Dudley said. 'And don't go worrying about Frank. If he's done nothing wrong the police can't keep him.'

'What do you mean, *if* he's done nothing wrong?'

Everyone laughed, but Lily Dudley looked aghast. 'Oh, my giddy aunt. I didn't mean it to come out like that. Our Frank wouldn't commit murder, but I might the next time I see that Godfrey McGann. I could tell you a thing or two about him when he was a young 'un. It's more luck than judgement that he's ended up on the right side of the law.'

'Save it for next time, Mother. We need to make a move,' Bill said, helping her into her coat, before helping Margot into hers.

'Time we went too,' Claire said. 'We need to pick Aimee up from Mitch's grandmother's house. She loves it there, but she'll be upset that we've been up here without her.'

'Might be best not to tell her,' Bess said. 'You'll bring her next time you come, won't you?'

'Yes. She'd have been with us today, but we've been up north visiting Mitch's old commander.' Claire shot a look at her husband. 'We drove up on Friday and Mitch wouldn't let her have the day off school.'

'Mitch has been very quiet,' Bess whispered, when Claire's husband was talking to Bill in the hotel's foyer. 'Is everything all right between you two?'

'To tell you the truth, Bess, I don't know,' Claire said, with a catch in her voice.

'Oh, Claire. I thought you and Mitch were happy.'

'We were.' Claire looked at the door. 'I can't go into it now, there isn't time, but when he goes away again I'll come up,' she said quietly. 'And if it's a school day, too bad! What the eye doesn't see…' Bess put her arms around her younger sister and held her tightly. 'Don't Bess, you'll have me crying.'

'Just remember, I'm always here,' Bess said, walking with Claire to the door. 'We both have telephones, so ring me anytime, day or night.'

In a flurry of hugs and calls of goodbye the family left, leaving Ena behind with Bess.

'I feel like a drink,' Bess said.

'Me too. I'll put the kettle on.' Ena said, going into Bess's office.

'I mean a real drink,' Bess called after her. Ena said something that sounded like *I was joking* and the door closed behind her.

'How are you coping, Mrs Donnelly?' Maeve asked, when Bess approached the reception desk.

'I'm worried to death, Maeve, as you can imagine. But worrying won't help Frank. Keeping on top of things here will. Later, would you fill me in with what's been going on; bookings, arrivals and departures?' Bess stretched. 'I know I've been sitting down for the last couple of hours, but I feel as if I've done a night shift. I'm going to put my feet up and have something to dull the anxiety I'm feeling. Oh,' she said, turning back to Maeve from the office door, 'if Frank, or Henry telephone--'

'I'll put them straight through to your desk extension.'

Bess pressed her lips into a straight line and nodded her thanks. She was too close to tears to speak.

It was two in the morning when Frank got home. He found Bess in a hunched, half-sitting, half-lying position in her chair. 'You're freezing, darling. Let's get you up to bed.'

Bess squinted at him and grimaced. 'Got a crick in my neck,' she said, in a voice thick with sleep.

'It's no wonder, falling asleep down here in the chair.' Frank gently massaged his wife's shoulders.

'What happened?' she asked, still not fully awake.

'I'll tell you in the morning.'

'But--'

'No buts, Bess. For once you are going to do as you're told.'

There was a knock on the door. Bess turned over and groaned. Frank jumped out of bed, pulled on his trousers and opened it. 'Maeve?'

'When I read your note saying you were late getting back last night, and asking for an alarm call at seven, I thought it might be nice for Mrs Donnelly - and for you too of course - if I brought your tea and toast up, instead of putting it in the office.'

'Room service with a smile,' Frank joked. 'Thank you, Maeve.'

'Thank you, Maeve,' Bess mumbled into her pillow.

'I'll be down shortly,' Frank said, taking the tray.

'I'm sure there's no rush. None of the guests are down yet, the kitchen is in full swing - Mrs Green is looking after things there - and the waitresses are preparing the dining room for breakfast. The post hasn't come, but the newspapers have. I've taken one to the smoking lounge, one to the library, and put one on Mrs Donnelly's chair in the office.'

'Thank you, Maeve. Well,' Frank said, 'as you have everything under control, I shall stay up here for another ten minutes and have breakfast with my wife. Oh, Maeve?' Frank said, when the receptionist turned to leave, 'would you ask Mrs Bramley's son, Davey, to clean the ashes from the grate in the office. Ask him to lay a fire, will you, but not to light it. We'll do that later, if we need to.'

'I've already asked him, sir. I noticed the ashes hadn't been cleared when I took the newspaper in. Young Davey's a good boy, but he can be forgetful.' With that Maeve left.

Frank poured the tea, putting Bess's cup on her bedside table. He drank his while he finished dressing. Bess sat up and yawned. 'Thank you.' She took a sip of her tea. 'Now, pass me my dressing gown and come and sit on the bed. I want to know what you meant yesterday when you told Sergeant McGann you had proof that David Sutherland was alive on the second of January.'

'Because I had a letter from him on that day.'

'Why would David Sutherland write to you?' Frank draped his wife's dressing gown round her shoulders and looked into her eyes. 'Frank?'

'Because he was blackmailing me.'

'What?' Fear, like a hot blade, stabbed at Bess's heart. 'I don't understand. What could David Sutherland possibly know about you that was so bad you needed to pay him to keep quiet?' Frank put Bess's cup back on the bedside table, sat on the bed, and took her hands in his. She gasped when the realisation hit her. 'It wasn't you he was blackmailing, was it?'

'No,' Frank confessed. Bess slumped back against the headboard and closed her eyes. 'Your name isn't on the letters, so McGann doesn't know they're anything to do with you.'

'He isn't stupid, Frank. He knows I knew Sutherland in London. He'll put two and two together.'

'He won't, darling, not now.' Bess looked questioningly at her husband. He lifted a stray curl of auburn hair from her face and put his finger to her lips. 'Don't shout at me.' Bess rolled her eyes, as if to say what now. 'I told him that I'd had a brief affair with a woman, a fling, and that Sutherland had found out about it and was threatening to tell you unless I paid him to keep quiet.'

'Frank what have you done? You've lied to the police. If McGann finds out, he'll put you in prison for perverting the course of justice.' Bess turned away and, as if every ounce of strength in her body had suddenly left her, fell sideways and cried into her pillow. Frank climbed onto the bed and lay next to her. Still crying, Bess brought up her knees. Frank brought his up too, until they were lying as close as two spoons in a cutlery drawer. With Bess safely in his arms, Frank stayed there until she calmed down.

'I'm sorry Frank,' Bess said, when she stopped crying.

'You have nothing to be sorry for. All that matters is you forgive me.'

'Forgive you? For what?'

'For having an affair with an imaginary woman.'

Bess couldn't help herself and laughed. 'I might.' She turned over and looked at her husband. 'Did McGann keep the letters?'

'No. He got so cheesed off with me repeating

the same story over and over again that he eventually stormed out of the interview room. When he didn't come back I gathered them up and slipped them into my pocket.'

Frank leant back thoughtfully. 'You know, I was going to burn them after Sutherland's body was found. I thought, if the police discovered he was blackmailing me, it would look as if I had a motive for shoving him into the lake. But there was so much going on that week I forgot all about them.'

'It's a good job you did. If you'd burned them, you'd have no proof Sutherland was alive in January.'

'I'm not sure the letters prove that, or that they were written by David Sutherland, because he didn't sign them. They are only initialled.'

'Where are the letters now?'

'Locked away in the safe. And that's where they are going to stay until this damn enquiry is over. Then I shall take great pleasure in lighting the fire with them.'

'Frank?' Bess said. Then she stopped and took a shuddering breath.

Frank laid his head on her shoulder and whispered, 'What is it?'

'Did McGann read the letters?'

'No. He glanced at the first and the last, which he said were so ambiguous they could have been written to anyone, by anyone, about anyone. Then he left the room. He came back brandishing a pocket diary that he said had been found in the lining of a suitcase in Sutherland's room at Hawksley's place. Sutherland had written D. and a financial amount on the first day of every month for six months. McGann checked the dates and amounts on the blackmail letters with the entries Sutherland had made in his diary.'

'And did they match?'

'Yes, within a day or two, all but the last envelope. The letter I received on January the second didn't have a stamp on it, so there was no post mark or date. And the fifty pounds I left under the bench in the walled garden was never deposited at Sutherland's bank.'

'Surely six out of seven letters with matching deposits are enough to prove your innocence.'

'The letters only prove Sutherland was blackmailing me, and if the last letter he wrote was on January the second it goes part way to proving he couldn't have died on New Year's Eve - when he thinks I had an alibi. McGann made it quite clear that I was still his main suspect.'

Bess looked up at Frank. Her face was red from crying, but her eyes were bright and questioning.

'What is it, darling?'

Bess swallowed hard and took a deep breath, garnering the strength and willpower she needed to ask Frank the question she had wanted to ask him since he first told her that Sutherland had been blackmailing him. 'I'd like you to tell me what Sutherland said about me in the letters.'

Frank lowered his gaze and shook his head. 'Why, Bess? What good will it do?'

'I need to know Frank. I have to know! What did he say?'

Frank exhaled and thought for a moment. 'In the first letter he said he knew your dirty secret

106

from your time in London. If you paid him £50 it would go away.'

'So you paid him?' Frank nodded. 'But it didn't go away?'

'No. He wrote and threatened to expose you every month, so I paid him every month.'

'But it was only the first and last letters that you showed McGann?'

'Yes.'

'What about the others?'

'They were similar to the first, getting progressively worse. In some he said you loved it, loved him. But don't worry, McGann didn't see any of them,' Frank assured her.

'You know none of what Sutherland said in those letters is true, don't you?'

'Why would you even ask me a question like that, Bess?' Frank held her in his arms a while longer, and then said, 'As much as I would love to stay here with you all day, I think I should go down.'

'Couldn't we stay in bed for just a little longer?' Bess whispered. 'Ena and Maeve are quite capable of looking after things. Besides, I'm ever so tired,' she teased.

Frank laughed. 'How about an early night tonight? Catch up on the sleep we missed last night. What about it?'

'Now there's an offer I can't refuse.' Bess laughed, brought her feet up and kicked Frank off the bed.

CHAPTER EIGHT

'What is it, Frank?'

'No wonder McGann didn't believe me when I said I hadn't killed Sutherland.' Bess walked across to the back of the desk and looked over her husband's shoulder. 'Look? This is the first letter; the one I told you about, the one that I showed him - and this is the last letter.' Frank laid the letter that he had received on January the second on the desk next to the first, flattening it with the palms of his hands. 'What do you see?'

'Two letters.'

Frank tutted. 'That's not what I meant. Look again.'

Bess screwed up her eyes and looked closer. 'Sorry, I can't see anything. Both letters are addressed to D. There isn't a signature on either of them, but they are both initialled, DS.'

Frank stood up, took Bess by the hand and sat her down in his chair. 'Now read them both again - every word - and look closely at the writing.'

'Apart from the fact that the grammar isn't correct in the last letter, I-- Hang on. Good Lord, his grammar hasn't only worsened, it's almost as if he's written it badly on purpose.' Bess picked up the first letter and scrutinised it. Then she picked up the last letter. 'The writing is slightly different too, but the initials...' Bess looked up at Frank, 'they really are different when you look closely, aren't they?'

'And that is why McGann didn't believe me when I said Sutherland was alive on January the second. I don't think he's bright enough to have noticed the deterioration in Sutherland's grammar, but you can bet your life he noticed the difference in his initials.'

Bess took a bundle of receipts from the drawer in her desk. 'Look, I put my initials on receipts when they've been paid, before I file them, and mine aren't identical.'

'Of course they're not. Sutherland's wouldn't be either, but this is just the thing McGann will be looking for. The man's desperate to solve this murder before the inspector from London does - and he's doing his damnedest to pin it on me.'

'Did Henry say anything to you at the police station?'

'No, only that he had to go somewhere this morning. Follow up on another line of enquiry... He said he'd call in this afternoon. I'll show him the discrepancies in the letters as soon as he arrives.'

'You know what this means Frank?' Bess looked from the letters to her husband.

'Yes. Whoever sent this letter on January the second was in on the blackmail. If they weren't, they were close enough to Sutherland to know he was extorting money from me.'

Bess took a sharp breath and put her hand up to her mouth. 'Which means they knew Sutherland was already dead.' Frank's brow furrowed. He looked questioningly at Bess. 'Think about it. Why else would they go to the trouble of demanding money, copying Sutherland's handwriting and forging his initials, if not to make you - and later the police when his body was found - think

Sutherland was alive on January the second?'

'To cover up the fact that *they* had murdered him on New Year's Eve.'

Maeve had asked for a few hours off so Ena was on reception. She waved to Jack to take over from her. Maeve had been training the likeable young man to be a receptionist, but until another day-porter could be found, Jack had agreed to work as a porter in the mornings - meeting and greeting guests on arrival, taking their luggage up to their rooms, and bringing down the luggage of those who were leaving. She looked at the clock. If she didn't go soon Katherine Hawksley might have gone home for the day.

Ena put on her coat as Jack arrived at reception and, after filling him in on who was where, she took the keys to Frank's Ford Anglia from the desk drawer. Leaving by the back door, she walked out into the sunshine. It felt warm on her face. She crossed the courtyard and, breathing deeply, caught the familiar smell of manure and wrinkled her nose.

As Ena turned onto Mysterton Lane, she saw her husband driving towards her. She stopped and wound down her window. 'Hello, you,' she said, when Henry pulled up alongside the old Ford in his new cream coloured Hillman Minx. 'Where have you been?'

'The Vicarage in Kirby Marlow, where Maeve O'Leary is lodging. I'll tell you about it later. Where are you going?'

'To see Katherine Hawksley at her stables.'

'What's your cover story?'

'I'm looking for somewhere to stable a horse, so I'm driving around the area comparing stables to see which have the best facilities at the most competitive prices.'

'She might recognise you from New Year's Eve.'

'I doubt it. Claire and I were in the background most of the time she was in the hotel.' Henry raised his eyebrows. 'The last thing she'd have done was look at who was there. Even if she did, it's been six months. I doubt she'd remember anything about the evening after the set-to between Sutherland and her father.'

'I expect you're right,' Henry said, putting the Hillman into gear.

'Of course I am.' Ena laughed, and waving out of the window with one hand she steered the Ford onto the Market Harborough road with the other.

She drove through the quaint village of Kirby Marlow. A black and white fingerpost pointed to the junior school on the right, and another to the market square and St. Peter's Church on the left. Paved with cobblestones the square was surrounded on three sides by double-fronted buildings. There was a newsagent and pub on the left of the square, a cobbler and blacksmith on the right - and along the top, facing the road, a baker and a butcher on either side of a general store. There was no market.

The Hawksley Stables was on the outskirts of the village. Ena pulled off the main road, not into the driveway leading to the stable block, but into a tractor-made lay-by a few yards south of an open five-bar gate. Blast! She was too late.

111

She watched Katherine Hawksley lock a small barn and run across the yard to her father's silver Bentley. She opened the passenger door, dropped onto the seat, and the car pulled away. At the gated entrance the Bentley stopped and Katherine jumped out. She closed the gate, secured it with a chain attached to the gatepost and padlocked it.

Ena ducked down. She heard the car door slam and, turning left, the Bently accelerated away in the direction of Market Harborough. When Hawksley's car had disappeared over the brow of the hill, Ena drove back to Kirby Marlow.

As she approached the school, Ena stopped and waited for several children and their mothers to cross the road. When they were safely on the opposite pavement, Ena noticed a woman put her hand up in a gesture of thanks. She looked through the windscreen and smiled - and then she looked again. The woman who had thanked her was Maeve O'Leary, and she was holding the hand of a little girl. Shocked to see Foxden Hotel's receptionist with a child, Ena almost drove into the back of a parked car.

She pulled out and cruised along the road, slowing down to a crawl every now and then, so she didn't overtake Maeve and the child. At St. Peter's Church, Maeve knocked the door of the house adjoining the ancient building. A short middle-aged woman appeared in the doorway and the girl reached up to her. The woman leaned forward and gave the child a welcoming hug. As Maeve walked down the path the woman and child went into the house.

If she hadn't already driven past the Church,

Ena would have stopped and offered Maeve a lift. She thought about going back for her, but the traffic was slow moving due to a tractor. She looked in the reverse mirror. Maeve was at the bus stop. Ena opened the window and waved her hand as high in the air as she was able. It would only have taken Maeve a few seconds to run to the car, but she didn't see her.

The tractor turned off the road onto a narrow lane leading to a farm. Ena glanced in the mirror again. The bus had arrived and Maeve was boarding. With the tractor gone the traffic started to move quickly. Ena put her foot down and was soon out of the village, slowing only when she approached a bend - and there were plenty of bends along the Market Harborough to Lowarth road.

Ena flew into the hotel by the kitchen door. 'Look out, here comes a whirlwind,' someone shouted as she ran through. She dashed into the cloakroom and looked in the mirror. She looked fine, there was no need to delay by combing her hair. She smoothed her skirt over her hips with the palms of her hands and pulled on the hem of her jacket. Then she walked calmly across the marble hall to reception nodding and smiling at guests who she assumed had just come back from one of Frank's excursions, and were waiting for the keys to their rooms. Ena acknowledged Jack, Maeve's male counterpart and, unable to wait a second longer to tell Bess that she had seen Maeve with a child, she burst into the office. 'Claire?'

'Auntie Ena!' Aimee called, running across the

room to Ena who immediately dropped onto one knee to welcome her niece.

'Good gracious, but you've grown,' Ena said, holding Aimee at arm's length before hugging her. 'What a lovely surprise it is to see you.'

'Daddy has gone to Canada on an aeroplane,' Aimee told her solemnly.

'Oh my goodness,' said Ena, taking hold of her niece's hand as she led her to the window seat where Claire and Bess were sitting. 'When was this?' she asked, directing the question at Claire.

'Yesterday. He's there for a week this time.'

'Daddy said we might be going to live there.'

'Oh?' Ena said. 'Would you like that, do you think?'

Rocking from side to side the little girl looked under her eyelashes at her mother.

'It's all a bit up in the air,' Claire said. 'Mitch didn't tell me the military were sending him to Canada this week until we were driving home at Easter, let alone him wanting to live there.'

'You don't sound keen.' Then, aware that Aimee was listening to every word, Ena said, 'I'm sure you won't be away for long, if you do decide to go. Right, Aimee? How about you and I go and find Uncle Frank and ask him if we can see old Donnie the pony?'

Aimee clapped her hands. 'Yes please!' she shouted, and was at the door before Ena had time to ask Claire if it was okay to take her.

Thank you, Claire mouthed. 'See you later?'

'Where do I start?' Claire said, when she and Bess were on their own. 'Mitch has changed. He isn't the husband and father he used to be. It's as if

114

he's two people. One minute he's caring and loving, the next he's shouting and angry.'

'He hasn't hurt you, has he?' Bess asked.

'No.' Claire shook her head. 'He would never do anything to hurt us - at least not physically. It's hard to explain. For much of the time he's normal and loving - my Mitch - and then he changes and he's cold and distant. He goes from being elated to being almost morose, in a second.'

Absentmindedly Claire twisted her wedding ring round and round on her finger. 'When he has these… mood swings, he changes so much I hardly recognise him. He isn't the man I fell in love with, Bess, or the man I married.'

'You've never spoken about your time in France, when you and Mitch first met and fell in love.'

'We met before we were sent to France.' A smile spread across Claire's face and her pale blue eyes sparkled as if she was seeing Mitch for the first time. 'We clashed at first. I don't think Mitch liked me very much. And I certainly didn't like him.' She laughed despite herself. 'We were opposites, which was probably part of the attraction, but we respected each other.' Claire blew out her cheeks. 'He made me jump through hoops when we were training to go overseas. But I wasn't going to let him beat me. The harder he drove me the harder I worked. I got it into my head that it was because he didn't like me that he worked me so hard. But I was wrong. He made me work because he did like me. I think he was a little in love with me even then. But whether he liked me or not was irrelevant. Mitch knew the work

115

we'd be doing in France was dangerous and difficult - and if I was going to survive, I needed to be both physically and mentally strong. And thank God he did push me. I don't think I'd be here today if he hadn't.'

Shocked by what her younger sister was telling her, Bess caught her breath.

'When we parachuted into France we were met by the sons of our friend, Edith Belland. They were part of the Resistance movement.' Claire looked out of the window, her eyes full of sorrow, as if the memory of that time was too much to endure. 'Mitch and I saw things that were so terrible, so inhumane, and--' Falling silent she shook her head as if she was trying to shake the awful memories from her mind. 'You see, when we were first in France - after the initial meeting with the Resistance - we only had each other. There was danger around every corner. We could have been caught, or killed, at any moment. We lived on our wits, and our emotions. For the most part our emotions had to be stifled, which only intensified the feelings we had for each other.

'Our assignments with the Resistance were dangerous. While we worked with the cell we ate, drank and slept the job. The problem was, after each mission we had no way of letting off steam, no way of getting rid of our excess energy, or of blocking out what we had done and seen. Then, one night, Mitch and I were hiding from a German patrol in a hay loft. We'd seen them earlier, drunk and bragging about the girls they'd brought to the farm, so we stayed hidden in case they came back.

'It was a freezing night. I couldn't stop

shivering. I'm not sure whether it was with fear or from the cold. Anyway, Mitch put his arms around me and we huddled together to keep warm. It was that night that the inevitable happened. Against the rules of the SOE, we gave in to our needs and made love.

'As time went on, more and more Germans flooded into Gisoir, the town where we lived, and life became even more dangerous.'

Claire could no longer hold back her tears. 'I'll never forget the day Mitch was arrested by the Gestapo. I had to stand in the crowd and watch them beat him before they dragged him off to Gestapo Headquarters. I wanted to go to his defence, but Madame Belland's youngest son stopped me - and thank God he did. If the German's had arrested me and tortured me, I'm not sure I'd have been brave enough to withstand it. It was only the fear of putting the lives of every Resistance member in Gisoir in danger - and the members of several other cells that I'd worked with - that stopped me.'

'What did you do?' Bess asked.

'Nothing. There wasn't anything I could do.' Claire wiped her tears. 'No one knew Mitch and I were in love, so I buried my feelings deep inside and got on with the job I'd gone there to do.'

'Good Lord, Claire, I knew you were doing dangerous work, from the letters your friend Eddie forwarded to me, but I knew nothing of this! And you had to endure it on your own.'

'Edith Belland, who I lodged with, knew I loved Mitch. She was like a mother to me. I wouldn't have got through the following years without her.'

'And all that time, Mitch was in a prisoner of war camp?'

'Yes. And he won't talk about it.'

'Do you remember, when we were little, Mam used to tell us to be quiet because Dad was having one of his turns? She used to say he'd been ill since he was invalided out of the Great War at the beginning of 1918.'

'And we assumed it was because of the wound in his knee, where he'd been shot, that was making him grumpy.'

'But it wasn't that at all,' Bess said. 'Dad had shellshock.'

'Overly protective one day and almost uncaring the next?' Bess nodded. 'For years Dad had awful mood swings,' Claire said. 'Like Mitch, normal one minute and angry the next - and for no reason.'

Bess took hold of Claire's hand. 'It sounds to me as if Mitch has shellshock.'

CHAPTER NINE.

Hand in hand, Ena and Aimee left the hotel by the back door. No sooner had they reached the cobbled courtyard, they saw Frank coming out of the stables. Aimee let go of Ena's hand and ran to him. Putting on a look of surprise, Frank bent down and swept Aimee off her feet, swinging her round as if she was an aeroplane. When he put her down she shouted for more, and Frank picked her up again.

'You are a pushover, Frank Donnelly.' Ena called to him.

'I know,' he said, putting Aimee down and pretending to be out of breath.

Aimee put up her hand and Frank took hold of it. 'What now?' he said, as the child began pulling him towards the stables.

'Please can I see Donnie the pony?'

'I've just put him to bed,' Frank said. Ena saw the smile on Aimee's face disappear and her bottom lip begin to quiver. 'Of course you can sweetheart. He won't have settled yet.' As Aimee skipped off ahead of him, Frank turned to Ena and winked.

Waving, Ena watched her brother-in-law and niece make their way to the stables.

'Aimee has her uncle wrapped around her little finger, doesn't she?' Maeve said, suddenly at Ena's elbow.

'She certainly does. The poor chap was coming in after bedding down the pony, but Aimee wanted to see it, so he's gone back with her.'

'At Aimee's age children are lovely,' Maeve

sighed.

'Especially little girls, don't you think?' Ena hoped her response would lead Maeve to talk about the child she saw her with in Kirby Marlow. It didn't.

They walked into the hotel together. Ena said, 'Do you have any children, Maeve?'

'No. When I was young I hoped that one day, if I found Mr Right, I would marry and have a family, but it wasn't to be. Do you want children, Mrs Green?'

'Yes, one day. Henry's older than me, so I expect it ought to be sooner rather than later.' Ena caught Maeve glancing at her sideways. 'I know the man's age doesn't make a lot of difference - to a woman conceiving, I mean, but Henry said he wants to be young enough to kick a football about on Sunday mornings.'

'It's going to be a boy then?'

Leaning back, Ena feigned a look of surprise. 'Of course, Henry has a plan. What about you? Girl or boy when you find Mr Right?'

'Boy. The world is too cruel to girls.'

This was the opportunity Ena had been waiting for. She would ask Maeve why she thought the world was cruel to girls, which would lead her into asking about the little girl she saw her with in Kirby Marlow. But when she turned, Ena saw such a depth of sadness in Maeve's eyes that her voice faltered, and she could only think to say, 'I'd like a girl.'

'One of you will be happy then.' Maeve opened the door of the staff cloakroom. 'If you'll excuse me, Mrs Green, I must hang up my coat and tidy my hair before I start work.'

'Yes, of course. I'll see you later.' Feeling guilty that she had awoken some deep rooted sadness in Maeve, Ena blurted out, 'I'm sorry.' The receptionist looked back at her. She had tears in her eyes. 'If I said something that upset you.'

'You didn't Mrs Green. I'm just a little tired. My niece hasn't been well.'

'Your niece?' Ena repeated, as she felt the heat of embarrassment develop in her cheeks.

'Yes. The child you saw me with earlier. Today was her first day back at school after being off with a summer cold. I thought she looked pale and was worried that I may have sent her back too soon. Was there anything else?'

'No. Except, if you ever want to talk, you know where I am.'

'Thank you.' Maeve turned and went into the cloakroom, closing the door firmly behind her. Ena's smile changed to a worried frown. There was something not right. She could feel it, sense that Maeve was deeply unhappy. But there was nothing she could do to help unless Maeve opened up to her - and Ena didn't think she would do that.

'Henry?' Ena called, as her husband entered the hotel. They walked towards each other, meeting in the middle of the marble hall. 'How did you get on at the Vicarage?'

Henry looked around. 'Come into the office, I'll tell Bess and Frank at the same time.'

'Claire's in there with Bess. She was near to tears earlier, so I expect Bess is giving her sisterly advice - and Frank's showing Aimee the animals.'

'Oh well, what I found out can wait. It isn't that

121

important.'

'What I found out is,' Ena said. At that moment, Maeve appeared from the direction of the cloakroom. 'I know you're a married man,' Ena whispered, 'but would you like to come up to my room?'

Henry laughed. 'Are you inviting me to your room for a secret assignation?'

'Perhaps,' Ena teased. She caught her husband by the hand and led him upstairs.

There were two single beds in Ena's room, Henry sat on one and Ena on the other, facing him. 'Right,' she said, 'what did you find out at the vicarage?'

'That Maeve O'Leary is staying there. The vicar's wife told me that Maeve was billeted at the Vicarage during the war and they had become good friends.'

'What did she do in the war?'

'Communications.' Ena knew from experience how all-embracing that word had been during the war. 'The vicar's wife said the facility where Maeve worked was just outside the village, and she had visited them regularly since the war ended.'

'Do you think she worked for one of the subsidiaries of Bletchley Park?'

'I don't know. Thousands of people all over the country worked in communications. It was the standard job description for any secret work. And there wasn't only Bletchley, there were other facilities. I'll try and find out more.'

'Why? I mean, why does it matter if Maeve worked in communications during the war?' Ena took a sharp breath. 'You don't think she's a spy, do you?'

'No…'

'What then?'

'I told you I had to cover David Sutherland's funeral.'

'Yes, and you saw Bess there. So?'

'I saw Miss O'Leary there too.'

'What? Maeve was at Sutherland's funeral? Have you told Bess?'

Henry shook his head. 'No. And I'd rather you didn't. I mentioned the funeral to the vicar's wife. I said it was a sad affair when someone dies and there were so few mourners in the church. She said, if it hadn't been for herself, Miss O'Leary and old Dolly Hinson, two women who worshiped at St. Peter's, Mr Sutherland wouldn't have had anyone at all to bear witness to his passing.'

'He had Sir Gerald and Katherine Hawksley.'

'Did you talk to Katherine Hawksley today?'

'No. Her father was there. They left almost immediately I arrived, so I didn't get the chance. I do have something to tell you. Though it isn't as surprising as Maeve going to David Sutherland's funeral.'

'What is it?'

'Maeve has a niece.'

Ena waited for her husband to react, but he only said, 'Nothing unusual in that.'

'I suppose not, except all the time she's worked here she has never mentioned a niece. Who's to say the child isn't hers. If she'd had her in the war and there wasn't a father in the picture, the vicar and his wife could be bringing her up. That would

123

be a good reason for Maeve to visit Kirby Marlow regularly, don't you think?'

'It would.' Henry got up and sat next to his wife. 'And if that is the case, it is none of our business. Leave the poor woman to get on with her life,' Henry said, kissing Ena.

'Shall we go down and tell Bess, or…?' Giggling, Ena laid back on the bed and stretched.

Henry checked his watch. 'There's plenty of time,' he said, laying down next to her.

Maeve wasn't on reception when Ena and Henry went down for tea. The office door stood open so Ena called, 'Coo-ee?' and they entered.

Maeve was bending down talking to Aimee, or rather listening while Aimee told her and Bess about the pony and the pigs - and how she had looked for eggs with Uncle Frank. 'Tea time is the wrong time of the day,' Aimee explained, with the authority of a seven-year-old going on forty. 'I shall have to get up early in the morning if I want to collect the eggs.'

Maeve stood up and acknowledged Ena and Henry with a smile. 'I had better get back to my post,' she said, and left the room.

'Maeve has a niece,' Bess said, with surprise in her voice. 'Her name is Nancy and she's going to bring her over to play with Aimee. So, because Aimee won't be here on her actual birthday, she's going to be like a fairy queen and have two birthdays, aren't you darling?' Aimee nodded. 'I thought, as there are a couple of children in the hotel this week, we'd have a tea party. We've decided on Thursday afternoon, after school, so

Nancy can come. What do you think?' Bess looked from Ena to Henry.

'I think it's a lovely idea,' Ena said, 'don't you, Henry?' Aimee squealed and clapped her hands before Henry had time to answer.

'That's settled then. I think you should send out some invitations, Aimee,' Bess said. 'Why not write to Nancy first, then her aunt can take it home with her when she finishes work today.'

Aimee ran over to the seat beneath the window to where she had left her paper and pencils. 'I shall draw Nancy a birthday cake,' she announced.

Bess savoured every minute of the hour she had off on Saturdays. When the hotel's guests who were leaving had vacated their rooms, which was any time between breakfast and eleven, the cleaners and chamber maids went in to prepare the rooms for new guests who were booked in from twelve.

Bess strolled around what was left of the old Foxden Estate: the park, the walled garden, and the lake. This morning because Aimee was with her it was, as always, the lake first to see the ducks.

The sun's reflection on the still water looked like silver silk. 'Don't go near the edge, Aimee,' Bess called to the excited child.

Bess kicked off her shoes, picked them up by their heels and ran across the peacock lawn, catching up with Aimee on the north side of the lake. She sat down on the grass and stretched out her legs. Aimee ran to her, sat down next to her and did the same. Looking at Bess's feet, and then her own, she began to take off her sandals. 'Where are the ducks?' the little girl asked, undoing the buckles.

'They must be in the rushes on the other side of the lake,' Bess said. 'Don't take your shoes off, Aimee. The grass is long over there, you might step on a thistle or a stinging nettle.'

Aimee frowned. She opened her mouth, but before she had time to argue that if Bess was barefoot, why couldn't she be, Bess slipped her feet back into her shoes. Checking the leather straps across Aimee's instep to make sure each was safely caught in the pin of the buckle, she stood up. 'Ready?'

Strolling round the lake with Aimee reminded Bess of the Land Girls that she had worked with during the war. In the winter, as soon as the lake froze, they would be skating on it. Three of them were accomplished skaters and when the village children came up to Foxden to skate on the lake, they acted as lifeguards. Bess smiled remembering the fun they'd had.

She had worked and lived with the Land Girls for five years; it was no wonder that they had become like sisters. She looked across at the grazing meadow on the other side of the drive leading down to the River Swift. It had once yielded root vegetables and beyond that there had been fields of wheat and corn.

Turning Foxden's fields and meadows into arable land had been hard work. The women were up before dawn to start work as soon as it was light and rarely, if ever, did they finish until dusk - and often in appalling conditions. From potato picking and digging up vegetables in torrential rain, breaking the ice on water troughs for the livestock in the outer meadows in winter, to getting burned in the mid-day sun and being stung by all manner of flying creatures at harvest time - they never complained.

Bess, suddenly aware that Aimee was calling her, looked to where the child was standing. Riveted to the spot, her back as straight as a poker, with an expression on her face that was somewhere between excitement and terror, Aimee stood in the middle of a family of ducks. Bess approached slowly so she didn't frighten the two adult ducks who were protectively leading their family of downy ducklings around the little girl to the lake.

When they were in the water Bess saw Aimee gasp for breath. 'Did you see them, Auntie Bess?' she said, panting. 'Did you see the baby ducks? They came right up to me. I shall tell Uncle Frank when I get back to the hotel. I bet he won't believe they came that close.'

Bess crouched down to Aimee's height and together they watched the raft of ducks gliding effortlessly across the water. 'Come on, let's see if we can get to the other side of the lake before they do.' Aimee skipped on ahead, turning every now and again to make sure her aunt was keeping up.

When Bess passed the spot where David Sutherland had drowned she looked away. She was determined not to let one bad memory spoil the many good ones she'd had over the last ten years, first at Foxden Hall and now at the Foxden Hotel. Despite the tragedy of a man losing his life, Bess smiled remembering how she used to walk her horse Sable round the lake and trot her through the woods before riding her at a gallop down to the River Swift.

Before the war, Lord and Lady Foxden who lived at the Hall, bred horses. In 1939, when the grooms and boys were called up and the horses were taken to Lord Foxden's estate in Suffolk, the Foxden Estate was farmed. Since then, some of Foxden's land had been leased to the tenant farmers, but most had been sold off to finance the Hall's transformation from stately home to hotel. Only the private grounds remained: The lawns around the lake, the small wood that bordered Shaft Hill, the parkland and the old walled garden which, during the war had been a kitchen garden, but had been restored to a picturesque flower garden with rose arbours and benches, where the hotel's guests could sit and relax.

CHAPTER TEN

Dressed for her party in a pink dress with a darker pink ribbon tied in a bow at the back, smocking on the bodice and a Peter Pan collar, Aimee sat in the old nursery waiting for her guests.

There was a small room off the nursery which had once served as a temporary bedroom where the nanny of the children who lived at Foxden Hall slept when they were ill. The rocking chair and single cot which Nanny slept in had been replaced by a table and two chairs, but apart from a lick of paint, toys and games for older children, as well as young ones, the room looked the same.

Brothers Matthew and Archie, who were staying in the hotel, were first to arrive. They gave Aimee a birthday present, which Claire suggested Aimee open when they had had their tea. Maeve and Nancy came later, after school. They went through to the small room off the nursery, where Nancy took off her school clothes - a burgundy blazer and grey dress - and put on a blue cotton shift with a white sailor collar. Replacing her school sandals with black patent ballerina shoes that had a bow on the front. Maeve combed Nancy's hair, adding a blue bow held in place by a Kirby grip.

Nancy gave Aimee a gift, which Aimee put with the others she'd received, and then took Nancy by the hand as if she had known her all her life. Bess and Maeve watched as the girls circled the boys. 'Safety in numbers,' Bess whispered to Maeve, when Aimee introduced Nancy to Matthew and Archie.

Watching the children playing with dolls and toy soldiers, trains and motorcars, Maeve commented on how Aimee and Nancy had hit it off. 'I was worried that Nancy would sit on the sidelines and watch the other children having fun,' Maeve said. 'She has spent most of her life with grown-ups. First my mother, and then Reverend and Mrs Sykes. Don't get me wrong, my mother worships Nancy, and the Reverend and his wife are lovely people. I don't know what Nancy and I would have done without them, but they are quiet folk. Kind, and generous to a fault, but they're of the older generation. And because they haven't had children of their own, Mrs Sykes is over-protective and the Reverend is very strict. Between them they don't allow Nancy much freedom to express herself.'

'Not like Aimee, you mean, who can be loud when she's excited?'

Maeve laughed. 'That wasn't what I meant, but yes, I would love to see Nancy jump about and get excited - and shout occasionally like Aimee. Nancy's shy and not usually comfortable around children she doesn't know, but she has really taken to Aimee.'

'For better or worse, Aimee is a Dudley. And we Dudley girls have never been shy.'

'Perhaps some of Aimee's confidence will rub off on Nancy.'

'She has plenty of confidence, does our Aimee,' Frank said, suddenly standing behind the two women.

'Now Mr Donnelly is here, I'll go down,'

Maeve said.

'You don't have to leave because I've turned up,' Frank joked. 'I'll go on reception. It's time I did some work today.' He winked at Bess.

'Thank you, but I'd rather keep to my hours. Be a good girl, Nancy,' Maeve called, but her niece was watching the boys dismantle a wooden-block railway engine and didn't hear her.

'She'll be fine. I'll be down shortly. I'll leave Frank up here with the children while I get the birthday tea sorted. There's cake and sugar mice. Tempted?'

'Yummy,' Maeve said, and left the old nursery laughing.

Bess watched Maeve walk along the landing to the staff stairs. Strange, she thought, but she had never seen Maeve laugh before. Bess liked Maeve. She felt lucky that when she was looking for a receptionist, someone as experienced in the hotel business as Maeve was looking for a job. Not only did she work hard, she was good with people. She was always polite and patient, even with the most demanding guests - and she used her initiative.

Bess's attention returned to the nursery when she heard the words, 'Have you got a poorly eye?' Frank was sitting between the two girls trying to mend a doll whose arm had come out of its socket. He was used to being asked about his eye. Because it was glass it didn't move like his own eye, which was often a source of curiosity when he met a child for the first time.

'It was poorly,' Aimee informed Nancy, 'but it's better now, isn't it Uncle Frank?' Aimee scrabbled to her feet, put her hands on Frank's shoulders and kissed him on the cheek.

'Thank you, Aimee,' Frank said. When his niece sat down again and had finished wriggling to make herself comfortable, Frank turned to Nancy. She was still looking at his eye. 'It's a special eye,' Frank explained. 'It was made for me by a clever doctor. I'm very lucky,' he said.

'Why?' Nancy asked.

'Because no one in Foxden, Lowarth, or even Kirby Marlow, has an eye like mine.'

Nancy got to her feet, bent down, and kissed Frank on the cheek as Aimee had done. Then she stroked the fading scar that was still visible on his left temple. 'Better now, Uncle Frank?'

'Yes, thank you, Nancy. Now,' he said, tears threatening to fall from his good eye, 'let's make this doll's arm better.'

Leaving the two girls dominating Frank's time and the boys, Archie and Matthew or was it Matthew and Archie - they looked so alike she couldn't tell - playing with the train, Bess went down to the kitchen to finish Aimee's birthday fare.

She took four trays from the kitchen cupboard. One for the birthday cake, one for plates of egg and cress, corned beef, and cheese sandwiches. One was needed for the sponge fancies and fairy cakes, and the last for the pink and white sugar mice, nibbling pineapple flavoured boiled sweets that pretended to be chunks of cheese. 'That's it!' she said aloud. She was miles away when she heard someone say, 'Need a hand?'

'Margot? You made it.'

Margot helped herself to a quarter-square of

cheese sandwich. 'What can I do to help?'

'Stop eating the food,' Bess said.

'You've made so much, no one's going to miss a couple of...' Margot leant forward to pick up another square and Bess tapped her on the hand with a spoon.

'Blimey, you are tight, our Bess. Cruel too. How could you deny your little nephew or niece a teeny-weenie piece of bread?'

Bess laughed. 'Put your bottom lip away, sister, and let me check we have everything.' Holding up her fingers, Bess said, 'Six adults and four and a half children.' Giggling, she went over to her younger sister and gave her a hug. 'You can eat as much as you like when the food's upstairs.' She backed away from Margot and placed the flat of her hand a few inches from her tummy. 'May I?' Margot nodded. 'Goodness, you're getting big.' Bess beamed, 'I can't wait until this little one is born. What a party we'll have then.'

Margot blew out her cheeks. 'I can't wait either. I'm counting the days. I feel like an elephant, a tired one. I haven't slept for a month.'

Bess laughed at her sister who was clearly exaggerating. 'Go and get Claire and Maeve.'

'Maeve?'

'Yes, Aimee invited Maeve's niece to her party.'

'I didn't know Maeve had a niece.'

'I didn't either. But then, why would I? Anyway, Maeve and Nancy are lodging with the Vicar and his wife at St. Peter's in Kirby Marlow. You'll like Nancy, she's lovely.'

Margot, miles away and deep in thought, said

wistfully, 'One of the children who comes to dance classes is called Nancy. When she first came, I couldn't say her name without thinking of my beautiful mentor at the Prince Albert Theatre, Nancy Diamond.'

'It's hard, isn't it? I don't think we ever get over losing someone we love. Accept it eventually, but there'll always be names, people, places, to remind us of those who have died, especially in the war. Come on,' Bess said, 'think of how lucky you were to have survived the Blitz, and go up and meet her.

'Aimee also invited little two boys who are staying here. Nice lads. Their parents have gone into Coventry for the afternoon. Their mother was born there, lived close to the city centre until she married. They've gone in to see the damage the Luftwaffe did to the Cathedral.'

'So you're babysitting,' Margot said.

'Not really. They'll only be away for a couple of hours. Besides, it wouldn't be much fun for Aimee if the only guests at her birthday party were her aunts and uncles.' Bess gave Margot a selection of cutlery in a tea towel. 'Put these on the table, will you? Oh, and Margot?' Bess called after her, 'Smile!' Margot pulled a comical face and left Bess arranging plates of food on the trays.

A breeze wafted into the hot kitchen. Bess turned and saw her brother-in-law Bill. Welcoming him with a kiss, she gave him a shopping bag containing bottles of lemon and barley, Vimto, lemonade and a dozen small tumblers.

'Margot's gone up to the old nursery. Will you take the drinks, and ask Frank to come down to help me carry the food? Oh, hang on.' Bess took a clean table cloth and a dozen napkins from the linen cupboard. 'Can you manage these?' she asked, pushing them under Bill's arm.

No sooner had Bill left than Frank arrived. He staggered across the kitchen and fell into Bess's arms. 'I'm puffed out from blowing up balloons.'

She kissed him, then playfully shooed him away. 'You have quite a fan club, *Uncle Frank,*' she teased.

'Is that what you call them? I thought Aimee was a handful, but with Nancy as well…'

'Go on with you, you love the attention. Oh, we'll need music to play musical chairs.'

Frank looked horrified at the suggestion. 'There isn't room for musical chairs!'

'Oh, all right then, scrap the idea.' And putting a tray of food in each of his hands, she sent him back upstairs.

Claire and Maeve arrived at the same time. Bess gave Claire the birthday cake. 'Don't take it up yet,' she said. 'Oh, we need matches to light the candles.' She ran over to the chef's store cupboard and helped herself to a box of Swan Vestas. 'Right!' Bess said, and giving Maeve the tray of individual cakes she led the way to the nursery. Outside Bess and Claire held back. Bess lit the candles on the cake and Claire carried it in to a rousing round of "Happy Birthday To You". When they had finished singing there were calls for Aimee to blow out the candles. She did, in one breath, to more cheers.

Bill and Margot had put the tablecloth on the table and laid out the food. Because so much was still rationed the party food was no different to what they would have eaten for tea any other day, but with a little rearranging it looked appetising enough. Bess realised there weren't any small plates and set off downstairs to get some while Frank poured everyone a soft drink. When she returned she put the plates on the end of the table and told the adults to help themselves.

'Children?' she called to Aimee, Nancy, Archie and Matthew. 'Would you like egg sandwiches, corned beef, or cheese?' It seemed they all wanted one of each, which suited Bess. 'If you want more, come and tell me. And when you've eaten your sandwiches we'll cut the cake.'

The party was in full swing. Margot was telling Maeve about her pregnancy, how she had tried to eat sensibly, to keep her figure in some sort of shape, but had failed miserably. 'Eating for two,' Bess heard her say.

Frank was telling Bill about the hotel's bookings, and how the summer differed from the winter. 'In the winter the guests seem to be older. And there are more city folk wanting to get away from the hustle and bustle of trains and trams and spend a relaxing time in the country. In the summer the hotel attracts families. The children love the animals,' he said smiling. 'In the winter, it's brisk country walks over the Rye Hills and visiting the farms. In the summer, it's days out to Warwick Castle, or trips to Coventry, to see what's left of the Cathedral. Some people, couples mostly, drive as far as Stratford-upon-Avon.'

Bess noticed Aimee picking at the corner of a box gift-wrapped in pink paper. She caught

Claire's eye and was about to suggest Aimee open her birthday presents when she realised Claire wasn't looking at her, she was gazing past her at the door.

Bess turned to see who Claire was looking at. 'Mitch?'

'Hi, Bess. Hi, honey,' he called to Aimee.

'Dadd-ee!' Aimee ran to her father. He picked her up and hugged her. 'I'm having a birthday party like the Queen of Hearts,' she said, wriggling to get down. 'This is my friend.' Nancy smiled up at Mitch, but stayed close to Frank. 'And these are my friends Archie and Matthew.' In turn the boys approached Mitch, shook his hand and said, 'Pleased to meet you.'

Mitch was welcomed warmly by his brothers-in-law and joined in with their conversation.

By the time Aimee had opened her presents - a doll dressed as a ballerina from Margot and Bill - a pad of drawing paper and a set of paints and brushes from Bess and Frank - a dress from her mummy - a colouring book and crayons from Nancy - and a box of liquorice allsorts from Matthew and Archie - the party had come to a natural end.

The boys' parents, back from their afternoon out in Coventry, thanked Bess for letting their sons join the party and took them off to get ready for bed. Maeve said she had better make tracks too, as the Reverend and Mrs Sykes would be expecting them anytime. She thanked Aimee for inviting Nancy to the party and Aimee, who had been laughing all afternoon, suddenly frowned. She ran to Nancy and put her arms around her. 'Can she

137

come and play again tomorrow?' Aimee asked, looking up at Maeve.

'Not tomorrow, honey,' Mitch cut in, 'We're going home tonight. It's school tomorrow, right?' Aimee's bottom lip began to quiver. 'We'll let Maeve know when we're next coming up to see Grandma and Aunt Bess, and she'll bring Nancy over to play then,' Mitch said, looking at Maeve for conformation.

Maeve looked shocked, as everyone in the room did, by the sudden change of plan that Mitch had made for Claire and Aimee, and said, 'Of course.'

That's it then, Bess thought, her sister and niece are going back to Oxford tonight. Bess didn't say anything, nor did she allow her face to show surprise, as Maeve's had done. She didn't want to cause trouble between her sister and her husband. Though she had a feeling trouble was brewing.

The two children, clearly not wanting to be parted, stood facing each other but didn't speak. 'Bye-bye, Nancy,' Bess said, breaking the silence. 'We'll see you another day.'

Nancy looked up at Bess with big eyes, whispered goodbye, and said, 'Thank you for having me, Mrs Donnelly.' She looked at Frank, 'Thank you, Mr Donnelly.' Then turning her attention to her new friend, she said, 'Goodbye Aimee,' and kissed her on the cheek. 'See you another day.'

Bess could have cried watching the two little girls saying goodbye to each other. She wished her niece and her sister lived nearer. She didn't see them often enough. Her gaze crossed to Mitch. If her brother-in-law had his way, she'd wouldn't see

138

them at all.

As the party descended the stairs, Frank closed the nursery door. 'We'll clear up tomorrow. I don't know about you, but I'm exhausted. I need a rest before the guests start coming down for dinner.' Bess yawned. 'Are you tired?'

She shook her head. 'Not tired exactly, but I'd like an hour to myself. I mean the two of us,' she clarified, 'before we start work again. Everything all right, Jack?' she called, passing reception.

'Fine, Mrs Donnelly.' He glanced over his shoulder at the pigeonholes where the room keys were kept. 'Everyone's in.'

Bess acknowledged Jack with a smile. He was getting to be as efficient as Maeve. Well, almost. 'We'll be in the office if you need us,' she said, pushing open the door. 'Hello, sweetheart.' Aimee was kneeling against the window seat with a blue crayon in her hand, colouring in the sky, and doing her best to stay within the lines of the colouring book that Nancy had given her.

'Tonight's float needs to go to the bar,' Frank said, taking the petty cash box from the safe and removing several material bags of coins from it. 'I'll check Simon has everything he needs and come back. Put the kettle on, love, I won't be long.' As he passed Aimee, Frank ruffled her hair.

Bess flicked the electric kettle switch, before sitting down at her desk. 'Is Mummy packing?'

Concentrating on filling in yellow stars in the sky, Aimee nodded.

Bess was wondering about her brother-in-law's sudden arrival and the family's imminent departure, when her thoughts were interrupted by loud voices in reception. Aimee turned to the door at the same time as Bess. It was her father who was raising his voice. Aimee left her colouring, ran to the door, and looked back at Bess.

'You stay here, sweetheart, I'll see what Daddy wants.' Aimee ran back to the window seat, but, instead of continuing to colour, she swiped the book to the floor, climbed onto the seat, folded her arms and set her face in a frown. Bess couldn't decide whether her niece was frightened or angry.

Annoyed with her sister and brother-in-law, Bess left the office. 'Aimee can hear you two arguing and it's upsetting her. Why don't you come in and discuss your differences without shouting? Let your daughter see there's nothing for her to worry about.' Claire went into the office ahead of Bess. Mitch, like a petulant child, sauntered up to her and waved her in first. Bess felt like slapping him. Instead she clenched her fists and kept her arms down by her side.

Bess returned to her desk and Mitch closed the door. Claire was kneeling with her arms around Aimee who pulled free of her mother when she saw her father and ran to him crying.

'Hey honey, why the tears?' A stupid question Bess thought. She got up remembering she had earlier put the kettle on, and with one ear on the conversation between her sister and brother-in-law, busied herself making tea.

'Claire, I don't want Aimee missing school. It's the one place we know she'll be safe.'

'What? You mean she isn't safe here, with me and my family?'

'That's not what I meant and you know it!'

'Then what did you mean?' Claire asked, unable to keep the exasperation out of her voice. 'Mitch - look at me?'

Bess poured tea for Claire and coffee for Mitch and set them down on the small table next to the hearth. 'I'm going to see to the kitchen; it's almost time for dinner, the guests will be coming down soon. Are you two staying tonight or not?' Claire shook her head. 'But you'll stay for dinner?'

'I'm afraid not,' Mitch said. 'Thanks anyway, but we need to leave for Oxford soon. Aimee will be late going to bed as it is.'

'We'd better find Uncle Frank, then,' Bess said. 'He'd be ever so upset if you left without saying goodbye to him.' Aimee took Bess's hand without speaking. Bess looked down at her niece and smiled. She looked very small. Aimee looked up at Bess with sad eyes. The usual bounce had gone out of her step as she walked with Bess to the kitchen.

'Hello, you two,' Frank called from the dining room. 'Have you come to help me check the menus?'

'Not tonight. Aimee's come to say goodbye, haven't you sweetheart?'

Aimee stretched out her arms for Frank to pick her up, which he did. Hugging his niece, Frank looked over her shoulder. 'They're staying for dinner, surely?'

Bess rolled her eyes. 'Mitch wants to get off.'

'Do you want me to have a word?'

'No. I think it's best we leave it for today. They've got a fairly long drive ahead. Margot will be having the baby soon. They're bound to come up then.'

'Right, young lady, we had better see if Mummy and Daddy are ready to leave.' Frank carried Aimee to the office and set her down. Claire had tidied her toys away and was holding Aimee's cardigan. Aimee put her arms down the sleeves and Claire buttoned it up. 'Have you got your case?' Frank asked.

'It's already in the car.'

The two men shook hands in what Bess could only describe as an uncomfortable atmosphere, one that she had never experienced before between any of her brothers-in-law. 'Come on honey,' Mitch said, picking Aimee up. 'Time we left or we'll be real late getting home.'

Bess had driven down to Oxford to visit Claire several times and the Sunday evening traffic could be bad. But, Bess thought, it was unnecessary and unfair to her sister and niece to leave this early.

Walking out to the car, Claire looked downcast. But Aimee, in her daddy's arms, had forgotten her tears and was chattering away. Scrambling onto the back seat of the car next to her mother, Aimee waved out of the rear window her normal boisterous self.

Bess and Frank stood in the courtyard and waved until the car was out of sight.

CHAPTER ELEVEN

'Is Claire and Mitch's marriage in trouble?' Frank asked.

'Yes. I think it is.'

'Anything we can do to help?'

'No, unfortunately. Mitch has to face the fact that he isn't well and see a doctor.'

'It's that serious, is it?' Frank said, shock resonating in his voice.

'From what I can gather he's behaving like Dad when he came home from the war in 1918. Mam said he used to have black moods. And when Margot and I were little, if we dared to talk when he was in one of those moods, he would get really angry. Luckily, our doctor was ex-military and had seen cases like Dad's when he was on active service. He helped Dad to understand what was happening, and how to cope with it.'

'And what was it?'

'Shellshock. Claire said Mitch has been getting progressively worse since they left France and came back to live in England.'

'But that's four years ago.'

'That's right.' Bess and Frank's conversation was interrupted by the clanging of pans and calls for this plate, or that dish. 'I'll tell you more later,' Bess said, 'once we've got this show on the road.' Leaving Frank in the corridor, Bess pretended to drag herself to the kitchen door.

'There's half an hour before dinner. I'll be in the office.'

Once in the kitchen, Bess slipped effortlessly

into professional hotelier mode. 'Everything all right, Chef?' Alfredo was as temperamental as ever and rattled off the usual list of unimportant complaints under his breath without lifting his head. 'That's good,' Bess said, ignoring what she was unable to hear. 'I'll be back by the time you start serving dinner. If you want me before then, I'll be in the office.'

'Tea,' Frank said, pouring Bess a cup as soon as she entered the office. Bess walked round the desk and sat down. 'Now tell me what's going on with Claire and Mitch.'

As she sipped her drink Bess relayed the conversation she'd had earlier with her sister, concluding with, 'I feel I should go down to Oxford, but we're fully booked next week.'

'Normally I'd say go, darling, but if he has got shellshock - and by what you've told me he has - it's a doctor he needs. Poor chap. Taken by the Gestapo, eh? He should talk to a psychiatrist and get it off his chest.'

'If he doesn't talk to someone, it'll eat him up inside.'

They drank their tea in silence. Thinking the same as each other, which they so often did, they found no need to speak. 'Aimee enjoyed her party, didn't she?' Bess said at last. 'She was so happy.'

'She was showing off,' Frank said.

'Of course she was. She was the centre of attention. I don't think she's had a very good time of it lately. What with her father being moody and changeable, and over-protective, she's probably confused. I think she's lonely, Frank.' Bess leaned back in her chair and thought how lovely it was that Aimee had other children to play with today - and what a nice child Maeve's niece was.

'Thinking about the children?' Frank asked.

'Yes, actually, I was. I was thinking how lovely it was that Aimee had a friend like Nancy to play with this visit.'

'Who'd have thought Maeve had a niece? A turn-up for the books, don't you think?'

'Yes. I'm surprised she hadn't mentioned Nancy before. Then again, why should she?'

'No reason at all, except that she's almost like family.'

Bess wasn't thinking about Maeve, her thoughts were about Nancy. 'She's a beautiful little girl, and so well mannered.'

'She'll be a good influence on our Aimee,' Frank said.

Bess felt a tingle at the back of her nose, swallowed to stop herself from crying, and tried to ignore the maternal feelings that reminded her that she didn't have children. 'I didn't have time to ask Margot how she was feeling,' she said, changing the subject. She swivelled round and looked at the wall clock. 'There isn't time now. I'll telephone in the morning.' She hauled herself to her feet. 'I'm nipping up to comb my hair and refresh my make-up. When I come down I'll do the kitchen and the restaurant if you do the money for the bank tomorrow.' Frank saluted her and Bess threw a teaspoon at him, before running out of the office.

'Watch it, or I'll do you for assault,' Frank joked. Bess didn't look back. She didn't want her husband to see her tears.

*

The following morning, Bess met Maeve running up the staff stairs while she was making her way down them. 'Mrs Donnelly, thank goodness!' she said, 'I tried phoning you, but your line is engaged.'

'Frank's trying to get hold of my mother. What's the matter?'

'Mrs Burrell,' she said, catching her breath. 'She's gone into labour. Mr Burrell has just telephoned. He said she was in a lot of pain, so he called for an ambulance and they've taken her to the Walsgrave Hospital in Coventry.'

'But she isn't due until the end of September, that's three weeks away.' Bess turned to go back to Frank, thought better of it and quickly turned round again. 'We'd better get over there. Would you go up and tell Frank, while I let the kitchen know I won't be working at breakfast or lunch? And, Maeve, tell him to bring the baby clothes down when he comes. We'll need to take them with us,' Bess said, reaching the bottom of the stairs.

The breakfast staff knew Margot and showed genuine delight that the baby was on its way. Bess checked the lunch menu. It was in order. Chef said that he and the head waitress would make sure the guests had everything they needed, and that Bess was to give Mrs Burrell everyone's best wishes.

Maeve was back on reception and Frank was in the office by the time Bess had finished in the kitchen. She grabbed her coat. 'Frank, did you bring down the baby clothes?' she asked, swinging her coat over her shoulders and pushing her arms down the sleeves.

'I brought this,' Frank said, passing Bess a large carpetbag.

'That's fine. There's no time to go back for the rest, this will do for now.'

'It will do?' Frank said laughing. 'The bag's so heavy, I thought you'd bought Kimpton Smith's entire baby department.'

'Not quite,' Bess grinned.

'Maeve, would you ring Ena and Claire, tell them what Bill told you. Tell them Frank and I are on our way to Coventry and I'll ring them as soon as I've got anything to report. Oh, and if Claire's husband answers the telephone, would you ask to speak to Claire? I think it's best if you tell her in person, instead of leaving a message with Mitch. He might forget. Right!' Bess said, 'we'd better get going.'

'Would you give Mrs Burrell this from me?' Maeve handed Bess a soft parcel.

'Of course. That's kind of you, Maeve.' Bess lifted her shoulders and grinned. 'I'm so excited. I never thought Margot would have children. I'm worried too, with the baby coming early.'

'It's amazing how tough babies are,' Maeve said. 'Don't worry, the little one will be fine.'

'Bess?' Frank called from the corridor leading to the back door. 'Are you coming?'

'You're right,' Bess agreed, 'I'm worrying for nothing. I'm sure everything will be fine.'

Maeve looked past Bess. 'I'm not sure Mr Donnelly will be fine, if you don't go soon.'

Running to catch up with Frank, Bess felt butterflies of excitement and anxiety flying around in her stomach. She calmed down when she saw

Frank's face. Maeve was right again. Frank wasn't fine. He looked impatient when she jumped in the car.

As they set off down the drive, Bess said, 'Mam! Oh, Frank, we haven't told Mam that Margot's gone into labour. She'll be furious if we don't tell her she's about to be a grandmother again, and offer to take her with us to the hospital.'

'I rang her when I went up for the carpet bag, but she didn't answer.'

'She never does. It was a waste of time having a telephone put in for her.' Frank pulled up outside Lily Dudley's cottage and Bess jumped out. She ran up the path and hammered on the front door. No answer, so she ran to the back door. No reply there either.

'She isn't in,' Bess said, climbing into the car. 'Let's go. We'll call in on the way back.'

The journey to Coventry took longer than it should have done. The traffic was heavy for the time of day and there were road works just outside the village of Brinklow. Once in Coventry it was plain sailing through the suburbs. The Walsgrave hospital came into view, Frank found a place to park the car, and he and Bess were in the hospital at ten o'clock.

Mrs Burrell, they were told, was in the maternity wing. 'First floor, ward 10, along the corridor on the right,' the woman behind the enquiries desk informed them.

The nerves on the top of Bess's stomach began to tighten. She took a deep breath to calm herself and held Frank's hand, interlinking her fingers in his. 'The baby is three weeks early, Frank.'

Frank gave her hand a reassuring squeeze. 'Don't worry love, she'll be okay; they both will, you'll see.' Hand in hand, Bess and Frank followed the overhead signs to Maternity, taking a flight of stairs at the end of the corridor to the first floor. Before they saw ward 10, they could hear Margot shouting.

'We're in the right place,' Frank said, laughing.

Bess hit him playfully on the arm. 'There's Bill,' she said, walking quickly on the balls of her feet, so her heels didn't click on the tiled floor, 'in the recess between wards nine and ten.'

'Bess. Thank God you're here,' Bill said, as Bess and Frank approached. 'I've been going mad on my own listening to Margot screaming. What the hell are they doing to her?'

'They're not doing anything to her, Bill. All mothers shout when they're giving birth.'

A nurse came out of a room next to ward 10. The rubber soles of her flat shoes squeaked as she walked briskly past without acknowledging Bill. A second later she was back with a midwife in tow.

'Excuse me?' Bill said, jumping to his feet. 'How is my wife? Mrs Burrell?'

'Doing fine,' the nurse said impersonally. And entering after the midwife, she left the door to swing shut on its own.

More screams, curses and grunts followed, and then, "Oh, Johnny! Oh, Johnny! Oh!"

'What the--?' Bill stood up, put his hands on his head and looked from Bess to Frank. 'She's singing,' he said, a look of incredulity on his face. 'She's bloody singing.'

The grunting started again, followed by a long

'Agh…!' and then, "Rule Britannia, Britannia rules the waves, Britain never, never, never shall be slaves." 'And I shall never let that damn man near me again. Can you hear me Bill Burrell?' Margot yelled at the top of her voice. 'Agh…!'

Bess couldn't speak for laughing. Eventually she managed to say, 'They're stopping Margot from pushing by getting her to sing.' Frank laughed too, but Bill looked astonished. 'Shush! Listen!'

'To what?' Bill asked. 'I can't hear anything.'

'Exactly!'

They sat in silence. Then a loud howl filled the corridor.

Bill sprang out of his seat and put his hands up to his mouth. 'He's here. The baby's here,' he cried, jumping up and down on the spot. Bess and Frank got to their feet. They each congratulated and hugged Bill, before hugging each other.

The midwife came dashing out of the room, her starched uniform rustling as she neared. 'What's going on?' Bill asked, his face pale and tear-stained.

'Nothing to worry about. Baby is fine. She has all her fingers and toes,' the midwife said, 'but because she's early, I'd like Doctor to have a look at her.' Some minutes later the midwife was back with the doctor. Bill approached the doctor who put up his hand. 'Doctor can't tell you anything until he has examined your wife and daughter, Mr Burrell,' the midwife said brusquely. 'You must be patient!'

'Fine! That's all they can say - and be patient!' Bill sat down. A minute later he stood up with a start. 'It's a girl. The midwife said, daughter.' Bill sat down again, but couldn't settle. 'The doctor's been in there a long time. You don't think there's anything wrong with the baby, do you, Bess?'

'No... You heard what the midwife said. The baby was early, so the doctor has to check her over. It's normal medical procedure.' Bill frowned, he didn't look convinced. Bess wasn't convinced either, but she carried on, 'They have to check all premature babies. It's just a precaution, there's nothing to worry about.' Bess had no experience with babies, premature or otherwise, she just hoped what she said to Bill was of some help.

'Mr Burrell?' Bill turned at the sound of his name. 'If you'd like to come in now, your wife is ready to see you.' Bess took a step forward and looked optimistically at the nurse. 'Husband only,' she said. When Bill went into the ward, the doctor and midwife left.

Passing Bess and Frank the midwife smiled. 'Mother and baby are doing well.'

'The child has a good pair of lungs. Takes after her mother, I gather,' the doctor said, winking at Bess.

'Yes,' Bess said, looking between the midwife and doctor. Her heart almost leapt from her chest with relief. 'She's doing well, Frank. Our little niece is doing well. Margot is too. She wanted a girl. She said she didn't mind, but secretly I knew she wanted a girl.' Bess looked along the corridor. 'Do you think we'll be able to see them today?'

'You're asking me? I have no idea about these things. Tell you what? I'll go and find a telephone, let Maeve know Margot's had the baby, so she can telephone Ena and Claire.' Frank gave Bess a peck on the cheek and set off down the corridor.

'Get Maeve to ring Mam when she's told the girls.' Frank waved in response. She probably won't answer the telephone, Bess thought. She looked down at the bag at her feet. It contained an assortment of vests, socks, and bibs, two pale pink nightdresses, and two lemon blankets with white satin edging. She was engrossed in her thoughts when she heard Bill call her name.

'Sorry, I was miles away. How are they both?'

'Wonderful. The baby is the most beautiful baby I have ever seen. She's very small,' Bill cupped his hands, 'but she's perfect. Margot's worn out, but she insists she wants to see you. The nurse said she'll be in trouble if the midwife catches you in there, so you're not to stay long, but she said to come in for a couple of minutes.'

Bess picked up the carpet bag and pushed open the door to Margot's room. The sight that met her filled her with the happiest, warmest, feeling... 'Hello, darling.' She tiptoed over to the bed. Margot was propped up by an elaborate arrangement of pillows that allowed her to hold her baby daughter in her arms.

'Say hello to your Auntie Bess, baby,' Margot said, gently pulling on the white sterile blanket that swathed the tiny child.

'Hello, beautiful girl,' Bess whispered. 'She's absolutely perfect, Margot.' Bess smiled at her niece through tears of joy, and then looked at her sister. Her hair was stuck to her head with perspiration. Her eyelids were red and looked heavy. 'What about you? How are you feeling?'

'Sore and tired. I expect I look a fright, but,' she said, looking down at her daughter, 'I don't care. The only thing that matters is this little one is here and she is healthy,' Margot cooed.

Bess was aware that the nurse, who had been hovering at the back of the room, had slowly made her way over to her patient's bed and was standing at Bess's side. 'I'd better go and leave you to get some rest, darling. I'll be back to see you as soon as you're allowed visitors. Bye, bye, sweetheart,' she said, blowing her little niece a kiss.

'There are some things in here for the baby,' she said, handing the bag to Bill. At the door, Bess looked back at Margot. She was already asleep. She mouthed thank you to the nurse and quietly left.

'The baby is perfect,' Bess said, falling into Frank's arms. 'She is gorgeous and Margot is amazing. She's so… so motherly.'

Frank laughed. 'Come on, let's go home.' As they turned to leave, Bill came out of Margot's room.

'Thank you for being here. And thank you for this.' He lifted the carpetbag to waist height. 'Margot needs some undies and another nightdress, so while she's sleeping, I'm going to go home and get washed and changed, and pick up some clean clothes for her. I'll take this with me, so it's waiting for them when they come home.'

'Do you want me to take anything to wash?' Bess asked, 'I could bring it back when I come in next.'

'No need. Margot bought new nightdresses, and she's got drawers full of underwear.'

Outside the hospital, before going to their respective cars, Bill promised to telephone Bess that evening to give her an update on Margot and the baby's progress, and to tell her when she could visit again.

Waving goodbye to her brother-in-law, Bess slipped her hand into Frank's hand and strolled by his side to the car.

Bess called at her mother's cottage on the way back from the hospital. There was no sign of life in the front or the back of the house. 'Mam's still out,' she said, sliding into the passenger seat of Frank's car. 'I'll leave her a note.' She rummaged around in her handbag, found a pen and a scrap of paper and scribbled, *Ring me at the hotel, Bess*. She then dropped the note through the letter box of the front door.

Returning to the car, Bess's face brightened. 'I can't wait to tell Maeve about the baby. And I'll telephone Ena and Claire, keep them in the picture.'

Walking into the hotel, Bess saw her mother sitting behind the reception desk like Lady Muck, telling Maeve how big her children were when they were born. 'The agony I went through having our Bess,' she said, 'And I can't tell you what it was like having Margaret.'

'That's good, because there isn't time, Mam,' Bess said, shaking her head. 'We get bigger every time she tells the story, Maeve.'

Maeve pressed her lips together to stifle laughter. 'How's Mrs Burrell and the baby?' she asked when she had recovered.

154

'If I told you that *Miss* Burrell was the most beautiful baby I have ever seen, would you think I was ever so slightly biased?' Maeve didn't hide her laughter this time. 'But she is.' Bess relayed every second of the time she spent at the hospital, from the moment she and Frank arrived, to the moment they left. 'Did you have time to telephone Ena and Claire?'

'Yes, and I telephoned them again, after Mr Donnelly rang. They both asked if you'd telephone them on your return and let them know how Mrs Burrell and the baby are doing.'

'I'll do it now. You coming through to the office, Mam?' Bess asked, 'or would you rather have a bite of lunch?'

'I am peckish,' Lily Dudley said, hauling herself out of the chair. 'I mean, there's no point me coming into the office with you, if you're going to be on that contraption talking to the girls for the next goodness knows how long. I might as well go and have something to eat.'

'All right. You go to the dining room and order what you want, and I'll join you as soon as I've spoken to Ena and Claire.'

When her mother was out of earshot, Bess told Maeve how the only way the midwife could get Margot to stop pushing, was to get her to sing. Maeve bit her lip and smiled sympathetically. 'I didn't want to tell you in front of my mother, or it would soon be added to her collection of embarrassing stories about *her girls*. I'm not sure Margot would approve of me telling you. Bless her, she is more sensitive than the rest of us Dudley sisters.'

155

Bess went into the office humming, "Oh, Johnny! Oh, Johnny! Oh!"

CHAPTER TWELVE

Still humming, Bess turned at the sound of a knock on the door. 'Come in, Maeve.'

'It isn't Maeve,' Sergeant McGann said, pushing open the door to Bess and Frank's private office and marching in as if he owned the place.

'Sergeant?' The hairs on the back of Bess's neck stood on end at the arrogance of the man. 'If you're here to see my husband, you should have telephoned. We've been out this morning and have only just returned.' Bess was damned if she was going to share her good news with the unpleasant man. 'Frank is rather busy.'

'It isn't your husband I've come to see, Mrs Donnelly.' McGann paused and looked around - for effect, Bess thought - and sucked his teeth.

'Sergeant McGann, I don't mean to be rude, but I am also busy. Would you get to the point of this intrusion, please?'

'Of course.' He took his notebook from his top pocket. 'All right if I--?' He pointed to the chair in front of Frank's desk.

Grudgingly Bess nodded. The tedious little man lifted the chair and plonked it down directly in front of her. Sitting, he slowly turned the pages of the notebook. 'Ah!' he said at last, 'got it!' He cleared his throat, laid the book on her desk, and resting his hands on the top of it, made a steeple of his fingers. 'Mrs Donnelly, how well did you know David Sutherland when you lived in London?'

Bess's heart almost leapt from her chest, but the self-satisfied smirk on McGann's face, reminded herself to stay calm. 'I didn't know him at all. I met him once at a first night theatre party given by my friends, Natalie and Anton Goldman. I had never seen him before that night, and I never saw him after that night - until he turned up here on New Year's Eve.'

'Several people that I have interviewed, since finding David Sutherland's body in your lake, told me that on that night Mr Sutherland threatened to expose you by telling your guests something that happened when you lived in London.' McGann glanced at his notes. '"What you got up to in London" was the phrase Mr Sutherland used.' McGann leaned across Bess's desk. 'What did he mean by that? What did he know about you that you wanted to keep secret?' Bess didn't answer.

'Did he have some sort of hold over you? Was that why your husband knocked him to the ground, to stop him from divulging something unsavoury, immoral perhaps, about your past?'

'My husband only did what any loyal husband would do if his wife was being threatened by a fascist bully like Sutherland.'

'Protect your honour?' Bess didn't answer. 'Very noble of him, I'm sure,' McGann said, making no attempt to hide the sarcasm in his voice. 'Your husband must love you very much, Mrs Donnelly. Does he love you enough to kill for you?'

'What? My husband didn't kill David Sutherland, you know he didn't.' McGann raised his eyebrows, as if to say he was no longer sure. 'If you'd had any proof that my husband killed Sutherland you would have charged him at Easter.

I told you then, and I'm telling you now, on New Year's Eve Frank stayed in the hotel. He didn't go outside until all the guests had left. By which time, according to you, Sutherland was already dead.'

Bess picked up the telephone, and dialled 9 for reception. 'Maeve, have you seen Frank?'

'He's taken Mrs Dudley home.'

Bess tutted. 'I thought my mother was staying for lunch.'

'She said she didn't fancy anything on the menu, so Chef made up a plate of cold meat and she took it with her. They've only just left. Do you want me to see if I can catch them?'

'No, it's all right, Maeve.'

'Is something the matter, Mrs Donnelly?' Bess could hear concern in Maeve's voice.

'Yes,' she said, barely able to keep the emotion out of her own voice. 'Ask Frank to come to the office as soon as he gets back, will you?' she said, and placed the telephone on its cradle.

Ignoring Bess's explanation as to where her husband was on New Year's Eve, and appearing not to have taken any interest in the conversation she'd just had with the hotel receptionist, McGann said, 'Several witnesses heard your husband threaten to kill Mr Sutherland if he came near you, or the hotel, again.'

'He lashed out in anger. But he wouldn't have killed him. My husband is a war hero. He went through hell in Africa. But even after the fighting, watching his friends get killed, and being shot in the temple and losing an eye, he is still the most decent and gentle man I know.' Bess swallowed hard, forcing down emotion that threatened to

159

engulf her as she remembered how grateful Frank was when, because the army surgeon had acted quickly, the doctors at the Walsgrave Hospital were able to save his other eye.

'My husband had been blind for months, not knowing whether he would ever see again. When his bandages came off, and the sight in his good eye gradually returned, and he was able to see,' Bess said, pointedly, 'Frank swore that he would never again hurt a living soul.'

'But he did, Mrs Donnelly. He punched a man and threatened to kill him!'

'He hit Sutherland because Sutherland was threatening me.'

'But why was he threatening you, Mrs Donnelly?'

Bess felt her pulse pounding in her temples. Her heart was racing. She put up her hands. 'Stop!'

McGann didn't stop. 'What did David Sutherland have on you? What did he know about you? Did you have a relationship with him?' McGann shouted.

'No! How many times do I have to say it? *I did not have a relationship with that monster.*'

'What then?'

'He raped me!' Bess screamed into McGann's face. 'Are you satisfied now? That--- That vile excuse of a man raped me. You want to know if I killed him? If it was me who bashed him over the head and shoved him into the freezing lake?' Bess looked at McGann, her eyes blazing with anger. 'Believe me I wanted to kill him. I have wanted to kill him many times. I was so ashamed after he violated me that I turned my back on the man I loved. I wanted to kill him then!

'Because of him I lived a solitary existence for years, when I could have, should have, been happy and loved. I spent those lonely years feeling dirty and used - unworthy of the love of a decent man. David Sutherland all but destroyed me. He took away my self-respect and left me feeling disgusted with myself.'

A heart-breaking smile spread across Bess's face. 'It wasn't until the man I loved, who loved me, made me realise that what David Sutherland did to me was not my fault. It was only then that I allowed myself to love, and to be loved.'

Bess exhaled a long breath. 'Sutherland hurt Margot's friend so badly that she almost died. He hurt me so badly that I wanted to die. Did I kill him?' McGann lowered his gaze to his notebook. 'Look at me!' Bess screamed. 'You were happy to look at me when you were accusing me of having a dirty secret in my past. The least you can do is have the decency to look at me now!'

McGann lifted his head and looked into Bess's eyes. His own, Bess thought, showed no sympathy, no remorse. 'No. I did not kill David Sutherland. Nor did my husband. But you can be sure that whoever did, would have had a damn good reason for seeing that evil bastard dead.'

There! She had done it! She had answered the question that she had dreaded being asked since New Year's Eve. With an overwhelming sense of relief, Bess burst into tears.

Frank crashed through the door, Henry hard on his heels. 'What the hell is going on?'

Bess held her arms out to her husband, tears

streaming down her face. 'Get him out of here, Frank. Get him out of here!' she sobbed.

McGann jumped up and came face to face with Frank. 'What have you done to her?' Frank shouted, stopping Bess's interrogator in his tracks. He elbowed McGann out of the way, dropped to his knees at Bess's side and put his arms round her.

Furious that McGann had interviewed Bess without him, or Inspector Masters, being present, Henry said, 'You'd better go, McGann.' Without his usual need to have the last word, the police sergeant left. Henry followed him out of the office and across the marble hall to the hotel's main entrance. He put his arm out and barred McGann's exit. 'Your card is marked,' Henry hissed. 'If Masters doesn't have you kicked off the force for this, I will.'

Back in the office, Frank told Bess she needed to rest. 'Come on love, I'm taking you upstairs for a lie down. You're exhausted.'

'But I need to---'

'You don't need to do anything, except take it easy for an hour or two. Come on, darling.'

Frank helped Bess to her feet and walked her to the door. 'Wait a minute Frank, I must look dreadful. I don't want the staff to see me looking a wreck. And what will the guests think if they see me like this?'

Frank opened the office door and stuck his head out. 'There's no one about.' He took Bess by the arm, walked her quickly past reception, across the hall and past the kitchen to the staff stairs.

'He knows, Frank. McGann knows about London.'

'Confound the man!'

'He suspects me of killing Sutherland. That's why he came here, to accuse me.'

Frank took the key to their suite of rooms from his pocket and opened the door. Bess went in ahead of him and dropped onto the settee in the sitting room. 'I think it would be best if you had a lie down on the bed,' Frank said, from the doorway of the bedroom. 'Come on love, have a proper rest.'

Bess forced herself off the comfortable settee and went into the bedroom. Frank had pulled back the eiderdown. 'You're right. I feel emotionally drained. I'm so tired I think I might even sleep. I'll try anyway.' Kicking off her shoes Bess fell onto the bed.

Frank lay beside her and held her until she dozed off. She slept fitfully, her eyes moving beneath their lids. She twitched, and a minute later jolted herself awake. Then she sighed heavily and, safe in Frank's arms, drifted into sleep.

When he was sure Bess had settled, Frank slid off the bed, pulled the eiderdown up around her shoulders and quietly left the bedroom.

The last thing he wanted to do was leave Bess, but he needed to attend to the new arrivals, make sure the kitchen was prepared to feed eight extra people at dinner - none of whom had been in the hotel at lunchtime when everyone else had ordered their evening meal, and, more importantly, he needed to speak to Henry.

Arriving downstairs Frank acknowledged Jack,

who was on reception with Maeve. 'I didn't realise you were on duty today?'

'I'm not officially, sir, until tonight.'

'I rang Jack and asked him to come in early,' Maeve said. 'I thought if he was here and you or Mrs Donnelly needed anything, I'd be on hand… I'll leave when the guests go into dinner.' Maeve looked anxiously at Frank.

'She's sleeping,' Frank said. 'I need to check everything's okay in the kitchen, make sure the dining room's ready for tonight, bring some wine up from the cellar, and take the float to the bar. Is Simon here yet?'

'Just arrived.'

'Right. I'll do his float first.' Frank went into the office, appearing minutes later with bags of change for the till in the public bar.

When Frank had finished in the kitchen he took a tray through to Maeve on reception. 'Would you take this up to Bess? She probably won't want to come down for dinner. She hasn't eaten all day, so if you could get her to eat this soup and bread, it would be something. If she refuses, I'm sure she'll enjoy a cup of tea.'

Frank left the tray with Maeve and set off to the cellar to choose a small selection of wines. Not many guests had wine with their evening meal, but Frank liked a variety of wines in the rack, in case. Besides which, he needed to keep busy.

Maeve took the tray up to Bess and Frank's rooms and gently knocked on the bedroom door. 'It's Maeve, Mrs Donnelly. Are you awake?'

'Yes, Maeve. Come in.' Bess called.

'I hope I'm not disturbing you, but Mr Donnelly thought you might like some soup.' Maeve set the tray down on the dressing table.

'He is a dear, but I'm not hungry. I'd love a cup of tea though,' Bess said, seeing the teapot and smiling. 'But there's only one cup. Aren't you going to join me?'

'No, I'm fine. I've not long had my break.'

Bess pushed herself up into a sitting position and accepted the hot drink that Maeve had poured. 'I needed that,' she said, after taking several sips. 'I suppose you heard what went on in the office?'

The receptionist's cheeks flushed pink. 'I wasn't listening, but I did hear the odd word.'

'I'm not surprised. I don't mind you knowing what that bloody man said, but I hope none of the guests heard.'

'There weren't any guests around at the time. And to be honest, it was only when you gave Sergeant McGann a good telling off that your voice was loud enough to hear in reception.'

Bess couldn't help but laugh. 'I did tell the little b off, didn't I?'

'From what I could hear it was no more than he deserved. He's a horrible man. I've a young brother in Ireland who would knock him down a peg or two. He'd soon wipe that smug grin off his face.' Both women laughed. 'That's better,' Maeve said. 'You're too good for the likes of him to bring you low. Right! I'd better go and let you get some rest.'

'I've rested for long enough. You don't have to go, not if you don't want to.' Bess craned her neck and looked out of the window. 'The afternoon light is fading, so I must have slept. And your shift ended some time ago,' she said, concerned that she was delaying Maeve. 'I'm sorry, I'm being selfish. You get off home.'

'I have nothing that will spoil at the vicarage. Mrs Sykes was taking Nancy to a school friend's birthday party this afternoon and picking her up this evening. She'll be in her bed by the time I get home, so I've nothing to rush back for. Would you like more tea?'

'Yes please. I feel mean enjoying my tea when you haven't got a cup.'

'I don't want tea, but if you'd like me to stay a while, I'd be happy to.'

'Thank you, Maeve, I would,' Bess said, tears welling up in her eyes. 'Argh!' she clenched her fists, trying her hardest not to give in to tears that she was powerless to stop. 'I'm silly letting that awful man upset me like this,' she cried. 'It's just that he kept on and on about the man who drowned in the lake.

'He knew the man who caused the trouble on New Year's Eve, David Sutherland, had threatened me, and that Frank had hit him. McGann quoted the exact words that Frank had said to warn Sutherland off. He said a witness had told him that Frank had threatened to kill Sutherland.' Bess let out a long breath. 'The problem is, Frank did say he'd kill him. But he only said it because Sutherland provoked him. Frank would never have done it. McGann's so-called witness had taken what Frank said completely out of context. Of course you know all this because you were there.'

Maeve nodded.

Bess took her handkerchief from beneath her pillow and dried her eyes. 'McGann kept asking me how long I'd known Sutherland, and if I'd had a relationship with him when I lived in London. He asked me over and over again. He didn't stop until I broke down and admitted that I had known David Sutherland in London.' Maeve gasped. 'No, no,' Bess said, 'not in that way.'

Bess couldn't let this kind, decent woman think that she had wanted to be with David Sutherland. 'I didn't have a relationship with that vile man.' Bess looked squarely into Maeve's face. Dare she tell her what Sutherland had done to her? She ached to share the secret that had been the source of her nightmares for so many years. She was desperate to talk to someone about the pain she lived with. A pain that was as raw today as it had been ten years ago. But more than that, Bess wanted someone other than Sergeant McGann to know what David Sutherland had done to her. She took a calming breath. 'He raped me,' she said.

Maeve held Bess's hands in hers. 'I am sorry. So very sorry.'

'I hope you don't think badly of me, Maeve?'

'Why would I think badly of you? Men like Sutherland, wicked men, bullies, take what they want from women--'

'Sutherland did that all right. And I wasn't the only woman he took from and ruined.' Maeve gave Bess an enquiring look, but Bess shook her head. 'It's a heart-breaking story, but it isn't mine to tell.' Maeve nodded, accepting Bess's decision to keep a confidence.

'It's because of Sutherland that I can't have

children. Poor Frank, he wanted children so much, we both did.' Tears fell silently from Bess's eyes. 'As soon as we were married we began trying for a family. When it didn't happen, I knew something must be wrong. We'd been married more than two years when I went to see our family doctor. He asked me a lot of questions and afterwards said that he could see no reason why I hadn't conceived. Trying too hard and worrying about it can stop a woman from conceiving, he said, and told me to go home, relax, and enjoy my husband.'

Bess took a long deep breath. 'It was then that I told him that I'd been raped. He was the first person I'd told since Frank.' A loving smile spread across Bess's face. 'I told Frank when he asked me to marry him. I thought it was right that he should know. Most men have an idealistic view of the woman they marry. A single woman walking down the aisle in white illustrates to her husband, and to the world, that she's a virgin - and I wasn't.

'I also thought that telling Frank before we announced our engagement would give him a moral excuse to back out of the marriage proposal.'

'But he didn't take it,' Maeve said.

'No, he didn't.' Bess felt the fine wings of butterflies stirring in her stomach. 'And I love him for that. But sometimes, when I see him with Aimee, or with children staying at the hotel - and that bloody pony,' Bess said, laughing in spite of herself - 'I wonder if he now regrets his decision.' Bess dried her eyes. 'Anyway, the doctor first thought my problem was psychological, but I knew it wasn't. The following day I had an internal examination, after which I was told that due to the amount of damage that had been done, I would probably never conceive.'

'Do your sisters know?' Maeve asked.

'I told Margot when she told me about a friend of hers. I don't want to break a confidence, but a talented young dancer at the theatre where she worked was beaten up by David Sutherland.' Maeve dropped her gaze and slowly shook her head. 'I know it's a huge coincidence, but it's true. Sutherland almost killed her.

'I didn't tell Ena or Claire, I thought they were too young at the time.' Bess flicked her hair back. 'I was training to be a teacher and living in London when it happened.'

'Was Mrs Burrell in London then?'

'No, I was there three years before the war, at a teacher training college. I came back in September thirty-nine, when the children in the school where I taught were evacuated. Margot moved to London the year after to be with Bill. He was a motorcycle courier with the MoD by day and a volunteer ambulance driver in the evenings. By then I was turning the Foxden Estate into farmland with half-a-dozen Land Girls.' Bess sighed thoughtfully and looked into the middle distance. 'It feels like a very long time ago.'

CHAPTER THIRTEEN

Bess had her hand poised on the handle of the kitchen door. She had abandoned her duties for long enough and had decided when Maeve left it was time she went back to work. First on her list of jobs was to look in on Chef and the kitchen staff. A daily ritual to make sure they had everything they needed.

'Mrs Donnelly? Telephone for you,' Maeve called.

The kitchen would have to wait. Bess turned, let her shoulders sag in an exaggerated fashion, and walking across the hall pointed to the office.

Maeve beamed her a smile. 'Mr Burrell,' she whispered.

'News of Margot and the baby?' Bess dashed into the office, picked up the phone and waited until she heard the dull click of the main telephone on the reception desk. 'Bill?'

'Hello Bess. I thought I'd better let you know that both my girls are doing well, and you can visit them tomorrow. Visiting hours are from two until four. The hospital only allows two visitors in at a time - and for the first few days it's only for an hour.'

'That's wonderful. I can't wait to see them. Shall I come in at three o'clock? Give you some time on your own with Margot and the baby first?'

'Yes. Good idea. See you tomorrow.'

Bess heard the pips. 'Give them my love,' she shouted, but the phone went dead. Replacing the receiver on the cradle of the telephone, Bess relaxed back in her chair. She was just going to get up and return to the kitchen, when there was a tap at the door and Maeve's head appeared.

'I'm off now, Mrs Donnelly,' Maeve said, already wearing her coat and hat. 'But I just wanted to give you this.' She crossed the room to Bess's desk and placed a scrap of paper with a telephone number on it. 'I hope you don't think I'm being forward, and I know you see me every day, but if you ever need to talk when I'm not on duty, you can reach me on that number.'

'Thank you, Maeve. And thank you for spending time with me earlier. I appreciate it.' Bess looked at the office clock. 'Oh dear, you really are going to be late now.'

Maeve flicked the suggestion away with her hand. 'I'll be off then. Good night.'

'Good night, dear. Oh, Maeve?' Maeve turned and looked over her shoulder. 'I won't keep you a second. During the time that you have worked here we've become friends - and today I have entrusted you with my most private, most personal, secret.'

'I won't tell a soul, Mrs Donnelly,' Maeve closed the door. 'What you told me today stays between us. I would never divulge a confidence, never! I give you my word.'

'I know you wouldn't, Maeve. You misunderstand me.' Bess felt embarrassment flush on her cheeks. 'What I'm trying to say is, because we are friends I should like you to call me Bess.'

A kind but serious expression crossed Maeve's face and she thought for a moment. 'I'm honoured that you trust me. And I should like very much to be your friend. But when I'm working with Jack it

171

wouldn't be fair for me to call you by your Christian name when he, quite rightly, has to call you by your married name. He's young and might see it as favouritism. I would also prefer to call you Mrs Donnelly in front of the guests. Let them see the moment they walk into the Foxden Hotel that it is a professional establishment.'

Maeve gave Bess an endearing smile. 'Good night, Mrs Donnelly, I'll see you in the morning.'

The more Bess got to know Maeve O'Leary the more she liked her. She was right of course, it was best to be professional while they were at work. She was right about Jack, too. He was charming, hardworking, and the guests liked him, but he was young. It definitely wouldn't be fair on him if Maeve called her by her Christian name.

Bess left the office. 'Everything all right, Jack?' she asked, in the casual manner that she used when talking to Maeve.

'Yes, thank you, Mrs Donnelly.'

'If anyone wants me, I'll be in the kitchen, and then the dining room. Oh, and if anyone telephones and asks to speak to me, would you take their telephone number and a message, and tell them I'll call them back as soon as I am free.'

'Yes, Mrs Donnelly.' Jack straightened up and stood with his shoulders back, as if he was on parade. He looked smart in the jacket Frank bought him to wear on reception. He was a good looking boy with a welcoming smile. He deserved his recent promotion to assistant receptionist from day porter, which had been his job since the hotel opened.

Bess knew she and Frank were lucky to have

the staff they had working for them and was counting her blessings as she approached the kitchen.

Shouting brought her to a halt. Instead of opening the door, Bess stood in the passageway between the restaurant and the kitchen and listened. The chef, his voice usually high and slightly effeminate, had taken on a deep, masculine tone. 'How dare you speak about Mrs Donnelly like that?'

'You didn't hear what she said after Sergeant McGann left - after he had interviewed her. I did,' a woman boasted.

'What did she say? Go on, Joan, tell us?' a younger woman asked.

'"He knows, Frank," she said to that nice husband of hers, "McGann knows."'

'Well I never!' the second woman exclaimed. 'Was she saying the police knew she'd killed the bloke they found in the lake, then?'

'Sounded like it. I thought it was her all along,' the woman called Joan said.

'Mrs Sharp? Hold your tongue and keep your opinions to yourself,' the chef shouted. 'I will not have malicious gossip in my kitchen!'

'I was only saying…'

'Then say it in your own time. Better still, don't say it at all,' he bellowed, 'Get out and don't come back!'

'You can't sack me!' Joan Sharp spat. 'I'll report you to Mrs--'

'Donnelly?' the chef said, with irony. 'And tell her what? That you think she is a murderer? Now go!' the chef hollered.

At that moment the door opened and Bess ducked to dodge a flying plate. 'What on earth is going on?' she shouted to the chef who, with his arm still raised, stood open mouthed on the opposite side of the kitchen.

'I think you had better leave,' Bess said to Joan Sharp, who had side-stepped the chef's missile and, struggling to stand up, had fallen sideways into Bess.

'I'm sorry, Mrs Donnelly.' Bess raised her eyebrows. 'I weren't saying you did kill that man,' Joan Sharp fawned.

'Of course you were, Mrs Sharp.' Bess held the door open for her. 'You were saying exactly that. You overheard a small part of a conversation between my husband and me, put two and two together and came up with five.' Joan Sharp looked daggers at the chef, hung her head, and manoeuvred her stout form past Bess and out of the kitchen.

'I am sorry about the plate,' the chef said, picking up the broken pieces at Bess's feet. 'I did not intend it to hit Joan--- Mrs Sharp, or you.'

'Well that's all right then,' Bess said, unable to keep sarcasm out of her voice. 'But accidents happen, and if you had hit Mrs Sharp the hotel would have been a chef short tonight, because you'd be in a police cell - and I would have a law suit on my hands.'

Bess gave the chef time to digest the implications of his actions before saying, 'Are you calm enough to carry on with your work, or shall I take over?'

'No!' Red-faced, Chef's fat cheeks wobbled

and the sagging skin around his jowls and chin quivered. 'With all due respect, Mrs Donnelly, you are not, not…'

'Capable?' Bess offered.

'Qualified,' the chef said. He clasped his hands in front of his considerable paunch and, leaning his head on one side, gave Bess a self-satisfied grin.

Bess looked at the chef and her insides groaned. It had been a day of extreme emotions. From joyous to distressing, followed by an outpouring of feelings. And although she had slept for a short time during the afternoon, she was tired and her nerves were frazzled. But if she was going to get this damn man back to work, Bess knew she would have to play his game.

'No, I am not qualified. And between you and me,' she whispered, 'I am not even a very good cook. But, Chef, it is my intention to give the guests in my hotel the dinner they are expecting tonight. So, someone has to clap their hands and shout, "Come people! Back to work!" And that I could do!' Bess looked sternly at the fifty-year-old man who, if anyone upset him in *his* kitchen, reverted to being a belligerent child, and waited for him to decide whether he was going to work or throw another tantrum.

'Mrs Donnelly?'

'Chef?'

'If you will excuse me,' he said, with a courteous nod, 'I have work to do.'

'Of course, Chef.' As she closed the door on the hot kitchen, Bess heard the chef clap his hands and shout the familiar words that the kitchen staff both admired and ridiculed him for, 'Come people!

175

Back to work!'

Feeling satisfied that she had won yet another battle with the excellent but exceedingly temperamental chef, Bess went to the dining room and walked among the tables. Crisp, white, and perfectly ironed tablecloths had been placed on the tables in such a way that ensured the same amount of fabric hung over the four sides of each table. Looking about her to make sure she wasn't being watched, Bess straightened a couple of uneven place settings on the table nearest to the window, before counting twelve porcelain *Reserved* markers.

Most guests found a table on their first night and stuck to it for the time they were staying at the hotel. Tables nearest the windows were favourite, because of the views. Tonight, every table with a view was taken, which was academic because the sky was already darkening. By the time the guests came down for dinner there would be little or nothing of the grounds or the lake to see.

Checking for dust, Bess ran her fingers along the window ledge - a habit she had picked up while working in a hotel in Leicester. She glanced at her finger. There was no dust! Before leaving Bess cast her eyes over the room. Everything was in its place, everything was just as it was supposed to be.

CHAPTER FOURTEEN

'Mrs Donnelly?'

The nerves on the top of Bess's stomach tightened at the sound of Detective Inspector Masters' voice. 'Yes,' she said, looking up and putting on a smile.

'Do you have room for one more at dinner tonight? I'd be very grateful. I have been staying at the Denbigh Arms in Lowarth, but I had to go up to London for a couple of days and when I got back someone new to the job, the manager said, had let my room and there isn't another. The hotel is full.'

It flashed through Bess's mind that the inspector was lying. The Denbigh might be full on a Friday night, but if someone had let his room by accident, surely the manager would have offered him dinner. He owed him that much. Bess gave the Detective Inspector a cautious smile. If he was lying she could easily find out. She looked around the room and pointed to three tables that hadn't been reserved. 'Where would you like to sit?'

'Here will be fine,' the inspector said, his hand on the back of the chair of the nearest table.

Bess went to the chest of drawers and took a *Reserved* sign from it. 'This is your table, then,' she said, handing him a menu. 'Dinner is served from seven for guests who have pre-ordered. If you decide what you want now you'll be served then, or just after. If you order when the dining room opens at six forty-five, you'll have a wait for your meal. The meat is already in the oven, for obvious reasons, but everything else is cooked fresh.'

'Home-made vegetable soup, and lamb casserole,' the inspector said.

'Good choice. I'll give your order to Chef. If you'd like to go up to the smoking lounge. Have a look at today's newspaper, perhaps?'

'I was wondering if I could have a word with you and your husband in private?'

Bess's heart plummeted, but she said, 'Yes, of course,' and on the way to the office, popped her head round the kitchen door. 'One more for dinner tonight, Chef. Vegetable soup and lamb casserole. Is that all right?' The chef put up his hand. 'If you need me to help with the washing up later, let me know. I'll be in the office.'

'Do you have to work in the kitchen as well?' the inspector asked.

'Only when Chef's short staffed - and he is tonight, he has just lost his washer-upper.'

Inspector Masters stopped at the reception desk. 'I won't be a moment,' he said, 'I wasn't sure I'd be welcome, so I only made a temporary booking for tonight. I had better confirm.'

Bess pointed to the door with brass plaque on it that said *Private* and left the inspector with Jack.

'Inspector Masters wants to talk to us.' Bess kissed her husband as she passed him and sat down at her desk.

'Now what?'

'No idea, but I don't think there's anything to worry about. He has just ordered dinner and now he's in reception booking a room for tonight. He wouldn't be doing that if he was going to accuse

178

either of us of murdering David Sutherland, would he?'

'I suppose not. I wonder why he's staying here?'

'He said the Denbigh was full.'

'That doesn't surprise me. Henry was saying there's a Masonic do on somewhere. He said the town's heaving. Apparently Freemasons from all over the county have descended on Lowarth for the weekend.'

Bess wrinkled her nose. 'Oh, and Chef has sacked Mrs Sharp.'

'What for?'

'Gossiping. She saw McGann leave this morning, then she saw me in tears. She heard me say, he knows, and decided I meant McGann knew I'd killed Sutherland. I'm only telling you because I might have to do a stint of washing up later.'

'It'll be all over Woodcote by this time tomorrow,' Frank said.

'Tomorrow? You underestimate Mrs Sharp's ability to spread bad news.'

'Does Chef have a replacement in mind? We're busy next week.'

'No idea.' Bess groaned. 'I had to kiss Chef's backside earlier - metaphorically speaking. I'll probably have to do the same to Mrs Sharp to persuade her to come back, if Chef can't find anyone to do her job. Washing greasy dishes isn't exactly a sought after career.'

There was a knock at the door and Frank got up and opened it. He shook Detective Inspector Masters' hand. 'What do you want with us, Inspector? After the hell Sergeant McGann put my wife through earlier today, I'd have thought you had all the information you need.'

'I have no intention of asking any more questions about David Sutherland. I am satisfied that neither you, your wife, or Miss Dudley - I mean, Mrs Burrell - had anything to do with his death.' Bess looked quizzically at the inspector. 'I arrived back from London a few hours ago and went to the Denbigh to drop off my case. As you know, Mrs Donnelly, I wasn't able to do that because I no longer had a room. While I was there, however, I bumped into Henry Green. He told me that McGann had been here today and that he had interrogated you, so I went to see him at the police station.'

The inspector turned at the sound of chatter and laughter on the other side of the office door. A second later, Claire and Ena came giggling into the room followed by Henry.

'Excuse me, Inspector,' Bess said. Jumping up she ran to her sisters and hugged them.

'Is Aimee with you, Claire?' Frank asked.

'She's in the car asleep. Would you fetch her?' Claire gave Frank her car keys and when he had gone, turned on Inspector Masters. 'What are you doing here? Can't you give my sister a moment's peace?'

Masters put his hand up in a friendly gesture. 'I am not here to interview Mrs Donnelly, I am here to apologise for Sergeant McGann's behaviour today.'

'Inspector Masters knows the score, Claire,' Henry said. 'Go on, Inspector.'

'After speaking to Henry earlier, I went up to

Lowarth police station. McGann had clearly been waiting for my return because before I'd had time to take off my coat, he began making excuses for coming here today, and gabbled out the most preposterous lies.' The inspector turned and looked at Bess. 'As I said, I came here to apologise to you, Mrs Donnelly. And,' he looked at Henry and laughed, 'the Denbigh really did let my room to someone else.'

A dull thud on the door told Bess that Frank wanted to come in but had his hands full. Claire stood up, but it was the inspector who got to the door first and opened it. 'I'll take her up and put her in our bed,' Frank said, 'until you get a room sorted out, Claire.'

'What if she wakes up? She won't know where she is,' Bess said.

'I'll stay up there. I need to finish that paperwork,' Frank motioned with a nod of the head to a mound of papers on his desk. 'I can work on the table in the sitting room.'

'But you've had nothing to eat, Frank. You can't keep going without food.'

'I'll get Chef to make Frank something, and I'll take it up,' Ena said, leaving the office.

'I had better go up too, in case Aimee wakes,' Claire said.

'Bring the papers on my desk, Claire, and the reservations diary.'

'You go, Claire, I'll bring the papers,' Henry stacked dozens of bills and hotel receipts on top of the diary. 'When I've taken this lot to Frank, I'll go back to the Denbigh, see who shows up. I'll see you tomorrow,' Henry said to Inspector Masters, before kissing Bess on the cheek.

When the family had bustled noisily out of the office, the inspector turned to Bess. 'I was hoping I'd get to speak to you on your own.' Bess felt a surge of panic rise in her stomach. The inspector must have sensed her discomfort, because he said, 'It's nothing for you to worry about, but while I was in London I called on Mr and Mrs Goldman. There's nothing for you to worry about there either. Police procedure! Eliminate them from the enquiry.

'They made me very welcome, offered me refreshment and showed me around the theatre - backstage too,' he said excitedly. 'And of course, they verified yours and Miss Dudley's story at New Year. They are good people,' he said.

'Yes, they are.'

'They told me Miss Dudley, Mrs Burrell, has had the baby and they are both doing well.'

'I'm sorry I didn't tell you when you first came in.' Bess looked quizzically at the man sitting in front of her. 'I didn't realise you had a personal interest in my sister. I don't mean to be nosy, but you often call Margot "Miss Dudley." Did you know her in London? See her at the theatre perhaps, in one of the shows?'

The inspector smiled sheepishly, as a teenage boy might. 'Yes. I saw Miss Dudley in several shows at the Prince Albert Theatre. Whenever I was home on leave my uncle got me a ticket.'

Bess rocked back in her chair, open mouthed. 'Your uncle was the lovely stage doorman, Bert Masters?'

'Yes.' Inspector Masters smiled with pride.

'Uncle Bert told me about the girl Sutherland beat up at the time. He was very fond of all the dancers, especially those who didn't have family in London. He had no children of his own and saw himself as a father figure. From what I've since been told, my uncle never forgave himself for not being able to keep Miss Trick safe. It's for her--'

'And for your uncle?' Bess suggested.

'Yes, and for me. Sutherland slipped through my fingers in 1938 and I joined up in the summer of thirty-nine. I've thought many times since then that, if I'd stayed a copper and put him away, he wouldn't have been around to hurt Miss Trick, or anyone else.'

'But you couldn't have known Sutherland would do what he did. You left the police force to fight in a war that put an end to fascism and Nazism. You'll never know how many women you, and men like you, saved from fascists like Sutherland.'

The inspector raised his eyebrows. 'I'd like to think that's true,' he said, with concern. 'When I heard that Sutherland had been found dead in a lake in the Midlands - and he'd been an associate of Gerald Hawksley's - I was determined to investigate the case. Meeting Miss Dudley again was a bonus. Meeting you all was. I am not sorry that the Denbigh didn't save my room. I feel as if I'm among friends here. And I think the Foxden Hotel is splendid. I love the marble hall and the sweeping staircase. From the little I've seen so far, the hotel is full of old-world charm and character.

'It is probably because you and your husband have done so well for yourselves that Sergeant

McGann has got a bee in his bonnet about you.'

'We've worked hard to make the hotel a success,' Bess said, 'and we will have to work hard for many years to come. But it's worth it. When Frank was signed off as fit after losing his eye, he couldn't go back to the engineering factory where he had done an apprenticeship before the war; it would have been too dangerous. He got a security job at Bitteswell Aerodrome and I carried on working on the estate here at Foxden.

'When the war ended the Land Army didn't disband, but when the local lads were demobbed they naturally wanted jobs. Many of them been farm workers, and so the Land Girls moved on to other work. I thought about going back to teaching, but I'd missed the beginning of the school year, so I got a job in a hotel in Leicester. At that time, Lord Foxden's plan was to lease the Foxden Acres, which had been turned into farmland, to the tenant farmers and restore Foxden Hall to its former glory.

'The servants' quarters, kitchen and the library, were redecorated. And the ballroom, which had been a large open ward for recuperating servicemen after Dunkirk, was reinstated. The refurbishment of the rooms in the west wing, which was the main hospital wing, took a lot of work but they were eventually turned back into bedrooms.

'The rooms where Lady Foxden had spent much of her time during the war, while her husband was in London at the War Office, had been decorated to her taste and her carpets and furniture brought out of storage. Everything was pretty much ready for her return.'

'But she didn't return?' Inspector Masters said.

'No. When Lord and Lady Foxden visited the Hall, just after the work was completed, Her Ladyship announced that she could never come back to Foxden to live. The memories of her son, James, growing up here and then being killed, were too distressing. James was a bomber pilot,' Bess explained. 'He was shot down over Germany.'

Bess winced at her own painful memory, then forced herself to continue brightly. 'So, Lord Foxden entrusted the Hall to me.' Bess saw the inspector's eyes widen. 'James was my fiancé and Lady Foxden said if James had lived we would have been married by now and Foxden Hall would have been our home. Frank and I couldn't afford the upkeep of the Hall, even if I went back to full time teaching. So, Frank, Lord Foxden and I had a meeting and we came up with the Foxden Hotel.

'Obviously we couldn't do it on our own, we didn't have the money, so Lord Foxden became our partner. He still owns the Hall, and he loaned us our share of the refurbishment costs, which we are paying him back. So, yes, I am proud. The Foxden Hotel is our business, our responsibility, and it is our home for as long as we want it.'

Bess was brought out of her reverie by Ena poking her head round the door. 'Dinner's ready. I've taken beef sandwiches up to Frank and I've sweet-talked Chef into finding enough food for me and Claire.' Ena giggled. 'He threw his hands in the air and said, after the guests have eaten, he'll bring anything left over to the dining room and we

185

can do with it what we want.'

Bess laughed out loud. 'How did you manage that?'

'I said we would do the washing up afterwards,' Ena said, and ran.

Chef was as good as his word. When Bess and the inspector arrived in the dining room, there was so much food on the first non-reserved table that there was hardly room to sit and eat at it. A waitress brought in the inspector's soup and placed it on the table that Bess had reserved for him, and Bess joined her sisters.

'Any chance of me sitting with you?' the inspector asked, with his bowl of soup in his hands. Bess got up and smiled apologetically at an elderly couple who had been enjoying their meal in the quiet, tranquil, atmosphere of an old English country house, until Ena and Claire entered and put a stop to it with their chattering.

Bess took a chair from the nearest vacant table and placed it next to hers. At the same time, Claire pushed several dishes of food closer together to make space for the inspector's plate. 'This is fun,' the inspector said, to the grumpy couple on the next table who were looking down their noses at him. 'Dinner with all my wives at the same time is such a rarity.' Bess bit her lip, while Ena and Claire giggled. The miserable couple, Bess noticed, had found something interesting about their serviettes to talk about and were straightening them on their laps.

The inspector looked up at Bess from under bushy eyebrows. 'Sorry,' he chuckled, 'I hope I haven't lost you two future customers.'

Bess frowned at him and mouthed shush, but was unable to keep a straight face. 'Eat your food while it's hot, darling,' she said, wagging her finger.

'I'll make it up to you,' the inspector said, and called over a waitress. 'A bottle of your best--' He looked across the table at Ena and Claire who both suggested red, and Bess nodded in agreement. 'Your best red, please.'

'A good wine, Sylvie,' Bess said pointedly. The waitress nodded that she had understood her boss, and went off to get a bottle of medium priced red wine. After going to the kitchen, for Chef to uncork it, Sylvie returned with the bottle and four glasses. She poured a little wine into the first glass and gave it to the inspector to taste. He took a sip, swished it about in his mouth and nodded his approval. Blushing, Sylvie filled each glass to just over a quarter, removed a dirty dish from the centre of the table, and put the wine in its place.

'Excuse me, Mrs Donnelly,' Sylvie said, 'Chef would like to see you when you have a minute.'

'Thank you, Sylvie. Tell him I'm on my way.' Bess rose from the table with a sigh. 'What now? I'll be back in a jiffy,' she said, leaving the dining room.

Opening the door to the kitchen, Bess came eye to eye with Mrs Sharp. Ignoring the woman, she looked across the kitchen to the chef. 'You wanted me, Chef?' He raised his hand and flicked a limp wrist in the direction of Foxden Hotel's dish-washer.

'It's me as wanted to see you, Mrs Donnelly,'

Mrs Sharp said, looking down at her wedding ring and twisting it round her finger. Bess didn't speak, but waited to be enlightened. 'It's my husband you see. He sent me to ask for my job back.' Bess looked at the chef again, and he looked to the heavens and shrugged. 'It were unforgivable of me to say what I said. I don't know what come over me. But if you could find it in your heart to let me have my job back…'

'It isn't up to me, Mrs Sharp. Kitchen staff are Chef's responsibility. If he is willing to forget the trouble you caused tonight, I am. But, and I think Chef will agree with me on this, there must be no more malicious gossip.' Joan Sharp hung her head, but Bess felt she needed to drive the message home. 'Listening to another person's conversation, hearing only part of it and then repeating what you think they meant, can have terrible consequences. Apart from which, it is a very unkind thing to do.' Joan Sharp looked as if she was about to burst into tears. 'If it happens again, Chef won't be so lenient with you.'

'No-o, Mrs Donnelly.'

'Thank you, Mrs Donnelly,' Chef said, and Bess left the kitchen.

'What was that all about?' Claire asked when Bess returned to the dining room.

'Kitchen gossip and temperaments,' she said. The chef came out of the kitchen to do a walk-about, which he did on special occasions. What the man thought was special about tonight, Bess had no idea. 'Chef?' Bess called, after he had asked several of the guests if they had enjoyed their meal, and name-dropped the Savoy Hotel in

London a couple of times. 'Everything all right with Mrs Sharp, now?'

'Yes, thank you, Mrs Donnelly. And thank you for letting the staff know who's the boss in my kitchen.'

Bess gritted her teeth for fear she would say something to burst the man's inflated opinion of himself. 'So, my sisters and I are let off the washing up now Mrs Sharp has been reinstated?'

Chef gasped and put his hands up to his fat cheeks. 'No!' he said. 'She dashed off to tell her husband she'd got her job back before he left for work. He's on nights at a factory in Lowarth, you see.' With that the chef puffed out his chest and strolled out of the dining room smiling and waving his podgy hands as if he were royalty.

To Bess's informed knowledge, Joan Sharp's husband, Sid - a bookend to the chef in stature - had never done a day's work in his life.

Ena and Claire, who had been listening to the conversation, left the table and began to clear it. 'We have to work for our supper,' Bess said to the inspector. Picking up several plates, she followed her sisters.

No sooner had the women started washing the dishes than Inspector Masters came into the kitchen with another bottle of wine. Scurrying behind him was Sylvie with four glasses. She put them down and giggled at Bess. The inspector had won Sylvie over. 'Budge up girls,' he said, grabbing a drying up cloth. 'I am a bachelor, and therefore an expert at this sort of thing.'

Bess, Ena, Claire and Inspector Masters laughed their way through the washing and drying

189

of every dish, pan, pot, plate and glass that had been used that night. When they had finished, Bess threw a dozen or more tea towels into the laundry basket and led the way to the office, where the four red-handed skivvies kept laughing while they drank the inspector's wine.

Inspector Masters was the first to leave, saying he had an early start and would see them at breakfast.

'Well?' Ena said, 'Who'd have thought a detective inspector from the Metropolitan police would be staying here and eating and drinking with us?'

'And washing up for the privilege,' Bess said, laughing with her sisters. 'He was also the bearer of good news, for a change. He told me earlier that he now knows that neither Margot, Frank, or I, had anything to do with David Sutherland's death.'

'What a relief,' Ena said.

'About time,' said Claire.

Bess gave Claire the key to her and Frank's rooms and, after checking with Mr Potts that all the guests were in the hotel, she made him a cup of hot chocolate and checked the back door was locked. Chef lived in, his room was a couple of doors along the corridor from Bess and Frank's. He was meant to be the last person to leave the kitchen at night, put out the lights and lock the door. On one occasion he had been on the cooking sherry and went to bed leaving the kitchen lights blazing and the door wide open. Bess hadn't trusted him since.

There was no need to go back and check the kitchen tonight, because she had been the last to

190

leave after the washing up marathon. Satisfied that all was well downstairs, and delighted that neither she nor anyone else close to her would be badgered again by the odious Sergeant McGann, Bess started up the staff stairs.

She paused half way. If the inspector knows it wasn't Margot, Frank, or herself who killed David Sutherland, who did kill him?

CHAPTER FIFTEEN

Beckoning Bess and shushing her at the same time, Claire stood in the corridor outside Bess and Frank's rooms. 'Come and see Frank and Aimee,' she whispered, leading Bess through the sitting room and into the bedroom.

Aimee, snuggled up against her Uncle Frank with her thumb in her mouth, was fast asleep. Frank, also asleep, was lying on his back fully dressed, clutching one of Aimee's story books and her old teddy bear to his chest.

'They're both out for the count,' Claire whispered. 'Aimee looks so content cuddled up to Frank, it would be a shame to wake her.'

Frank doesn't look comfortable though,' Bess said. Taking the book and teddy out of his hands, Frank stirred and let out a long sleepy sigh. Claire looked at Bess and they both held their breath. Frank rolled onto his side, didn't wake, and was soon breathing rhythmically again. Aimee, as a small animal would do, wriggled forward until she was leaning against Frank's back.

Bess didn't know whether to laugh or cry at the sight before her. Her husband would have made a wonderful father. 'We'll leave them,' she said. Taking a blanket from the chest at the bottom of the bed, Bess put it over them, turned out the light and crept out of the room behind Claire.

Bess dropped onto the settee. 'I'll sleep in here.' She swung her feet up, but wasn't able to straighten her legs, and when she tried to turn over she almost fell off.

'Come and sleep with me. It'll be like when we were kids.'

Bess laughed. 'All four of us had to bunk together, top to tail, when Granny visited.'

Claire pretended to shiver. 'She used to scare the life out of Ena and me, always dressed in widow's weeds.'

'She was all right. She was just Victorian in her ways, that's all.'

'Come on,' Claire said again, 'it'll be fun.' She looked disparagingly at the settee. 'This thing can't be comfortable to sleep on, it isn't big enough.'

'You're right,' Bess said. 'I'll be with you in a second.' Creeping into the bedroom, Bess took her dressing gown from the back of the door and a clean blouse from the wardrobe. The nightdress she would have worn was under Aimee's pillow, so she took a clean one from the chest of drawers along with knickers and stockings, and slipped out of the room without disturbing her niece or her husband.

By the time Bess had collected toothbrush, hairbrush, and other toiletries that she'd need in the morning and made her way to Claire's room, her sister was in bed.

'How's Mitch?' Bess asked, cleaning her teeth.

'The same. He doesn't sleep much, so he's often irritable. When he does drop off he has awful nightmares, which wake him up, so he's more irritable. He's jumpy and nervous. The slightest things upset him, and he worries all the time about mine and Aimee's safety. It's like living with an unexploded bomb, never knowing when it's going to go off. The doctor said he's suffering from nerves.'

'Same as Dad was when he came home from the Great War,' Bess said, taking a glass from the shelf above the hand-basin, filling it with water and rinsing the toothpaste out of her mouth. 'Some of the lads who came back from Dunkirk had the same symptoms. They had a hell of a time, saw some terrible things, and some of them couldn't shake off the experience. They probably still haven't.' She took off her clothes, pulled on her nightdress, and jumped into bed next to her sister.

'Mam said our Tom was like it when he came back.'

'He was,' Bess said, leaning on her elbows. 'Meeting Annabel and spending time with the lads in the hospital wing helped for a while, but then he started to drink.'

'He always liked a pint,' Claire said.

'He did, but this was different. He was getting drunk every night and offending people he cared about. It was as if he was on a merry-go-round and didn't know how to get off.'

'But he's all right now, so what changed?'

'He did. He had to. Mr Hands from The Crown in Woodcote telephoned me and said Tom was drunk and crying, and telling everyone that he had killed his best friend at Dunkirk. He asked me to go down and pick him up. He was frightened Tom would harm himself.'

'Had he killed his best friend?'

'No. The two of them had found a motorboat and Tom got it going. They were waiting for it to get dark, and then Tom, his best friend, and half a dozen other soldiers were going to escape. The

194

boat was full when a couple of lads, carrying their injured mate, asked Tom's friend to take him. There wasn't any room, so Tom's friend got out of the boat and put the injured lad in his place. Not long after they'd left the harbour it was blown up. Tom couldn't forgive himself for being alive when his brave friend was dead.'

Bess and Claire sat in silence. It was Claire who spoke first. 'How did Tom get over it?'

'As I said, it was a combination of things - falling for Annabel and helping in the hospital wing. But the turning point was that night Mr Hands asked me to take him home. Tom was so drunk he couldn't speak. I made him strong coffee and literally poured it down his throat until he was sick.' Bess wrinkled her nose at the memory. 'When he stopped being sick, he began to talk. He talked about his friend, how selfless and brave he was. Jock!' Bess said, his name suddenly coming to her. 'That was his name, Jock.

'He talked about how scared he'd been, about the horror of seeing men his own age wounded and dying on the beach, and dead bodies floating in the sea.' Bess stopped speaking and took a deep breath. 'I think talking it out with someone he trusted helped, I really do. I happened to be there for Tom at a crucial time,' Bess said. 'Can you think of anyone Mitch trusts; who he could talk to without feeling inadequate or embarrassed?'

Claire thought for a moment. 'The only people we know are in the military, and he'd never talk to any of them, he'd worry that they'd see him as weak.'

'What about his father?'

'He hasn't seen him for years,' Claire said. 'No, not his father, but our friend Edith Belland, the woman we lived with in France. Edith is the only person in the world Mitch would trust with his fears - and she is the only one I can think of who would understand what he's going through.'

The following morning Bess and Claire looked in on Frank and Aimee. They weren't there, which meant they had already gone down to breakfast. Aimee's old French teddy was propped up between two pillows on the bed. And on the table in the sitting room, in place of the pile of receipts Frank had brought up to work on the night before, was a note. "Good morning lazy Auntie Bess. Uncle Frank and me have been up for ages. We've collected the eggs and are now having breakfast." The note was signed "Aimee." Bess laughed. Her niece's handwriting had developed quite a sophisticated style overnight.

Maeve was on the telephone. She lifted her hand in a welcoming gesture as Bess passed. There were no newspapers on the reception desk, so they had either not arrived, or Frank had dealt with them. No post either, which Bess assumed her husband had taken to the office. She popped in and skimmed through half-a-dozen open envelopes. There was nothing urgent, so she dropped them back onto the desk and went to the dining room for breakfast.

As she passed reception, Maeve was on yet another call. Frank was right, it looked as if the coming week was going to be busy.

Bess poked her head round the kitchen door and

196

saluted the chef. 'I'm going in to breakfast,' she shouted. He muttered something in reply that Bess couldn't hear above the clatter of pots and pans, so she left.

Sylvie, on her way to the kitchen balancing a stack of empty plates took Bess's order. Two eggs and bacon, toast and tea. She was always hungry the morning after a late night, especially if she'd had too much to drink, which she'd definitely had last night.

'Morning, darling,' Bess said to Frank. She looked at Aimee, pretending to frown. 'Who slept in my bed last night?'

'I did!' she squealed.

Bess put her forefinger to her lips and pulled a wide-eyed face. 'Not too loud darling. People are eating.' She looked at the half-eaten piece of toast on a side plate next to Aimee. 'Where's Mummy?'

'Taken Nancy to the lav,' Aimee piped up, loudly. Bess looked prudishly at Frank and bit her bottom lip to stop herself from correcting her niece.

'Well you did ask,' Frank said. Leaning down until his mouth was level with Aimee's ear he whispered, loud enough for Bess to hear, 'She did ask didn't she, Aimee.' Aimee looked at Bess very seriously and nodded.

'Stop encouraging your niece to be cheeky,' Claire said, returning to the table with Nancy. Claire pulled out Nancy's chair and the little girl sat down.

'Hello, Nancy,' Bess said, looking across the table at Maeve's niece who was waiting for Claire to push her chair nearer to the table. 'How nice to see you again.' When she was within reaching distance of her toast, Nancy looked up at Bess with big eyes, whispered hello and turned to Frank for what looked to Bess like approval.

Aimee took a slice of toast from her plate and ripped it in two, giving one piece to Nancy who, still looking at Frank, said, 'Thank you.'

'Jam?' Aimee asked. Pulling a small glass dish on a silver tray towards her she stuck in a spoon.

'I think I'd better do that,' Frank said. 'It wouldn't do to get jam on your clothes, would it?'

As Sylvie brought in Bess and Claire's breakfasts, Ena and Henry arrived. Seeing what her sisters were having, Ena asked if she could have the same.

Sylvie looked enquiringly at Henry. 'Not for me, thank you.' When the waitress had left, Henry turned to Bess and Frank. 'Inspector Masters pushed a note under the bedroom door, asking me to meet him at Lowarth police station. I'll have something to eat afterwards,' he said, and, kissing Ena, dashed out.

'Have the children had something savoury to eat?' Bess asked, wrinkling her nose as Frank spooned a dollop of strawberry jam onto Nancy's toast.

'Boiled eggs,' her husband replied.

'And I collected them. You have to get up ever so early to collect the eggs,' Aimee informed Nancy.

Bess looked at Claire and raised her eyes. The two women shook their heads and laughed.

When they had finished eating, Claire said, 'I'll take the girls up to the nursery. While they're

198

playing, I'll write to Edith Belland, ask her if we can visit.'

'We'll talk about how best to approach the subject with Mitch later.'

'Mm. That's a conversation I am not looking forward to,' Claire said.

'Coffee?'

'Lovely,' Bess murmured, absentmindedly, as she listed figures in the accounts ledger.

'What time are you going to see Margot and the baby?' Frank asked, putting Bess's coffee on her desk.

Bess lifted her head from the pile of receipts that Frank had planned to enter the night before. 'What's the time?'

'Just gone twelve.'

'I'd better make a move.' She picked up the telephone, 'Maeve, would you give the kitchen a ring and ask Chef to get one of the girls to make a selection of sandwiches?' She put her hand over the mouth piece. 'Are you having lunch in here, or in the dining room, Frank?' He pointed to the work in front of him. 'Six rounds should be enough. As soon as possible, please.'

'What fillings do you want in them?' Maeve asked.

'Whatever Chef's got. And some cake if there is any.'

'See what I can do.'

'Thank you. Oh, Maeve?' Bess said quickly, before the receptionist had time to put down the telephone, 'have you seen either of my sisters?'

'They're still in the nursery with the children.'

'Thanks, I'll go up.' Bess put down the receiver. 'I'd forgotten Aimee and Nancy were going to be here today when I told Bill I'd go to the hospital this afternoon.'

'I don't see the problem.'

'There isn't one. It's just that Margot will be expecting me, but with Claire and Ena having come up specially to see her and the baby, they ought to go in my place. I'll stay here and take care of the children. I'll visit Margot next week.'

'You go with your sisters,' Frank said, 'I'll look after the children.'

'You!' Bess declared, slapping her hand down on the mound of papers on her desk, 'can finish what you started, or rather didn't start, last night. Enter this lot into the accounts ledger, and then file it.'

Frank lifted the pile of receipts from Bess's desk, plonked them down on his own desk, and saluted. Bess left him to it and went upstairs to her sisters.

'I've ordered sandwiches. You'll need something to eat before you go to the Walsgrave to see Margot,' she said. 'Bill's expecting you at three o'clock.'

'Aren't you coming?'

'No. I can go anytime. Claire's going home tomorrow, so you go with her today and I'll stay here with the children. Oh, and Mam's expecting to go today too, so will you call and pick her up on the way. If she's dressed for the occasion, take her with you. If she's forgotten, tell her I'll take her on Monday. Who's hungry?' Bess called to Nancy and Aimee. Both girls jumped up, discarded their

200

toys and led the way downstairs.

'Now girls, what do you want to do?' Bess asked, when Claire and Ena had left to visit Margot and the baby. Aimee lifted her shoulders and swayed from left to right. Nancy copied her. 'Shall we… play with the doll's house? You could take the furniture out of each room and put it back where you think it looks best.'

Neither child was impressed by Bess's idea. 'Or, we could get the train set down. I bet Uncle Frank would put the railway tracks together for us.' Bess looked at Frank for support, but didn't get any. 'We could go on a magical journey. Hooray!' Bess clapped her hands. 'What do you think? Is that a good idea?' she asked, nodding madly in the hope that her enthusiasm would rub off on the two girls and they would agree to play with the train. They didn't.

'I want to go outside and play,' Aimee said, 'I want to see the pony.'

'And the pigs?' Nancy said. 'Can we play outside, please?'

'Er… Yes, of course we can.' The pony was one thing. Bess loved horses and was more than happy to lead old Donnie round the paddock, but she would do anything to avoid the pigs. 'The pony it is then!'

'And the pigs,' Nancy reminded.

'And the pigs.' Bess grimaced. 'I know,' she said, as if a sudden thought had just popped into her mind. 'We'll get Uncle Frank to come out with us.' The girls cheered and ran to Frank. 'How about it, Uncle?' Bess put her hands together, as if in prayer.

'But my paperwork,' Frank said, raising his eyebrows.

'Touché!' Bess said, laughing. 'Tell you what, I'll help you with your work later, if you'll help me with mine, now.' She looked from Aimee to Nancy. 'Besides, you're much better than I am with the pigs.'

'You mean I don't mind getting my boots mucky.'

'What a cheek! How many years was I a Land Girl?'

Bess and Frank followed the two chattering children outside. It was a lovely afternoon. An Indian Summer the BBC's newsreader had called it. It hadn't rained for several weeks so the ground was dry. Frank forked hay into the pony's manger and filled the water trough in the small stable. 'We'd better leave Donnie to eat in peace.' There was a moment of complaint until Frank said they would go back to the pony. 'Now,' he said, 'we need to give the pigs some water.'

'Do the hens need water?' Aimee asked.

'Yes. All animals need water. Same as us humans.'

Aimee wrinkled her nose and Nancy copied her. 'By the time we've fed and watered the other animals, Donnie will have finished eating and be ready for a walk round the paddock.' Both girls shouted their approval.

CHAPTER SIXTEEN

Hand in hand, Bess and Frank followed Aimee and Nancy across the peacock lawn. Rounding the north side of the lake and strolling down the east side, the children disappeared every now and then to collect leaves. In contrast to the neatly mown lawn, which had been tailored since the days of the present Lord Foxden's great-grandfather, the grass on the east side of the lake was left to grow to encourage wild flowers.

'Don't go near the water, girls,' Bess called to the children. 'Come on, let's catch them up.' Still holding Frank's hand, Bess started to run. Frank pulled her back, put his arms around her and kissed her. Bess looked up at him, 'What was that?'

'Has it been so long you've forgotten?'

'No!' Bess laid her head on her husband's chest. 'We've been so busy lately we haven't had time for us.'

'Then we'll have to make time,' Frank said, kissing her again.

Bess giggled. 'Stop it, the girls will see us.' She looked over her shoulder. The children were engrossed in making patterns with different coloured leaves. 'We are going to have to organise our time better.' Frank pulled her close. 'I mean it, Frank. Because it's half-term this week the hotel is full, and with Maeve taking the week off we're going be busier than ever.'

'Do you think Maeve would change her week?'

'No. She specifically asked for next week off because it is half-term. The Reverend and Mrs

Sykes are somewhere up north visiting a sick relative and Nancy will be at home every day. Maeve doesn't have anyone to look after her.' Bess looked up at Frank and kissed him on the cheek. 'We'll be all right. Claire has to go home and sort things out with Mitch, but Ena will be here. I'll work on reception and Ena can oversee the kitchen and dining room.'

'Chef will love that,' Frank said sarcastically.

'He will actually. He has a soft spot for Ena. His cheeks go pink like a china doll's when she's around. And Ena likes it because he does as she asks, instead of debating every issue, which is what he does with me. Chef is putty in our Ena's hands.'

Bess turned at the sound of someone calling her name. Maeve was running across the peacock lawn. They walked back to meet her. 'What on earth's the matter, Maeve?'

'My holiday, Mrs Donnelly. I booked the week off starting on Monday, because it's half-term and the Reverend and Mrs Sykes are away. However, I have just taken a phone call from my brother in Ireland. My mother is seriously ill. She had a stroke yesterday and has been rushed to hospital. Would it be possible for me to start my holiday today? The doctor told my brother it's touch and go. He said she only has a fifty-fifty chance of recovering. I need to go to Ireland urgently.'

'Of course. You must go straight away. Is there anything Frank and I can do? One of us will drive you to the station, or wherever you need to go, won't we, Frank?'

'Yes, I'll take you,' Frank said.

Maeve nodded her thanks, and then turned to Bess but didn't speak. She closed her eyes as if she searching for the right words. 'What is it, Maeve?'

'I have no one to look after Nancy. I was hoping, praying, that she could stay here with you and Mr Donnelly for the week. Mrs Sykes is in Yorkshire and there isn't anyone--' Maeve caught her breath and began to cry.

'They're away until the weekend,' she said, taking a handkerchief from her pocket and wiping her tears. 'I should be back by then. If I'm not, Mrs Sykes will look after Nancy - take her to school and pick her up. They're getting old and taking care of a child twenty-four hours a day is a bit too much for them. Well, maybe not for Mrs Sykes, but it is for the Reverend. Oh dear,' Maeve said, 'Mother taking ill couldn't have come at a worse time.'

'Frank?' Bess looked at her husband, willing him to say yes. She would love to have Nancy stay with them for a week, but their marriage was one of equality. To have a child living with them, when they were going to be busy, had to be a joint decision.

'Yes. As long as it won't be too much for you, Bess?'

'It won't. You go and see your mother, Maeve. Nancy will be fine here with Frank and me.'

'Thank you, Mrs Donnelly, Mr Donnelly.' Maeve shook their hands in turn. 'I'll go and tell her,' she said, running to where the children were playing.

'You are sure about this, Frank?'

'If it's what you want?'

Bess thought about making light of it by saying *if it will help Maeve or it's only for a week...* The truth was, looking after Nancy was what she wanted more than anything. Bess had never lied to Frank and she wasn't about to start now. 'Yes, it is what I want. She's a lovely little girl.'

Frank put his arms around her, kissed the top of her head, and rocked her gently. 'Just promise me you won't get too attached to her, Bess. She is lovely, but she will be going back to live with Maeve when she returns from Ireland.'

'I know,' Bess said, looking at Nancy as her Aunt explained the following week's arrangements. Bess watched Maeve and the two little girls as they walked towards her.

Aimee broke away from the trio and ran ahead, arriving at Bess's side before the others. 'Can I stay with you and Uncle Frank next week, too?'

'You have to go home to your daddy, sweetheart.' Aimee's face crumbled and her big blue eyes brimmed with tears. Usually when she cried, Bess gave in to her, but not this time. That Claire went home and sorted things out with Mitch was of the utmost importance. 'We'll talk about it later, darling.'

Maeve looked at Bess, and then at Frank. 'I'll drop off Nancy's clothes and some of her toys on the way to the station.' Bending down so she was Nancy's height, Maeve said, 'Be a good girl for Mr and Mrs Donnelly.' Nancy nodded and wrapped her arms around her aunt's neck. Maeve eased the little girl from her and kissed her goodbye. 'I'll be back soon.' She thanked Bess and Frank, and ran back to the hotel.

'I'll take Maeve to Kirby Marlow to pick up Nancy's clothes, then I'll drop her off at the station,' Frank said, and followed Maeve to the hotel.

Bess thought it would take Nancy's mind off her aunt leaving if, instead of going back to the hotel, they carried on with their walk. She took each child by the hand and as they strolled along by the lake, she talked about the ducks and drakes, waterlilies and bulrushes. When they came to the south side of the lake, by the small wood that backed onto Shaft Hill, Bess had progressed to talking about her childhood. Reminiscing, she told them how she and her sisters used to visit the Foxden Estate with her father when they were Aimee and Nancy's age. She told them about the time she worked on the land with her friends in the Land Army - and she told them about Sable, the horse she'd loved, which from a young age she had exercised every day.

Eventually the girls lost interest and ran off to collect more leaves and watch the ducks on the lake.

As she walked along, Bess reflected on her decision. Looking after a child during one of the busiest times in the hotel's calendar was not going to be easy. It was what she wanted, and dare she think it was what Frank needed. She had wondered how Frank would feel about adopting a child. A lot of children were left without parents after the war, which she and Frank had talked about and which Bess had hoped would lead to a discussion about adoption. Then a disaster in the kitchen happened, or she was called away because of a double

207

booking. But if looking after Nancy for a week was a success - and she felt sure it would be - she would broach the subject of adoption at the end of the summer, when the hotel was less busy.

Bess watched Aimee and Nancy skip round the bend of the lake by the small wood and quickened her step. 'Aimee, where's Nancy?' Aimee pointed to the edge of the lake and the large clump of reeds that had hidden David Sutherland's body from New Year until the middle of March. 'Come away from there Aimee.' Bess took her niece by the hand, and led her away from the bank to higher ground. 'Stay there,' she said - and to Nancy she shouted, 'Don't go any nearer the water, darling.' Nancy, seeming to ignore Bess, pointed to the reeds at the water's edge.

Bess's stomach knotted as she slid down the short, steep incline the way Frank had done on the day Sutherland's body was found. Forcing herself to look, she saw the webbed foot of a duckling ensnared in the roots of the reeds. She slithered down further until she was able to reach the flapping creature. With one hand she managed to grab the frightened duckling without it attacking her, and with the other hand she picked the tangled roots from around its leg. She let go of the duckling as far from the reeds as she could safely reach and the little creature fluttered and splashed its way to freedom across the glassy lake.

Digging her heels into the soft earth at the lake's edge, and pushing down with the palms of her hands, Bess inched her way up the slope. Once she was in no fear of slipping into the lake and taking Nancy with her, she reached out to the child. 'Take my hand, Nancy.' The little girl turned her head to look back at Bess and slid nearer to the water.

'Don't turn round, darling. Keep looking forward. Just put your arm out to the side.' Nancy did as she was told and Bess clasped her hand around the child's wrist. 'That's it. I've got you. Now I'm going to pull you up the bank to me, but before I do that I want you to press the heels of your shoes into the ground.' Nancy nodded without turning. 'Good girl. Here we go, then.' As soon as Bess saw Nancy was digging her heels into the grassy bank, she pulled her arm. The slightly-built eight-year old weighed so little that it only took a few seconds for Bess to haul her to safety.

Trembling, Nancy flung her arms around Bess's neck and held onto her tightly. Bess was startled by her strength. 'There you are,' Bess said, 'you're safe now.' Bess felt Nancy's cheek brush her hair as she nodded, but she didn't lift her head, or take her arms from Bess's neck. When she did eventually relax her grip, she slowly turned and looked back to where the duckling had been trapped.

Icy fingers gripped Bess's heart and she gave a convulsive shiver. Nancy was looking directly at the spot where David Sutherland's body was found six months earlier.

'You saved the life of that little duck, didn't you, darling?' Bess said, trying to attract the child's attention. Transfixed on the water, Nancy only nodded. It struck Bess that there might be times during the coming week when she wouldn't be able to watch Nancy every moment of the day, so she must make it clear to her that if she went outside on her own, she must not go down to the lake.

'Nancy? Look at me, sweetheart.' The child's gaze slowly drifted from the reed's twisted roots, lying just below the water's surface, to Bess's face. Bess didn't want to frighten the child, but if she had fallen into the lake and become caught up in them... Bess's stomach churned. The consequences didn't bear thinking about.

'You must promise me that you will never go near the edge of the lake again,' Bess said, sternly. Nancy glanced over her shoulder at the water. 'Nancy!' The child's head jerked and she looked back at Bess, her eyes moist from the harsh tone of Bess's voice. 'I didn't mean to shout, but the water is deep and it is dangerous. Do you understand?' Nancy nodded. 'Good girl.' Bess hugged Nancy to her.

Scrambling to their feet, Bess and Nancy joined Aimee. Together the three of them watched the lone duckling, its feathers still ruffled, paddling for all it was worth across the lake to join a family of a dozen or more ducks by a large cluster of bulrushes on the far side.

Nancy looked up at Bess and slipped her hand into Bess's hand. Bess offered her other hand to Aimee and together they walked alongside the lake, but at a safe distance, up to the peacock lawn. As they neared the drive, Frank's car came round the corner of the hotel with Maeve in the passenger seat. Frank beeped the horn and Maeve waved out of the window.

Bess and Aimee returned the gesture. Aimee

shouted, 'Bye, bye,' while Bess called, 'Safe journey.' Nancy stood motionless and said nothing. She watched the car until it had disappeared around the bend to Mysterton Lane. Then, gripping Bess's hand tightly she said, 'Will Aunt Maeve come back for me?'

Bess knelt down on one knee and looked into the little girl's troubled face. 'Of course she'll come back for you, darling.' Nancy didn't look convinced, so Bess said, 'When we get back to the hotel, we'll mark the days that she'll be away on the calendar in my office. Then you can colour them in one day at a time until your aunt is back. All right?'

'All right,' Nancy said.

That problem solved, the two friends ran ahead of Bess, waiting for her to catch up with them on top of the hotel's steps.

'Any calls?' Bess asked Jack, as she and the children arrived at reception.

'One for Mrs Mitchell, from her husband. He said he'll ring again later.'

'Thanks Jack, I'll tell her when she gets back from Coventry.'

Bess suggested to her two small temporary wards that they all go upstairs, change out of their muddy shoes and socks, put on clean ones, and wash their hands and faces because it was almost time for tea. The reply from both girls was *can we tick the calendar first*? So into the office they traipsed, muddy shoes and all.

They followed Bess across the room like two shadows. She took the calendar from the wall and laid it on her desk. 'Who knows what day it is?'

211

'Saturday!' they both shouted, pointing to the square beneath the word.

'That was much too easy, wasn't it?' Bess said, laughing, and marked the square with an X. 'Your aunt Maeve has only just left for Ireland, so it isn't really the first day that she's away, is it?' Nancy shook her head. 'And next Saturday she'll be back.' Bess marked the day with an X 'So because tomorrow is the first day, write the number one in Sunday's square Nancy, and Aimee write number two in Monday's square.'

Bess watched the girls take it in turn to write the numbers in the squares, arriving at six the following Friday. 'There,' she said, lifting the calendar and admiring the neat numbers. 'Now every time you colour in a square you'll be one day nearer to seeing your aunt again, Nancy.'

Bess hung the calendar back on the wall and went to check on the kitchen leaving the girls with sheets of paper and crayons to make the important decision of which colour would be best for which day of the week. By the time she returned to the office, it wasn't only tea time, but Claire and Ena were back from visiting Margot and the baby.

'Jack said Mitch telephoned. Is it all right if I use your phone to call him back, Bess?'

'Of course. Ena and I will take the girls up to get changed. Can Nancy borrow a pair of Aimee's socks?'

'In the top drawer of the tallboy. Help yourself to anything.'

'Thanks. Come on you two, leave your colouring. You can finish it after tea.'

Upstairs, Ena and Bess took the children into

Claire's room. Bess took off Nancy's shoes and scraped the mud from them into a wastepaper basket, while Ena took off both girls' socks, giving them clean ones to put on. Aimee elected to keep her dress on as it was clean. Nancy's was soiled from where she had been sitting on the edge of the lake and although she didn't want to take her dress off, Bess persuaded her to wear one of Aimee's dresses until her own clothes arrived. Although Nancy was two years older than Aimee, she was small for her age. Aimee's dress was a little big round Nancy's waist, but with her cardigan on top she looked fine.

Bess and Ena returned to the office. Claire was waiting for them. 'We're going home tomorrow,' she said to her sisters. Aimee's face changed from happy to almost tearful, until Claire said, 'Daddy is taking us to France on Monday to see Grandma Edith.'

Bess and Ena looked at each other. They had discussed Claire's unhappy marriage and Mitch's shellshock. And they had agreed that if Mitch wasn't going to seek professional help through the Canadian Air Force, the best person for him to talk to was Edith Belland, but so soon--

'Close your mouths, you two,' Claire said. 'After all my agonising, Mitch agreed to see Edith the second I mentioned her name.'

'But I haven't seen Grandma Dudley,' Aimee whined, her bottom lip sticking out further than her top lip.

'We'll call in on our way home tomorrow,' Claire said, which seemed to satisfy Aimee.

'We took Mam with us to see Margot,' Ena said

to Bess.

'That's good. I'll get her to come up for lunch tomorrow, to meet Nancy. I might be calling on her to babysit during the week.'

Turning at the same time, Bess's sisters looked surprised. 'Long story, which I shall tell you about some other time, but Maeve has had to go Ireland. Only for a week,' she added, for the benefit of the child, 'so Nancy is staying here with Frank and me. Frank's in Kirby Marlow now, picking up Nancy's clothes. Then he's taking Maeve to the station.' She looked at her watch. 'He should be back soon.'

'Right, I'm parched. Who's ready for tea?' Ena called and, like the Pied Piper of Hamelin, she led the children out of the office.

'Where does she get her energy?' Bess said. Linking her arm though Claire's arm they followed their youngest sister to the dining room.

CHAPTER SEVENTEEN

The next morning after breakfast, Ena, Bess, Frank and Nancy, went outside to wave Claire and Aimee off. The sisters hugged and kissed each other. Claire said she'd let them know how long they'd be in France, and Bess and Ena wished her lots of love and luck.

While the grown-ups were chatting, Aimee and Nancy said goodbye. Aimee put her arms around Nancy and told her that she would see her soon. 'Best friends?' Aimee said, kissing her on the cheek as her mother had done to her sisters.

'Best friends,' Nancy reciprocated, kissing Aimee back.

Touched by the scene between the two children, Frank lifted Aimee onto the passenger seat of the car, tucked the car rug round her, and closed the door. Nancy reached up and took hold of Frank's hand and, with Bess and Ena, they waved goodbye to Claire and Aimee.

Walking back into the hotel, Nancy gazed up at Frank. 'Can I see the pony?'

'Yes, if it's all right with Auntie Bess. You didn't have anything planned, did you, love?'

Bess shook her head. 'Only a cup of coffee and a natter with Ena. See you two later,' she said, following Ena into the hotel to the office.

'What with one thing and another, I didn't get chance to ask you how Margot was last night,' Bess said, putting on the kettle.

'Blooming. She's bored of course, as you can imagine she would be. She says she wants to go home.'

'What, after only a couple of days?'

'Yes.' Ena brushed the air with her hand, as if to flick the idea away. 'You know what she can be like. The hospital won't let her go home of course, it's far too soon. Even if the baby hadn't been premature it would be too soon.'

'There isn't anything wrong with her, is there?'

'With Margot?' Ena laughed.

'No, the baby.'

'She's perfect. You said yourself, it's because she was early that the doctors are monitoring her, Margot too. Hospitals keep new mums and babies in for a week, even if they go full term. Margot knows that. She's worried that, because Natalie was three weeks early, they'll make her stay in hospital until the date she should have been born.'

'Natalie?'

'Yes. Natalie Elizabeth Goldie. Elizabeth's after you.'

'Natalie is after Natalie Goldman, and Goldie is the name of her dancer friend who she helped escape from David Sutherland in the war. I wonder if Bill had a say in choosing the baby's name?'

'I don't think he cares what she's called. He's so happy, he'd agree to anything.'

'He's a lovely man.' Bess poured two cups of coffee and took them over to Ena who was sitting on one of the easy chairs by the unlit fire. 'And what about your lovely man?' she asked, putting their cups on the small coffee table and sitting down in the chair opposite.

A frown crept across Ena's face. 'I don't know. He and Inspector Masters are somewhere up north on a job. That's all he could tell me.'

'As soon as there's anything to report, I'm sure he'll telephone you.'

'That's the worrying part. Henry always phones to let me know where he is.' She picked up her cup and took a drink. 'I shouldn't be telling you this, but if I don't tell someone I'll go out of my mind with worry. You mustn't say anything--' Bess shook her head. 'Sorry, I know you won't.

'They're hunting down Hawksley's associates; the chain of command that's in place along the route to South America. It's a massive organisation of seemingly innocent businessmen who are Nazi sympathisers. They each bring something different to the group. Some have safe houses, others are forgers, or arrange the forging of documents like birth certificates and passports. Many speak foreign languages. There's even a couple of high-powered bank managers among them who are able to hide large amounts of money to dish out when necessary.

'If MI5 and the Metropolitan Police are successful in capturing these people, the organisation will be shut down forever. If they don't succeed, and they're caught-- Well,' Ena inhaled deeply, 'it doesn't bear thinking about. Fascists are not the kind of people to say "Gotcha, now be good lads and skedaddle."'

Ena pushed herself out of her chair and stretched. 'I need some fresh air. Blow my worries away. I'll walk down to see Mam. Bill's parents are going to the hospital this afternoon, so shall I tell her that we'll take her in tomorrow or Tuesday?'

'Yes. Bring her back with you, will you? Claire was going to tell her to come up for lunch when she called in with Aimee. I'll make a start on this week's book-keeping while you're gone.' Ena left the office and Bess went over to her desk. She took a pile of receipts from one drawer and the accounts ledger from another. But before she had time to take out her pen, Ena was back.

'Bess, there's someone here to see you?'

The look on Ena's face told Bess that she was shocked by the arrival of the unexpected visitor. Bess flashed Ena a questioning look, but before she had time to introduce the person with her, Katherine Hawksley stepped cautiously into the room.

'I'm disturbing you,' she said nervously, her eyes flitting from Bess to the paperwork on her desk.

'Not at all, Miss Hawksley.' Bess made a wide arc with her arm dismissing the papers. 'Accounts are my husband's domain. I was only filling in time. It can wait.' Bess walked round the desk and offered Katherine Hawksley her hand. The young woman shook it. She was trembling. 'Won't you sit down, Miss Hawksley?'

Katherine perched on the edge of the chair that Ena had vacated, and Bess returned to the chair that she had been sitting in.

'I'll leave you two to talk,' Ena said, opening the door.

'Would you take Nancy with you to Mam's, Ena? Tell Frank not to worry about the accounts. And tell Jack to take a message if anyone rings for me.'

Smiling goodbye to Bess and including Katherine, Ena left the office, closing the door firmly behind her.

Katherine Hawksley sat with her head down and picked at the edge of her handkerchief. She was physically shaking. 'It's chilly today,' Bess said, taking a box of Swan Vestas from the shelf at the side of the fireplace. Striking a match, she put the small blue flame to the newspaper beneath the kindling in the grate. The paper caught instantly, igniting the dry wood, and Bess soon felt warmth emanating from it. 'Would you like a hot drink?' Bess asked, replacing the matches. Katherine shook her head.

Katherine leaned nearer to the fire and stretched out her hands, while Bess busied herself pouring a cup of coffee, which she took back with her. After taking a couple of sips, Bess put the cup on the shelf next to the box of matches. Whatever it was that had brought Katherine Hawksley to see her at the hotel, against McGann's wishes, must be important Bess thought.

'Feeling warmer, Katherine? I can call you, Katherine, can't I?' With her gaze fixed on the flames devouring the wood and licking around the coal, the girl nodded. 'And you can call me Bess.'

'Bess,' Katherine repeated.

Bess didn't want to push Katherine for fear she would clam up, but she could tell by her troubled expression that the poor girl was weighed down by something painful that she needed to get off her chest. 'Would you like to tell me what is making you unhappy, Katherine?'

'Yes,' she whispered. She looked at Bess

through red-rimmed eyes. 'He used to come into my room at night after my father had turned in and lay on my bed.'

'Who did, Katherine?' Bess asked, fearing she knew the answer to her question.

'David. At first it was just that. He would just lie next to me. Then,' she held her breath and buried her head in her hands.

'Take your time.' Bess reached out and gently touched Katherine's arm.

Katherine looked up, her eyes wide, tears falling onto her cheeks. 'Then,' she took a juddering breath, 'one night he-- touched me.' She fell silent as if the words were too distressing to say. 'The next night,' she said at last, 'he came to my room again. He got into bed with me and he touched me again. He asked me if I liked it. I said no. I told him to stop, but he laughed. He said when a woman says no, she means yes. I said if he didn't stop I'd scream, and he said there was no one to hear me. I told him Daddy would hear me. I said my father would come in and throw him out, but he laughed again and said, your old man's drunk, he won't hear anything until the morning.'

'Did you tell your father in the morning?'

'No. David said if I told him he would say that I had gone to his room and asked him to come back to mine. He said he'd tell him that I'd led him on, teased him, and that it was me who wanted--' She lowered her gaze and whispered, 'sex.'

'Surely your father wouldn't have believed him over you, his own daughter.'

'David said he was a hero, a respected officer in the Association, and that everyone would believe him over a silly girl.'

'Association?'

Katherine caught her breath and put her hands over her mouth.

'What is it Katherine?'

She shook her head. She had clearly said something she shouldn't.

'I've said too much. I've got to go.' Katherine jumped up. 'I shouldn't have come here, but I wanted to tell you that I was sorry about - what he did to you - in London before the war.'

'He told you that he raped me?'

'Yes, on New Year's Eve. He didn't use that word. He said you had wanted him to do it. He said you were asking for it, like I was. It was then that I knew he'd raped you, because I didn't want him to do it to me, but he did it anyway. He raped me, Bess, and he said it was my fault.'

Bess stood up and wrapped her arms around the girl. 'It was not your fault, Katherine. None of it was your fault.'

'I've got to go.' Easing herself out of Bess's arms, Katherine took a step backwards. Her eyes searched Bess's face, as if she was wondering whether she could trust her. Bess was sure Katherine wanted to tell her more, but the frightened girl ran to the door.

'You know where I am if you want to talk again, Katherine.' Bess called after her.

Katherine's steps faltered and she turned and faced Bess. 'You saw me, didn't you?'

'When, Katherine? When did I see you?' Katherine didn't answer. She had the frightened look of a cornered animal in her eyes. The same look that Bess had seen on the day Katherine ran in front of the car on Lowarth High Street.

Afraid that she would run away again, Bess went to her and slowly led her back to the chair next to the fire. When they were both seated, Bess said, 'Are you referring to the day you ran in front of the car, or to New Year's Eve?'

'New Year's Eve.'

'What did I see on New Year's Eve, Katherine?'

'Me, kill David Sutherland.'

Bess heart almost leapt out of her chest. 'I did see you on New Year's Eve, Katherine, but you didn't kill David Sutherland.'

Tears fell from the tormented young woman's eyes. 'Mrs Burrell saw me too, and that American.' Bess had to stop and think who the American was. Then the penny dropped. The American was a Canadian, her brother-in-law, Mitch. Bess didn't correct Katherine about the man's nationality. She hadn't told McGann about him when he questioned her on New Year's Eve. It would look suspicious if she acknowledged his presence now.

'Yes, Margot and I both saw you. You were running away from David Sutherland.'

'That was afterwards.' Katherine took a deep breath that made her thin frame shudder. 'Before that he said he was going to give me what he'd given that snotty bitch in there.' Katherine looked embarrassed repeating Sutherland's words. 'He meant you,' she whispered.

'I know,' Bess said, nodding sympathetically in an attempt to ease Katherine's discomfort.

'He grabbed hold of me and pulled me to him. I was so frightened I kicked out and the toe of my shoe caught his shin. He cursed and slumped, but he didn't fall down, so I hit him as hard as I could with my handbag and I ran.'

'But you didn't see him go into the water, did you?' Katherine shook her head. Looking at the thin frightened girl before her, Bess found it difficult to believe that she could hit anyone hard enough to knock them off their feet, let alone send someone the height and weight of David Sutherland flying into a frozen lake. Bess needed the poor girl to understand that. 'So,' she said, looking into Katherine's face and waiting until Katherine looked into hers, 'You can't be sure it was because you hit Sutherland that he fell into the lake and drowned. Well, can you?'

'No, but--'

'No buts, Katherine! I think you should go home now, but first I want you to promise me that you won't tell anyone what you have just told me.' Lines appeared on the young woman's brow. She looked confused. Bess couldn't tell her that Sutherland had also been stabbed, because when Henry told her, he had sworn her to secrecy. Even so, Bess felt it was her duty to make Katherine understand that she had not killed David Sutherland.

'Katherine, hitting a man as big as Sutherland with a handbag would have at worst knocked him off balance. He may even have slipped down the bank into the water. But a blow from you would not have knocked him unconscious, so that he drowned. He was a strong man, he'd have been able to climb out of the lake in seconds. Believe me, Katherine, you did not kill David Sutherland.'

Bess saw the worry noticeably lift from Katherine's shoulders and relief spread across her face in a thin drawn smile. 'Thank you, Bess.'

'There's no need to thank me, Katherine. That man put you through a terrible ordeal. Added to which, for nine months you believed you had killed him. I wish you had talked to me sooner.'

'I wanted to tell you that day at the bus stop, in the spring. I was desperate to tell you, but my father and Sergeant McGann had forbidden me to speak to you.'

'I understand.' Bess wanted to ask Katherine about her mother, but feared asking her outright would upset her more. She waited a moment, and then said, 'Do you have any one to talk to, other than your father? An aunt, perhaps, or a female friend?'

Katherine shook her head. 'My aunts abandoned us when my mother died. Dad said they had never liked him. He said they were jealous because he was rich. Once, when I asked him about my mother, he said she had only married him for his money, and if it hadn't been that she got pregnant with me, he would have divorced her.'

Bess saw in Katherine Hawksley's eyes the years of sadness and the pain that her vile fascist father had caused her by saying such wicked things. She watched helplessly as huge tears fell from them. 'Dad said my mother never wanted me.'

Bess could stand it no longer. She leapt out of

her chair, knelt in front of Katherine and clasped her hands. 'I want you to promise me that if you are ever frightened, worried, or just need someone to talk to, you'll come and talk to me.' Katherine nodded and with a sad, lost look in her eyes, sniffed back her tears.

Bess left Katherine by the fire and went over to her desk. She lifted the telephone. 'Would you put me through to Clarke's taxis, please, Jack?'

'Hello, Mr Clarke, this is Bess at the Foxden Hotel. Do you have a taxi available?' She waited. 'One passenger to be picked up here and taken to Kirby Marlow. Thank you.'

As they walked out of the hotel the taxi was coming up the drive. Bess gave Katherine one of the hotel's cards with her telephone number on it. 'Telephone me anytime,' she said, pressing the small white card into Katherine's hand. 'And,' she added, 'forget about David Sutherland.'

The taxi pulled up in front of the hotel and Katherine started down the steps. Halfway she turned and ran back to Bess. 'I told my father I thought I'd killed David and he told Sergeant McGann.' Katherine held Bess's hands so tightly her fingernails dug into the soft flesh of Bess's palms. 'My father would kill me if he knew I had told you this, but--' Katherine faltered. Bess held her breath in case she changed her mind and didn't tell her what was so important that she feared retribution from her own father. 'Beware of Sergeant McGann. He is a wicked man.'

'What do you mean, Katherine?'

'He said it didn't matter that I had killed David Sutherland, because he was going to pin the murder on you.' Bess felt a wave of heat like a knife slice through her and the sickly taste of bile rise from her stomach to her throat. She swallowed hard. 'He said he had a way to make it stick. But don't worry,' Katherine said, her expression one of stubborn defiance, 'I won't let him blame you. I won't let anyone blame you.'

Bess's stomach turned into a sea of nausea and cold sweat trickled down her back. The innocent daughter of the head of the Fascist Association in England was prepared to put her life in danger for her. Bess couldn't let her do that. 'I appreciate you telling me this Katherine, but you *must* now stay out of it. Do you understand?'

Katherine nodded and ran down the steps. 'Be careful!' Bess called, as she got into the taxi.

Bess watched the vehicle drive off and went inside. She couldn't tell Frank what Katherine had said, he would go after Hawksley and McGann - and not only would he get Katherine into trouble, he would more than likely get himself killed. She would tell Ena, and she would tell Henry and the inspector as soon as they returned from wherever it was they had gone.

In the meantime, she must do what she had advised Katherine Hawksley to do: put this business with David Sutherland out of her mind. She had work to do, Nancy to look after, her mother coming for lunch and her sister and new baby to visit in hospital. 'Any messages?' she asked Jack as she passed.

'No, Mrs Donnelly.'

'Thank God for that.'

CHAPTER EIGHTEEN

Frank picked Bess up and swung her round. 'We are three-quarters of the way through the first year of business and things are looking pretty good.' Setting her down, Frank took Bess by the hand and led her to the desk. He turned the accounts ledger round so it was facing her. 'And the bottom line is?'

'Hooray!' Bess shouted, throwing her arms around Frank's neck. 'I'm not crying, honestly,' she said, wiping her tears. 'These,' she lied, pointing to her eyes, 'are tears of happiness.' Bess picked up the ledger, ran her finger down the incoming column then the outgoing column and laughed loudly. 'We've broken even. I can hardly believe it.'

'It's all there in black and white. And,' Frank said, kissing Bess, 'by this New Year's Eve, we'll be making a profit.'

Bess blew out her cheeks. 'There have been so many problems that could have set us back.'

'But they didn't,' Frank said, 'and nothing is going to. Come on, you're on reception duty with Jack, and I have to feed the animals. I'll go and put my old togs on.'

'I'll check on the kitchen first,' Bess said, following Frank out of the office. 'I'll be with you in five minutes, Jack.'

Bess stuck her head round the kitchen door. 'Need anything, Chef?' she called, expecting the usual mutterings of, "A second pair of hands" or "A twin would be good."

Instead he sang 'All is *bravo* in my kitchen, gracias!' He was more Spanish than ever. 'Oh, the laundry was delivered this morning. If you would like to check it, I do not have the time.'

The laundry had been done well and stacked neatly as always. Bess ticked everything off the list. Leaving the laundry room, a pile of half-a-dozen new chefs' aprons caught her eye. 'Going into business selling pinnies, Chef?' she said, closing the door.

'Noooo!' the chef threw back his head and looked to the heavens. 'A mistake was made when they were ordered. By the supplier, of course.'

'Of course.'

'But I decided to keep them. I believe you have complained in the past about me going into the dining room in a dirty apron, so I thought you would rather me have a few spare.'

Resisting the urge to argue that, at the speed the Lowarth Laundry collected and returned the hotel's linen and kitchen-whites, Chef only needed one extra apron, not six, Bess said, 'Good!' and left.

As she neared the dining room door she heard Alice Arkwright, the senior waitress in charge of the dining room and its staff, ticking Sylvie off for coming to work in laddered nylons. Sylvie said she had snagged her stockings on a box in the staff room, but it seemed the senior waitress wasn't listening or, like Chef, didn't want to back down and admit she could be wrong. 'This once,' Alice Arkwright said, 'you can take a pair from my cupboard, but do not come to work in shabby attire again!'

228

Bess had thought about intervening, but thankfully didn't have to. As the sounds of, 'No, Miss Arkwright,' and 'Thank you, Miss Arkwright' grew louder, Bess realised the grateful waitress was near the door, so she moved away from it. Deciding to check the dining tables later, she turned on her heels and went back to reception to do her shift.

'Hello?' Bess said, beaming at Nancy who dropped Ena's hand as soon as she saw Bess and was running across the marble hall to her. 'Have you had a nice time at--' Bess wasn't sure what Nancy should call her mother.

'Yes. I played with Grandpa Dudley's pipes in the front room. And Grandma Dudley gave me some chocolate,' Nancy said, showing off by swinging from left to right. Something she'd picked up from Aimee.

Bess's mother strolled in behind them. 'Hello, love. I've brought a recipe for Chef. I'll pop through to the kitchen and give it to him,' Lily Dudley said, without pausing for breath.

'He's busy, so don't expect him to stop and chat.'

Bess's mother shrugged off her coat, gave it to Ena, and with her handbag swinging on her arm waltzed across the hall in the direction of the kitchen.

Bess pressed her lips together to stop herself from laughing. 'Are you hungry, Nancy?' she asked. Nancy shook her head. 'No, I didn't think you would be.'

'I did tell Mam not to give her cake, or she

wouldn't want her lunch, but she didn't listen,' Ena said.

'Cake? I thought she had chocolate?'

'She did. She had cake too, with a drink of milk. Sorry, I'm not very good at saying no to children, and there isn't a way of saying no to our Mam.'

'Ah, here's Jack.' Another heart won, Bess thought, as Jack arrived, leaning forward ready to pick Nancy up. 'My but you're getting a big girl. Is Mrs Donnelly feeding you too much cake?'

'No, but my mother is,' Bess said. Jack gave Nancy a wide-eyed, open mouthed look of surprise and she giggled. 'I'll take my lunch break now, Jack, if it's all right with you?'

'Of course, Mrs Donnelly. See you later, Nancy,' the young receptionist said, standing Nancy down.

Bess and Ena's mother came out of the kitchen as her daughters and Nancy turned from the hall into the passage leading to the dining room. Nancy took the extended hand of her new Grandma - and the sixty-eight year old and the eight year old walked into the dining room together.

Ena stopped short of the door and turned to Bess. 'What happened with Katherine Hawksley?'

'She's had a terrible life, poor kid. Her mother died when she was little, she has an aunt somewhere who hates her father.'

'I wonder why?'

'Exactly. He told Katherine that her mother didn't want her.'

'The bastard!'

'What are you two cooking up?' Frank called,

from the far end of the passage.

Bess waited for Frank to join her. 'I'll tell you later,' she whispered. And taking hold of Frank's hand, they walked into the dining room behind Ena.

By the time they'd finished eating the afternoon light was fading. Chef, in a pristine and newly laundered white apron, swanned into the dining room and began making a fuss of Bess's mother. 'Lily, lo-v-ely Lily,' he gushed, lowering his large frame onto the chair next to her. 'I have created a new pudding especially for you. She is called, Chef's Lily.'

Hardly able to stop herself from laughing, Bess left her mother to the chef's charms and returned to reception. Ena asked if she could make a couple of telephone calls from the office, and Frank took Nancy out to see the animals.

Reception was busy. It always was at weekends. Bess stood back so she could observe Jack, letting him deal with guests on his own unless two came to reception at the same time. He was polite, he listened, he answered their questions confidently, and was very patient with an elderly lady who was hard of hearing. Bess couldn't help but smile. The old lady made Jack repeat everything he said. He did, and he was charming without being sickly.

Jack was good at his job, Bess observed, but then he'd had an excellent teacher. Bess was wondering how Maeve was getting on when Ena stuck her head round the door and beckoned her.

'Will you be all right if I pop into the office, Jack? My sister wants a word with me. I won't be long. Call me if you need me.'

'There's no record of Katherine Hawksley's mother after Katherine's birth. It's as if she disappeared into thin air. Or she never existed.'

'What do you mean?'

'Katherine Hawksley's birth is registered at Somerset House. Father, Gerald Hawksley; mother, Dorothy Hawksley, nee Pemberton from Cumberland - and that's it! There's no wedding certificate or death certificate in the name of Dorothy Hawksley, or Dorothy Pemberton. Nor is there a divorce petition, or a decree absolute, registered in her name, or his name. I can't access some of the government's classified records from outside the building where I work in London, so I telephoned a pal who works in the same department, and asked her to look for me.' Ena shook her head slowly. 'There *is no* marriage, divorce, or death certificate.'

'Then what happened to her?'

'I'm wondering whether she ever existed. I managed to get hold of Henry and I told him what I'd found out. He wants me to go up to Cumberland to check out the Pemberton family who, like Hawksley, are wealthy business people. If Dorothy Pemberton was only a name on Katherine's birth certificate, it could mean the Pembertons are Nazi sympathisers too, in which case they could be involved with Hawksley.' Bess stood open mouthed. 'Don't look so shocked, it's work.'

'Is it?'

'Yes. And it's linked to Inspector Masters' investigation. But apart from that, there was once a woman in Katherine Hawksley's life when she was small who she called mummy - and if this woman is still alive I want to find her for Katherine.'

'But Henry wants you to find the woman for MI5.'

'It isn't quite as simple as that,' Ena said. 'If the Pembertons are part of Hawksley's Fascist Association, MI5 is worried that when the net starts closing in on Hawksley he'll do a moonlight flit and disappear to a bolt hole in the wilds of North West England.'

'Isn't Henry worried about your safety?'

'Of course he is. And I'm worried about his safety, but it's our job, Bess. It's what we signed up for after Bletchley.' Neither sister spoke for some time. 'So,' Ena said, first to break the silence, 'I shall have to leave early in the morning. Will you drive me into Lowarth?'

'Where to, the station?'

'No, I'm driving up. The office are arranging for a car to be brought from a company in Leicester. It should be at Burton's garage for me to collect at nine.'

'I'm glad you got to speak to Henry.'

'Yes.' Ena sighed loudly and blew out a long stream of air. 'He couldn't say anything about the operation, in case someone was listening to the call, but my pal at the London office said they're closing in on the men who provide the documents and money for the Fascist Association that Hawksley runs.

'Before they can shut down the escape route, they need to know the names and addresses of every member of Hawksley's organisation. They need to arrest them all at the same time. They can't risk one person falling through the net. It's going to be a huge operation. Don't look so worried, Bess, I'm not involved in any of that.'

'Maybe not, but going to Cumberland on your own could be dangerous.'

'Yes, well, as I said, it's part of the job.'

'I wondered what you did all day in that big flat of yours in London, when Henry was working.'

'I'm working too,' Ena said. 'I'm rarely at home these days.'

The sounds of guests arriving seeped through the door. 'I'd better get back to reception and help Jack.' Ena didn't reply, nor did she lift her head from the hotel's road atlas of the British Isles. 'I'll see you later,' Bess said, to which her sister mumbled an acknowledgement.

'Can I help you?' Bess asked a couple standing at the reception desk.

'No thank you, we're being dealt with.'

The new porter arrived a second later, Jack gave him the key to a room with a view on the first floor and, as smooth as clockwork, the porter swept up the couple's cases and led the way to the stairs.

Bess was feeling slightly redundant and a little unwanted when Frank returned with Nancy. 'We're going to take your mother home,' he said. 'It's getting dark, so we'll run her down in the car.'

'I'll get Nancy's coat.' Bess turned towards the office door.

'I'll get it. I'll get your mum's too. Did Ena put it in the office?'

Bess looked up at the ceiling, and then at her husband. 'Sorry, were you asking me?'

'Are you feeling left out? Or is it that you're a little under-employed?' Frank teased, opening the office door. Appearing with two coats over his arm, he said, 'If you are, there are plenty of maintenance jobs I can give you to do.' Bess ripped a sheet of notepaper from the jotting pad, screwed it into a ball and lobbed it at him. As Frank bent down to help Nancy into her coat the paper ball bounced off his chest onto Nancy's head, making her giggle. 'That's no way to treat your guests.'

'You are not a guest.'

'No, but Nancy is.'

'Take Uncle Frank away before I throw something heavy at him,' Bess said, winking at Nancy. She watched the little girl pull Frank, who pretended to resist, across reception to where Bess's mother stood talking to the chef. With a grand gesture of his arms, Chef took her mother's coat from Frank and like a matador swirled it in the air as if it was a capote. Then, with a deep bow, he held it for her while she slipped one arm at a time down each sleeve. Smiling like the proverbial cat who got the cream, Lily Dudley waved goodbye to Bess - and a second later she had gone. Chef, stamping his feet and clicking his fingers like a flamenco dancer, threw back his head and, after a dramatic bow to Jack and Bess, returned the kitchen.

'Alfredo's got a real way with him, hasn't he Mrs Donnelly?' Jack said, smiling with admiration.

'He certainly has,' Bess said. 'Watching that performance, you'd think he really was Alfredo from Madrid, not Alfred from Oldham.'

Bess yawned. It had been a long day. A disconcerting day in many ways. She laughed thinking about her mother and the chef. What a pair of old ducks. She didn't know who was the most comical. She was delighted that the hotel was at last holding its own. She had told Frank when Lord and Lady Foxden had insisted on standing guarantor for them, that if they hadn't begun to break even by the end of the first year, she was not prepared to borrow any more money using the Foxden name, and they would have to think of another way to earn a living.

Bess smiled. They had not only broken even, they had begun to make a profit. A small one, but apart from owing the bank a fortune they were at last in the black, as Frank called it.

Bess yawned again. She really ought to go to bed if she was going to be up early in the morning to take Ena into Lowarth. Bess worried about Ena and the work she did. She worried about Katherine Hawksley too. To think that poor child's mother might only have been a name on her birth certificate. Worse still, she may have been a Nazi sympathiser who was paid to nurse Katherine while she was a baby. Then, when Gerald Hawksley deemed his daughter old enough, the woman left leaving Katherine thinking her mummy had died. What a cruel man Gerald Hawksley was.

Bess closed her mind to all thoughts of Katherine Hawksley's evil father, but she wasn't able to shake off the sick feeling of guilt she had in the pit of her stomach when she thought about her sister Ena going to Cumberland to investigate links between the Pemberton family and the Fascists Association. If Ena gets into trouble, is hurt in any way, it would be her fault for telling her about Katherine Hawksley.

Being the oldest sister Bess had always felt responsible for her siblings. Except for Tom - he was older anyway. She leaned her head on the side of the bed and thought about her handsome older brother. She hadn't seen him, or his wife, Annabel, since before Christmas. Smiling to herself, Bess yawned again. She didn't usually wait up for Frank when he was working late, but tonight was different. Was it because she was comfortable relaxing on the floor in front of the fire, or was it that she loved watching the little girl she was looking after, while she slept?

Bess heard the door open and a pale shaft of light fanned across the room. 'What are you doing still up?' Frank whispered.

'Waiting for you.'

Frank knelt down beside Bess and looked at the sleeping child. 'She is lovely, isn't she?' Bess made a soft caring sound. Frank smoothed a stray curl at the side of Bess's head, and whispered, 'You remember what you promised?' Bess nodded and leaned against her husband, her head resting on his shoulder. 'Come on then,' Frank said, gently easing Bess away from him and standing up. He put out his hand, Bess took it and he pulled her to her feet. 'Time to get some sleep.'

CHAPTER NINETEEN

Bess flung her arm out of bed, walked her fingers along the top of the bedside table, found the copper alarm clock and hit the bell. 'Your turn to go down early, Frank,' she mumbled, without opening her eyes. 'And don't wake Nancy when you go through the sitting room, she was late going to sleep last night.' With no reaction from her husband, Bess turned over. 'Frank?' She opened her eyes and to her delight he wasn't there. 'Good-o!' she said aloud, and cuddling his pillow went back to sleep.

'Bess? Time go get up, love. I've put a cup of tea on the side for you,' Frank said, drawing back the curtains.

Bess opened her eyes. 'Is Nancy awake?'

'She certainly is. Our little guest was perched on her bed, fully dressed, when I crept through the sitting room at six o'clock. She nearly gave me a heart attack. I got as far as the door, quietly turned the knob, and a little voice, all matter of fact, said, "Is it time to collect the eggs yet Uncle Frank?"'

'And you said, yes.'

'What else could I say? I'd already told her they had to be collected first thing in the morning.'

Bess laughed. 'Ena was right, you are a pushover. Where is she now?'

'Eating one of the eggs that she collected, with bread and butter soldiers.' Bess raised an eyebrow. 'Sylvie made them for her. She has won the hearts of all the staff,' Frank said, making for the door.

'I'll be down in fifteen minutes to do the post

and the papers.'

'All done. But you're due to go on reception at ten.'

'Oh heck! I'd better get up then.' Swinging her legs out of bed, Bess took a drink of her tea. 'Thank you,' she called after Frank. When she'd finished, she went into the bathroom. Cleaning her teeth, Bess shook her head. If Nancy was already dressed and waiting for Frank when he got up, and they went straight downstairs, she wouldn't have cleaned her teeth or washed her face. She probably hadn't brushed her hair either and Frank wouldn't think to do it.

'Good morning, early birds.' Bess said, joining her husband and Nancy in the dining room. Frank pulled out a chair and Bess sat down. Nancy gave her an endearing smile. Her hair resembled a bird's nest, but as there was nothing Bess could do about it at the breakfast table, she thought it best not to say anything.

'What would you like for breakfast this morning, Mrs Donnelly?' Sylvie asked, suddenly at Bess's side.

'Scrambled egg on toast, please, and a pot of tea.' Bess glanced at Frank. He raised his cup. Leaning to her left, Bess looked at Nancy's empty glass. 'And what about you, darling? Would you like some more milk?'

Nancy shook her head. 'No thank you.'

'Just tea for one then, Sylvie.' When the waitress left, Bess said, 'I have to work on reception this morning, in place of your aunt Maeve, but this afternoon when Jack has had his lunch, would you like to go and see Auntie Margot and the new baby?'

Nancy's eyes lit up and she nodded vigorously.

'And we'll take--' Bess hesitated. She felt uncomfortable calling her mother Grandma Dudley, even though that was what her mother had told Nancy to call her.

'I'll telephone your mother,' Frank said. 'I'll tell her you'll pick her up at, what, two?' Bess looked at her husband and smiled. 'Ready sweetheart?' Nancy jumped down from her chair. 'She promised Donnie she'd draw his portrait.' Frank was doing his best not to laugh. 'See you in a while, love,' he said, following Nancy out of the dining room.

Sylvie brought Bess her breakfast and looked twice at the empty chairs. 'Surplus to requirements again,' Bess said, laughing.

When she had finished eating, Bess called into the kitchen to ask Chef if he needed anything. He didn't, so she went to reception. 'Everything all right, Jack?'

'Yes, Mrs Donnelly, all quiet.'

'I'll be back in a minute, then,' she said, and dashed into the office. 'Nancy, while the guests are having their breakfasts, Jack doesn't need me, so shall we go upstairs and wash your face and brush your hair?' Nancy left her drawing of the pit pony and joined Bess at the door.

On the left side of Bess and Frank's sitting room, Frank had put a single bed. And in the corner a tallboy that had four deep drawers and narrow wardrobe. Nancy took off her outer clothes and without being told scooped up her washbag and towel from the end of her bed and skipped off to the bathroom, a small room off Bess and Frank's bedroom.

When she returned her face was shiny-clean but her underclothes were wet. 'Right,' Bess said, 'clean undies and a pretty frock.' Bess took vest, knickers and socks, from the top drawer of the tallboy, and a blue dress and cardigan from the wardrobe.

She helped Nancy to dress. Then sat on the bed with the child sitting on the rug in front of her and brushed out the knots in her tangled curls. Bess had curly hair and as a child was never allowed to let it grow. With a new baby arriving every eighteen months Lily Dudley didn't have time to brush Bess's hair for the pleasure of it. She brushed it once a day before school, often so roughly it made Bess cry. It was Ena who, as soon as she was old enough, liked to brush Bess's hair. She would brush it until it shone. She never tired of putting ribbons in it, plaiting it, turning fine strands around her fingers to make ringlets. Bess smiled at the memory.

'There, all done.' Bess put down the brush and lifted Nancy's golden locks from her shoulders. Her hair was soft and curled easily. 'We'll tie it back with a ribbon, shall we, then it won't get in your eyes when you're drawing.' Bess took a length of blue ribbon from a box at the side of the bed, swept Nancy's hair up and tied a bow around it.

Bess and Nancy arrived downstairs as a group of people dressed in thick jackets and walking shoes were leaving. Bess opened the door to the office. 'You go and see Uncle Frank and finish your drawing, while I help Jack.' Closing the door, Bess heard complimentary words about Nancy's dress. Nancy replied, but Bess didn't catch what she said.

'The group that have just left are taking the public footpath down to the River Swift, and then over the bridge to the Rye Hills, and Lowarth,' Jack said. 'One of them has a distant relative in Bitteswell, so they're going to walk a far as the village and have lunch in one of the pubs.

'And I gave another man, a historian I think he said he was, directions to Market Bosworth. He wanted to see where the Battle of Bosworth took place. He said he wouldn't be back for lunch, because he's driving up to Nottingham, to see the castle.' Jack gave Bess a lopsided smile.

'I know that look! What have you done?' Bess teased.

'Nothing, only the young woman in the room next to the gentleman who asked for directions to Market Bosworth came down a few minutes after him and told me that she wouldn't be in for lunch either.' Jack lowered his voice. 'She followed him out and when she got to the door she turned and winked at me. I think she's the historian chap's fancy woman,' he whispered.

'If she is, she isn't very discreet, is she?'

'No,' Jack said, 'but I am.' Bess smiled and took her position behind the reception desk. 'Discretion is important in the hotel business. Take these two,' Jack said.

'I'd rather not,' Bess replied, and, smiling politely, asked the middle-aged couple who had aired their dirty linen over dinner twice during the week if they needed any help.

Other guests came and went. Two children asked to see the animals, so Frank and his eight-year old helper led them and their parents outside. 'Don't let Nancy get near the pigs in her clean dress, Frank,' Bess called after them.

'Did you hear that, Miss?' Frank turned and saluted Bess, and the little girl giggled.

After lunch, Bess and Nancy set off to see Margot and the baby, collecting Bess's mother on the way. Lily Dudley chattered all the way to the hospital about when she had her children. 'We had babies at home in the old days,' she told Bess. 'There was no way of getting to a hospital if you lived out in the country. I stayed in bed a day or two when I had our Tom, but when you girls were born your father was out at work all day, so I had no choice but to get up to look after you all.'

'I remember Granny staying at our house and looking after you when Claire and Ena were born. Surely she came and stayed when Margot and I were born too - and Tom.'

Lily Dudley looked out of the window. 'Yes, now I think of it, she did, but I still got up after a few days. Your granny was a good help. All the same…'

'We're here,' Bess said, putting an end to the conversation, which Bess had heard so many times and which always ended with "it's a wife's job to look after her husband and children."

The small room that Margot had given birth in was empty. 'Margot has been moved,' Bess said, leading the way to the maternity ward. From the corridor, Bess could see Margot, Bill and the baby

243

through the square panes of glass in the ward's door. A second later Bill came out and welcomed them.

Bess's mother went in to see Margot first with Bill, and Bess and Nancy waited outside. Half an hour later, Bill came out and beckoned Bess and Nancy. When they entered the ward, Bill and his mother-in-law left.

Bess waved as she and Nancy walked down the ward to Margot's bed. Bess stopped to greet her sister, but Nancy, letting go of her hand, tiptoed over to the cot and peered in.

'Hello, darling.' Bess kissed Margot's cheek. She craned her neck and looked over at the baby. 'Oh, Margot, she is beautiful.' And on the balls of her feet, so she didn't wake her niece, Bess skirted Margot's bed to join Nancy. 'Hello baby?' Bess cooed, when the tiny child opened her eyes and yawned.

'Hello baby?' Nancy said, emulating Bess. 'What's your name?'

'Her name is Natalie Elizabeth Goldie,' Margot said.

Nancy looked from the baby to Margot and back again. 'That's my mummy's name,' she told the baby, who was looking in her direction through unfocused eyes. Bess's heart beat heavily. The joy she felt at seeing her new niece was overshadowed by the pain she felt for her small ward. Standing behind Nancy, with her hands on the little girl's shoulders, Bess watched Margot's baby daughter's eyes slowly close.

'I think she's asleep,' Bess whispered. Nancy nodded, but made no attempt to move away from the cot, so Bess left her watching over the sleeping baby and returned to her sister. 'Did you hear what she just said?' Bess quietly asked Margot.

'Yes. I wonder which of the names she meant.'

'I'll ask Maeve when she gets back.'

'How has it been looking after an eight-year-old?'

'Frank's done most of the work.' Bess told Margot how Nancy helped Frank with the hens, how she collects the eggs for breakfast, about her feeding the pigs. At the word *pigs*, Nancy turned and smiled. 'And you love Donnie, don't you?'

'Donnie is a pit pony,' Nancy told Margot.

'I rarely see one of them without the other. Bath and bed are my duties, aren't they, Nancy?'

Nancy nodded. 'And reading me stories.' Then, turning her attention back to the baby, she said, 'Once upon a time,' in a hushed voice.

'So, asking the question again,' Margot said, pointedly, 'how has it been?'

'Wonderful. I love it. I didn't think I would. I thought I'd be worrying about work when I was with her, and feeling guilty when I was at work because I wasn't giving her the attention she needed. But everything has worked out really well, so far.' Bess lifted her hands and crossed her fingers.

She looked back at Nancy. 'You should see Frank with her; he's a natural.' Bess lowered her voice, 'I'm going speak to him about us adopting. I've raised the subject a couple of times already, but something has always stopped us from discussing it properly. I'm not sure Frank saw it as a possibility then, or would have wanted it, but

245

seeing him with Nancy has made me realise what a great father he'd make.'

'You'd make a great mum, too.'

Bess looked to the heavens. 'It would be a dream come true.'

No sooner had Bess given Margot the news about Claire going home to sort things out with Mitch than the nursing staff came marching through the ward doors. 'I think it's time we were going,' Bess said. 'Come on sweetheart, visiting time is over.' Nancy mouthed bye-bye to Natalie and with a puckered brow joined Bess.

'You'll see Natalie again,' Bess said. 'Won't she, Margot?'

'Of course she will.' Turning to Nancy, Margot said, 'You're Natalie's friend and you can visit her any time you like.'

That night, Bess was woken by a noise coming from the sitting room. She looked at the alarm clock and although it was dark, she could just make out the time. It was midnight. Worried that Nancy had got up and dressed again, to be ready to collect the eggs with Frank, Bess slowly turned back the bed clothes. So she didn't wake Frank, she slid out of their bed and pushed her feet into her slippers. Grabbing her dressing gown from the stool under the dressing table, Bess threw it around her shoulders and quietly opened the bedroom door.

By the night light, Bess could see Nancy sitting cross-legged on the floor surrounded by a pile of her old photographs. 'What are you doing, darling? It's ever so late. You'll be too tired to collect the eggs with Uncle Frank in the morning.'

Nancy gave Bess a photograph of Margot when she first went to London at the beginning of the war. She was dressed in her usherette uniform posing with some of the showgirls from the Prince Albert Theatre. 'That's Auntie Margot,' Nancy said, pointing to Bess's younger sister, 'And that's my mummy.'

CHAPTER TWENTY

'Bess wake up!' Bess had put Nancy back to bed and, after thinking about Nancy's mother, had fallen asleep beside her. She opened her eyes to see Frank was already dressed. 'If Nancy wants to come with me to collect eggs this morning, you'll have to get her up, love. We're running late. The alarm didn't go off.'

Bess wondered if she had accidentally knocked the tiny hammer that banged on the clock's brass bell when she looked at the time before going into Nancy in the early hours, but didn't say anything.

'Frank?' Bess pointed to the pile of photographs that Nancy had been looking through. 'Nancy was looking at those pictures in the night. One is of Margot and the dancers at Anton and Natalie's theatre--'

'Tell me later, darling, there's no time now.'

Bess shrugged, stood up, and still half asleep staggered across the room to the bathroom.

'Good morning, sleepy-head,' she heard Frank say. 'I'm going down to start work. We'll collect the eggs as soon as you're dressed,' he said, as he was leaving.

'Wait for me Uncle Frank,' Nancy called.

'Not without a wash, young lady,' Bess said, looking round the bathroom door and seeing Nancy pulling on a dress.

When she was washed and dressed, Bess brushed Nancy's hair and said she could go down to Frank. 'I should think he'll still be in the office sorting out the post. Look for him there first.'

Nancy ran out of the room and started along the corridor. 'If he's outside already, he'll be in the yard with the animals.' Bess was petrified in case she went anywhere near the lake. 'You know where to go, don't you?' Nancy shouted, *yes!* 'Don't go near the lake,' Bess called. As she disappeared down the stairs Bess heard Nancy shout, *no!*

Bess returned the photographs to the drawer, putting the one with the dancer that Nancy said was her mother on top of the pile. She then dashed back to the bathroom and washed and dressed.

Bess was desperate to tell Frank what Nancy had told her, but she wasn't on her own with him at all that day. She had spent the morning on reception, while Frank and Nancy were outside with the animals. After lunch, Nancy had been in the office with her, playing with her dolls, while Frank was fixing the plumbing in one of the first floor bathrooms. Later, when Nancy had had enough of her dolls and had put them to bed, she got out her drawing book. After tea, Bess returned to reception to allow Jack to have a break, and left Nancy drawing pictures of clowns and balls, stars and half-moon shapes that she carefully coloured in, staying within the lines. When Bess returned to the office, she took down the calendar and Nancy filled in another square.

'How many days has it been since Aunt Maeve went to Ireland?' Bess asked.

Nancy counted each day by tapping her finger on the coloured squares. 'Five!'

'And how many days until she's back?'

'Two.' Nancy sang out, without using her fingers.

Bess put Nancy to bed that evening and read her a story. When she was sure Nancy was asleep, Bess took the pile of photographs from the drawer, laid them on the floor, and looked through them. She then took several programmes from earlier shows that she had seen with her friends Natalie and Anton Goldman at the Prince Albert Theatre and, with the photograph that Nancy had been looking at the night before in one hand, she turned the pages of the programmes with her other until she found the same face. Looking down the cast list she spotted a name that matched both photographs, and Margot's baby's name. The pretty girl who Nancy had called her mummy was Goldie Trick.

Bess sat back on her heels hardly able to take in what she was seeing. In the hospital when Margot had told them that she was going to call her baby Natalie Elizabeth Goldie and Nancy had said that's my mummy's name, Bess had assumed she meant Natalie or Elizabeth. She hadn't. She had meant, Goldie. In a daze, Bess turned the next page over and there was a photograph of, Nancy Diamond, the Prince Albert theatre's lead dancer.

Suddenly it all made sense. Bess looked at the little girl sleeping soundly and wiped the flow of silent tears from her face with the back of her hand. She had been named Nancy Margaret after the two friends who had helped her escape London - and David Sutherland - by her late mother, Goldie Trick.

As she stepped onto the marble floor of the main hall, Bess saw Ena. She waved and her youngest sister retuned the gesture. 'Have I got some news for you,' Ena said, her voice high with excitement.

'And me for you,' Bess said. Opening the door to the office and standing back to let Ena enter first, she looked over her shoulder. 'Any messages, Jack?'

'Mr Donnelly is mending a lamp in the library. Other than that, no, Mrs Donnelly.'

'Problems?' The receptionist shook his head. 'Indiscretions?' He laughed. 'Well you know where I am if you need me,' she said, disappearing into the office before the receptionist had time to reply.

'Katherine Hawksley's mother isn't dead!' Ena announced, as soon as she and Bess sat down. 'She is very much alive and running the family's cotton business in a small town outside Carlisle. It took me a hell of a time to track her down. She changed her name some years ago, so Gerald Hawksley wouldn't be able to find her. After fifteen years, she is still terrified of him.'

'What's she like?'

'She's a very nice woman who comes from a well-to-do family in Carlisle. It was Gerald Hawksley who married her for her money, not the other way round, like he would have people believe. And she didn't abandon her daughter either. Hawksley was a big noise in the BUF and he threatened to have her killed if she didn't leave.'

'I still wouldn't have gone without my child,' Bess said.

'Nor did she. Dorothy told Hawksley that her father was ill and she wanted to take Katherine up to see him. But he wouldn't let her take *his* daughter, so she went up to Cumberland on her own. She didn't go to visit her parents because her father was ill, she went to ask them if they would take her and Katherine in, because she was going to leave her husband. They said yes, but when she returned to the marital home, Hawksley had gone and taken Katherine with him. She had no idea where they were.

'She went to the police and told them her husband had kidnapped their daughter. She told them that her parents had offered Katherine and herself a home, and that she wanted custody of Katherine.'

'And?'

'They said they'd look into it. But Hawksley must have had a copper, if not several, in his pocket, because a week later they informed her that she would not be getting custody of Katherine due to complaints that Sir Gerald had previously made, about her drinking. While Dorothy Hawksley was in Cumberland, Hawksley had told the police that he feared for his daughter's safety when his wife was drunk. He also said some of the men his wife took back to the house when he was away on business were unsavoury characters. He hadn't seen them himself, he said, but friends of his had.'

'She hadn't taken men to the house, had she?'

'No, but Hawksley provided the police with the names of several men who would swear in court that she had. He also had a doctor on his payroll who was willing to testify to Dorothy Hawksley's excessive drinking. He must have been planning to get rid of her, one way or another, for some time. Not only had he made a statement to the police, he had consulted a solicitor. The accusations he made were in black and white. Dorothy Hawksley didn't stand a chance of getting Katherine back.

'At the time, he told the police that he'd had to leave the family home and go into hiding with his daughter, because he feared his wife would become aggressive - again - and harm Katherine. The bastard even said he hoped his wife would get help for her addiction, and would one day lead a normal and fulfilling life. But regrettably, he said, it would not be with him and his daughter.'

Bess let out a long breath, blowing out her cheeks. 'The poor woman.'

'She employed a private investigating agency. They searched for months, but couldn't find Hawksley and the girl. It was as if they had dropped off the edge of the world. The agency concluded that Hawksley had taken Katherine abroad. Dorothy was heartbroken. She believed that if she stayed in the house, even though it held the most awful memories for her, her daughter would know where she was and would one day come back to her.

'Instead of Katherine coming back, two of her husband's thugs turned up. They gave her a one-way train ticket home and a message; Leave by train now, or in a box later.'

'How could Hawksley do that to the mother of his child?'

'Dorothy said he was unhinged, and the higher

he climbed up the fascist ladder the worse he became. She said if Hawksley didn't get his own way, lost a business deal, or had a fall-out with someone in the fascist movement, he'd bubble up like a volcano. She said he never took it out on the person he was angry with at the time - he was too canny for that - he would wait until he got home and take it out on her. He beat her regularly, but he never laid a finger on Katherine.'

Ena shook her head. 'Dorothy wouldn't have left Katherine with Hawksley when she visited her parents in Cumberland if she thought for a second he would harm her. He worshiped the child. It was Dorothy who he'd taken exception to. She told me that the only reason she took the train ticket that Hawksley's goons had given her was because, if she hadn't, they would have killed her - and she wouldn't be any good to her daughter dead.

'Dorothy Hawksley left the house that day in the clothes she stood up in. She had no money of her own, Hawksley had frittered away her inheritance. Once back in the north west she changed her name, got a job with a distant relative, and saved every penny she earned. Eventually she employed private investigators again. This time they found Hawksley and Katherine in London - and again when they moved to Kirby Marlow. Dorothy wrote to Katherine every week and sent birthday and Christmas presents. When Katherine didn't reply, she knew Hawksley had intercepted the letters and Katherine hadn't seen them. She kept writing to her daughter in the hopes that one day they would be reunited. From then on, whenever she took a holiday she stayed in the village or town nearest to Katherine's boarding school.'

'Did she ever see Katherine?'

'Yes, several times, but she never told her who she was. It was enough for Dorothy to know her daughter was alive and safe.'

'And Katherine believes her mother never wanted her, abandoned her when she was a child, and has since died.'

'Yes. Dorothy didn't know Hawksley had told Katherine she was dead. Until a few days ago, Dorothy's plan was to introduce herself to Katherine on her twenty-first birthday.'

'Because once she came of age, her father wouldn't have control over her.'

'Or his wife.'

'Wife? Dorothy isn't still married to the man, surely?'

'She is. If Hawksley ever intended to divorce Dorothy, he didn't go through with it. And she wouldn't dare divorce him, because then he'd be able to find out where she lived. After all this time she's still terrified of him. Which is why Henry and I think it's best if she stays in Cumberland until Hawksley has been arrested.'

'I agree.'

'Sorry for rabbiting on. What was it that you wanted to tell me?'

Bess looked down. She was still holding the programme from the Prince Albert Theatre in 1940. She showed it to Ena.

'When we visited Margot she told us the baby's name and Nancy said, that's my mummy's name. I thought nothing of it. I assumed her mother was called Natalie or Elizabeth. But in the early hours of the morning I was woken by a noise in the sitting room. I knew it could only be Nancy, so I got up and went in to her.

'She had opened the bottom drawer of the old dresser and was looking at my photographs. She pointed to one that Bill had taken of Margot when she was an usherette at the theatre. I think Margot sent us all one.' Ena nodded. 'Anyway, Margot was standing with some of the dancers and Nancy said, "That's my mummy." And this is the dancer she pointed to.' Bess gave the programme to Ena. 'Margot's friend, Goldie.'

'Who Sutherland beat up and almost killed?'

'Yes. And Maeve told me Nancy's mother was dead.'

'Which means, if Goldie is Nancy's mother, Goldie is dead. Oh my God.' Ena said, suddenly, putting her hand to her mouth. 'Henry saw Maeve at Sutherland's funeral.'

'He didn't tell me.'

'No, because the Vicar's wife said that, as members of the congregation, she had asked Maeve and another woman to attend the funeral or there wouldn't have been any witnesses to Sutherland's passing.'

'And Henry believed her?'

'He had no reason not to.'

'If Maeve is… was… Goldie's cousin,' Bess said, 'I suppose she had more reason than most to want to see him buried.'

'And more reason than most to want to see him dead,' Ena added.

'Not necessarily.' Bess felt the need to defend

Maeve, and herself for that matter. 'I went to his funeral too. It was stupid of me, I know, but at the time I thought seeing him interred would give me some sort of closure. I expect that's why Maeve was there.'

'She could have killed him,' Ena said. 'She was working on New Year's Eve.'

Bess shook her head. 'The only people Margot and I saw anywhere near where Sutherland's body was found in the spring was Sutherland himself and Katherine. We spent quite some time down there; we'd have seen Maeve. Besides, she was on reception. She brought us tea and coffee when the police arrived, remember?'

'Strange though, that she didn't tell you she knew Sutherland,' Ena said. 'I bet she knew he was living at Hawksley's place in Kirby Marlow when she applied for the receptionist's job here. Too much of a coincidence if she didn't know.'

'You're probably right. She worked in communications somewhere near Kirby Marlow in the war and was billeted with the Reverend and his wife. She told me she came back to see them quite often, so it's more than likely that they told her Sutherland was at Hawksley's. And yes, it's also likely that he's the reason she came here for a job, but none of that makes her a murderer, so stop assuming the poor woman is guilty by association.'

'Hasn't she said anything to you about her sister and Sutherland?' Ena asked.

'Goldie was her cousin,' Bess said, 'but no she hasn't mentioned a connection. She told me that her cousin, Nancy's mother, had died. It was tragic the way she--' Tears filled Bess's eyes. 'That man!

That bloody, bloody, man!' she shouted. 'I have never wished anyone harm, but Sutherland? He was the damn devil! Will the hurt and destruction that evil man caused never end?'

CHAPTER TWENTY-ONE

'Nancy?' Donnie lifted his head from his hay basket, gave Bess a weary sideways glance and shifted his weight from one leg to the other making it clear she was disturbing him. 'She's not here eh, boy?' Bess left the old pony in peace to eat his supper.

'There you are,' she said, seeing Frank and Nancy crossing the courtyard from the direction of the pigsty. 'Your aunt Maeve has just telephoned, Nancy. I told her you'd call her back.' Nancy ran into the hotel ahead of Bess.

'I'll check Donnie has fresh water, I'll be in in a minute,' Frank called after them.

In the office, Bess offered Nancy her chair and when she was seated dialled the number that Maeve had given her. When the telephone was answered, Bess passed the receiver to Nancy and left. She hadn't been in reception more than two minutes when Nancy peeped round the door and beamed a smile at her. Bess pretended to hurry back to the office to hear what Nancy's aunt had to say. 'Well?'

'Aunt Maeve will be back tomorrow teatime,' Nancy said, her cheeks flushed with excitement.

'Then you had better fill in the last square, hadn't you?' Nancy collected her coloured crayons from the seat beneath the window and returned to Bess's chair. 'What colour are you going to use for today?' Bess asked, taking the calendar down and placing it in front of the child.

Without a moment's hesitation, Nancy shouted,

259

'Red!' And, concentrating, she began to fill in the square. When Frank came in, Nancy looked up and waved her crayon at him. 'Aunt Maeve is coming home tomorrow.'

'Well, that is good news,' Frank said, looking from Nancy to Bess.

'Done it!' Nancy shouted.

Moving to stand next to his wife, Frank looked down at the calendar. 'That's very good. You haven't gone over the line once. We've got another budding artist in the family, Bess. I think we should buy Nancy pencils and drawing paper like we bought Aimee, don't you?'

Bess followed his gaze. The other squares had been lightly coloured in blue and green, yellow, orange and purple. The last square was a solid block of red, reminding Bess that Nancy's aunt Maeve was the most important person in her life - and the nearest thing she had to a mother. It also reminded her that Nancy would be going home to Kirby Marlow the following day. 'Excuse me,' Bess said. And standing up she edged out from behind the desk and left the room.

That night, as Bess had done every night when she put Nancy to bed, she read her a story. Halfway through she noticed the child had fallen asleep. Not wanting the time she had left with Nancy to end, Bess lowered her voice and read on. When she finished the chapter, Bess closed the book and put it on the rug at the side of the bed. Watching the little girl sleep, Bess thought of Aimee and the times she had read to her, either at Claire and Mitch's house in Oxford, or when Aimee had stayed with her Grandparents at Foxden. Bess smiled to herself. Aimee would fight to stay awake, only giving in to sleep when her eyes grew so heavy she could no longer keep them open.

Bess stood up and started to pack Nancy's suitcase. Except for the nightdress she was wearing, and a clean set of clothes for the next day, every item of Nancy's clothing had been washed and ironed. Folding her blue dress with the sailor collar brought back memories of Aimee's birthday party and how she and Nancy had become friends. Bess made a mental note to ask Maeve to bring Nancy over when Aimee next visited. Huh! she sighed. That will be when they get back from Canada. Probably not until next year.

Bess took the letter she'd received from Claire, which her sister had written the day they landed in Canada, from the mantle shelf. Mitch would be in hospital now, Bess thought. And taking the letter out of its envelope she wondered how he was responding to treatment.

She flicked open the letter and began to read. "It was all such a rush in the end," Claire wrote. "The Royal Canadian Air Force arranged everything. They flew us from France to Canada, with only a twenty-four-hour stopover in England to pick up our clothes and personal belongings. We expect to be in Canada for three months."

Three months felt like a long time. Bess had hoped with her brother Tom, his wife Annabel, and their daughter Charlotte coming to Foxden for Christmas this year, the whole family would be together for once. Three months, she sighed, would mean Claire, Mitch and Aimee would be in

Canada for Christmas.

Bess remembered Mitch saying the 'Fall' in Canada was similar to the autumns in England, but the winters were much harsher with lots of snow and the temperature below zero for much of the time. Bess hoped Claire had taken plenty of winter clothes for her and Aimee.

She looked back at the letter. "From the apartment," Claire went on to say, "where Aimee and I are living it's a short bus ride to Mitch's father and step-mother's house. And the military hospital, which specialises in men who have suffered mental breakdowns after what they have seen or been through in the war, is a couple of stops further on in the city centre.

"We took the bus to his father's house this morning. Aimee stayed with Mitch's step-mother and his father drove Mitch and I to the hospital in his car. The doctor said he was eager to start Mitch's treatment, which would begin as soon as Mitch had been assessed. He didn't say when that would be, so we'll have to wait and see."

Bess was apprehensive. She wanted to know more, but until her sister wrote again there was nothing she could do except hope and pray, and wait.

Bess put Claire's letter back in the envelope and slipped it into her pocket. She hated the idea of her sister being so far away, but she knew if Claire and Mitch were ever going be happy again, Mitch needed to have specialist treatment. Claire was strong. All the Dudley girls were, but Bess had always thought of Claire as being the strongest of them. If being hospitalised in Canada was what it was going to take for her husband to recover from the mental torment he has been suffering since being in a POW camp in Germany, then Claire would deal with it. And, Bess thought, so would Aimee. Her niece was a Dudley girl through and through.

Bess smoothed Nancy's clothes with the palms of her hands and closed the suitcase.

'Ena? Miss Hawksley?' Astonished, Bess strode across the hall to meet them. 'Won't you come into the office?' She looked at Jack as she passed. No words were exchanged. The young receptionist took a suitcase from Ena, and one from Katherine Hawksley, and pushed them up against the inside of the desk so they couldn't be seen.

'My father has been arrested,' Katherine cried, as soon as Bess closed the door. 'They took him away in handcuffs. That policeman from London and some other men.' Katherine shot a look at Ena.

'Henry and I were with them. Henry thought it best if I went along to take care of Katherine. Can she stay here?'

'Of course. I'm so sorry, Katherine.' Bess felt for the young girl. She wasn't sorry that her father had been arrested, she was delighted about that; she was sorry that the fascist movement and everything associated with it had ruined Katherine's life. What kind of man would expose his daughter to that? 'You look all in,' Bess said to the trembling girl. 'Can I get you anything?'

'I think it would be best if Katherine had a lie down,' Ena said.

'I'll ask Jack if there's a room at the back of the

hotel. One that looks across the fields,' Bess said, pointedly. She didn't want Katherine looking out of the window and seeing the lake. After the arrest of her father, the poor girl didn't need to be reminded that she was the last person to see David Sutherland alive - except for his killer. 'I'll see what we have vacant,' Bess said, making for the door.

'Hang on, Bess!' Ena stopped her sister in her tracks. 'My room is at the back of the hotel, and it has twin beds. Katherine could stay with me. That way if anyone comes looking for a guest who booked in today, there won't be one.'

Bess went out and asked Jack for the key to Ena's room. 'Except for Ena, no one but you and I, and Frank when he comes in, knows Miss Hawksley is staying here,' she said. 'And it must remain that way.' With a sympathetic smile, Jack nodded slowly, assuring Bess that he understood. Bess took Ena's room key into the office and gave it to her.

'I'll take Katherine up and stay with her until she's settled,' Ena said.

Bess followed Ena and Katherine out of the office and into reception. As she stepped behind the desk, Jack picked up Katherine's suitcases. 'I'll take these up, Mrs Donnelly,' he said, making light of the cases as he swiftly crossed the marble hall ahead of Ena and Katherine.

Jack returned as Frank and Nancy came in from feeding the animals. Apart from a little dirt on her shoes, Nancy was as clean as she had been when Bess dressed her that morning.

Because it was important that no one knew

Katherine Hawksley was staying at the hotel, Bess didn't want to tell Frank in front of Nancy. If I'm being melodramatic it's too bad, she thought, but an eight-year old child might innocently say a name, which, if overheard by the wrong people, could be disastrous.

Bess trusted Maeve and would tell her on Monday when she returned to work. To Frank she said, 'Ena has brought her friend from New Year's Eve to see us.'

'Good. The removal must have gone to plan.' Frank took hold of Nancy's hand. 'Let's get some tea and biscuits, shall we?'

Jack, professional and discreet, was busy writing something in the reservations diary. 'Can you manage on your own if I take a break, Jack?'

'Yes, Mrs Donnelly.'

With the hotel having been full during the half-term break, Jack had been busy most of the morning with guests paying and departing. Because the children were back at school on Monday, the majority of the guests had left soon after breakfast. Bess looked at the clock on the wall above reception. It was ten-forty-five. 'I'll be back at eleven.'

Bess turned to remind Jack to take messages, but he beat her to it saying, with a twinkle in his eye, 'Messages?' Bess laughed. She was still laughing when she entered the dining room.

'Chef has made me a cake,' Nancy said, smiling broadly, 'Do you want some?'

'Yes, please,' Bess said, and held her breath while Nancy cut through a sponge cake, with a cake knife. Trying to work out which way the cake would wobble off the knife if it fell, Bess lifted her plate. She needn't have worried. Meeting the plate half-way, Nancy turned the wide blade of the knife upside down and the cake tumbled onto Bess's plate.

Waving his hands in the air, the chef came into the dining room. 'Did you like the cake Chef made for you, little one?'

'Yes, thank you. Will you look after the rest, so I can give Aunt Maeve some when she comes for me?'

'But of course.' With a flamboyant swoop, he picked up the cake-stand and flounced out of the dining room.

Frank laughed and Bess shook her head. 'I need to go on reception now, Nancy, so Jack can have a break. When he comes back is there anything you'd like to do before lunch?'

Pulling a thoughtful face, Nancy put her finger to her chin and looked up at the ceiling. 'Say goodbye to Grandma Dudley.'

Bess felt a lump in her throat that she knew wouldn't clear by coughing. 'All right. We'll walk down. I shall need the exercise, if I eat all this cake,' she said, picking up her plate. She knew she wouldn't be able to eat it, but said, 'Thank you, Nancy, I'll take it with me. See you two later,' she called over her shoulder as she left.

At reception, Bess said goodbye to a middle-aged couple who had paid their bill, but were in no hurry to leave. Thanking them, she said, 'I hope you've enjoyed your stay?'

'Everything was perfect; the room, the food - and the staff,' the man said, 'couldn't do enough

266

for us, could they, dear?'

'No,' his wife agreed. 'And the view of the lake from the window in our room,' she swooned, 'with the ducks and drakes... That's what I loved best. It was spectacular.'

'We're city folk you see. Staying in a real country house like this, with its history and charm was a real treat. We shall recommend the hotel to our friends.'

'See you next year,' his wife called, as they were leaving.

While Jack was on his break, Ena came down. 'Katherine's asleep, so I thought I'd chance it and get a cup of tea.'

'You look as if you could do with a sleep,' Bess said, noticing the dark shadows under her sister's eyes.

'We had to pull an all-nighter last night. The operation was co-ordinated to take place at two in the morning. But it took hours to search every room in every fascist's home, as well as their places of work and the safe houses. Hopefully every building that is owned or rented by the British fascist movement has been searched by now. A lot of youngsters like Katherine will have had their worlds turned upside down and will be left wondering what has happened to their fathers - their mothers too, in some cases.'

'At least this Katherine is safe.'

'For the time being,' Ena said, her expression one of worry.

'The poor girl looked scared to death earlier. What if she wakes and you're not there? Won't she be frightened?'

'She won't wake up for a while.'

'How can you be sure?'

'She said she hadn't slept properly for weeks, so I gave her a light sedative.' Bess's mouth fell open. 'Don't look so shocked, it was only a mild one. It'll calm her down and help her to relax, so she can get some sleep.'

Bess put up her hand. 'I don't want to know any more.'

'It's for her own good. She'll be fine.'

'She'll be fine once she's reunited with her mother.'

'Hopefully.'

'She will be reunited with her mother, won't she?'

'Yes, eventually, but there's a lot to do before we bring her mother down.' Bess tutted. 'It's important that we find out how much, if anything, Katherine knows about her father's business - and I don't mean where he worked, I mean how he got his money.'

'And that's your job, is it?' Bess asked, a mixture of annoyance and apprehension in her voice.

'Part of my job, yes. But my main job is to keep Katherine Hawksley safe. Not for MI5 or Special Branch, but from her father's fascist associates. We're hoping they were all caught last night, but if any of them have slipped through the net they might think Katherine, being the head of the organisation's daughter, knows their names and roles in the fascist movement. They'd be wrong. Apart from the names of a few men who passed through Kirby Marlow last year bound for South America - and David Sutherland - she doesn't know the names of anyone involved in the organisation. The problem is, they don't know that. It's Hawksley's people who are a threat to Katherine, not us.'

'I see,' Bess said lamely, although she wasn't sure she did see.

'Anyway,' Ena said, 'how are you feeling? It's today that Maeve comes back, isn't it?'

'Yes, she'll be here around four. Then Nancy will go back to the Vicarage in Kirby Marlow.' Bess gave a sad smile. 'I've just asked her what she'd like to do before lunch and she said, say goodbye to Grandma Dudley. She's quite taken with our Mam.'

'And Mam's taken with her. We all are. And, here she is,' Ena sang, as Nancy and Frank appeared from the direction of the dining room. 'If you're going down to Mam's, I'll take the newspaper and a pot of tea up to the room. I'm so tired, I might even try to have a sleep. Bye-bye, Nancy,' Ena said, and made her way to the kitchen.

Bess got their coats from the office, helped Nancy into hers and put her own on. 'Jack shouldn't be long,' she said to Frank, who was already in position behind the reception desk. 'We'll see you later.'

'Say hello to Grandma Dudley for me,' Frank called, as Bess and Nancy got to the door. Nancy turned and waved, and then slipped her hand into Bess's.

CHAPTER TWENTY-TWO

Nancy jumped down each of the circular steps and, on the last, let go of Bess's hand and skipped down the drive until she came to the small wood that was once part of Foxden's parkland. 'Stay on the path, Nancy,' Bess called.

Catching up with her, Bess saw concern in Nancy's eyes. Standing very still she was staring into the wood at the gnarled roots of a giant oak tree. Bess knelt down beside her. 'There's nothing to be frightened of, sweetheart. The wood is quite safe. My sisters and I used to play in there when we were your age. We often saw rabbits and squirrels, or fox cubs. When I grew up I used to come here when I wanted to be on my own.' Bess laughed. 'When I wanted to get away from my chattering younger sisters. It was so quiet and peaceful,' Bess sighed. 'And in the summer when it was really hot, I used to walk my horse through the wood. Because of the trees it was shaded and cool. Then I'd ride her at a trot across the fields to the river.'

'What was your horse's name?'

'Sable.' Nancy wrinkled her nose, making Bess laugh. 'She was called Sable because her lovely warm, dark brown, coat was the colour of sable.'

'Where is she now?'

Bess hadn't reckoned on that question and didn't want to tell Nancy that Sable had died, in case it reminded her that her mother was dead. 'I'll tell you more about Sable another day,' Bess said, walking on to her mother's cottage.

Opening the gate, Nancy ran up the path to the front door ahead of Bess and knocked, unanswered questions about Sable forgotten for the time being.

'Well if it isn't our Bess. Come in, love.' Lily Dudley, pretending she hadn't seen Nancy until she entered the front hall, put her hands up to her cheeks. 'And our Nancy!' she exclaimed. 'Well this is a nice surprise.' Nancy, giggling, skipped down the passage at Lily Dudley's side.

'Who's for milk and cake?'

'Me!' Nancy shouted, running into the kitchen.

Bess was about to remind Nancy that she had just been eating cake, but seeing the fun Nancy was having with her mother, said, 'Please?'

'Please,' Nancy repeated, standing next to the cupboard where she knew Bess's mother kept the cake tin.

'That's better. We don't want your aunt to think you've forgotten your manners while you've been staying with Uncle Frank and me, do we?'

Nancy shook her head. 'Thank you,' she said, to the glass of milk Bess's mother poured for her. Then, clapping her hands, she beamed a broad smile as Lily Dudley put a plate with an iced fairy cake in front of her.

'Tuck in, love.' Then, turning her attention to the stove, she switched off the gas beneath the boiling kettle and made a pot of tea.

When she had finished her milk and cake, Nancy slid off her chair, stood in front of Bess and lifted her chin. 'All clean,' Bess said, after wiping the milk-moustache from Nancy's top lip with a clean handkerchief.

'Can I play with Grandpa's pipes?' Nancy

asked.

Bess was about to say no, in case you break them, when her mother said, 'Of course you can, sweetheart, you know where they are. But before you go.' Lily took a glass jar from the cupboard, took off the lid and offered it to Nancy. With a cheeky grin, Nancy chose a toffee, thanked Bess's mum, and skipped out of the room.

Bess raised her eyebrows.

'What?'

'You,' Bess said, 'you spoil her.'

'And why not? I can't spoil Aimee, she lives too far away, and it'll be years till Margot's baby is old enough to spoil. Anyway, why shouldn't the poor child have a treat now and again?'

'She isn't poor, Mother. And her aunt Maeve, and Mrs Sykes who they lodge with, give her plenty of treats.'

'That's as may be, but a child without a mother...' Lily tutted and shook her head.

For the next hour, Bess and her mother chatted about the hotel; how nice it was that Ena was at Foxden, but how worrying that Claire was in Canada. They talked about Margot and Natalie - the beautiful new edition to the Dudley family - and they talked about Nancy.

Lily got up and cleared the table putting the tea things in the sink with a clatter. Turning back to Bess, she said, 'You'll miss her when she goes back to Kirby.'

'I know. Frank will too. He was worried that I'd get too attached to her, and wouldn't want to give her back when Maeve returned, but I think he's become more attached to her than I have. I suppose

272

it's because she follows him about all the time.' Bess shook her head. 'Those bloomin' animals,' she said, laughing, 'I don't know who's the daftest with them, Nancy or Frank.'

Bess looked at her wristwatch. 'We'd better get back.' Standing up, she opened the kitchen door. 'Nancy? Time to go.'

'Have you put Grandpa's pipes back in the right order?' Lily asked when Nancy appeared in the kitchen.

'Yes,' she said, pushing her arms down the sleeves of her coat, which Bess was holding for her. As Bess knelt in front of her to button up the coat, Nancy said, 'The smallest first and the biggest last.'

'That's almost right.' Lily laughed. 'I shall leave them in that order until the next time you come to see me.'

Bess put on her own coat. 'Ready?'

Nancy nodded. 'Goodbye, Grandma,' she said, looking up at Bess's mother with big eyes.

'Goodbye, love. Promise you'll come and see me the next time you visit Auntie Bess at the hotel?'

'I promise,' Nancy said.

At the gate, Nancy stopped and looked back at the cottage. Bess's mother was at the front room window waving. When Nancy waved back, Bess saw the same unhappy look in Nancy's eyes that she had seen on the night the little girl looked at the photograph of her mother, Goldie. 'Goodbye, Grandma.' she called, her small chin jutting out and her mouth downturned.

Nancy walked back to the hotel in a sombre

273

mood, but the minute she stepped inside that changed. 'Aunt Maeve!' she shouted, dropping Bess's hand and racing across the hall to where her aunt was talking to Jack at reception.

Maeve fell to her knees and hugged her niece. She was early. Bess swallowed her disappointment and walked over to the desk smiling. 'Welcome back,' she said. 'Did you have a good journey?'

'I shouldn't complain, but the Irish Sea was choppy and the boat was crowded with noisy children going home after their holiday. I'm glad to be back on terra-firma - and,' she said, holding Nancy at arm's length, 'I'm really glad to see you.'

Bess was about to ask Maeve how her mother was, but decided to wait until Monday, when she came back to work. 'Would you like some lunch? We haven't had ours yet. I thought we had more time, but you're early,' Bess said, almost accusingly. 'I mean not that it matters.' It did matter, but only to Bess. She turned to Nancy, 'I know you've had cake and a toffee, so you're probably not very hungry, but I think you should have some proper food inside you before you go.' The little girl looked up at her aunt, waiting to see what she said.

With raised eyebrows Maeve nodded and Nancy nodded too. 'Good. Go through to the dining room and I'll get Frank.'

Bess took a deep breath and put on a smile. 'Coming for lunch?' she asked, entering the office.

'Yes, I'm starving.' Frank put down the papers he'd been working on and, crossing the room, met Bess in the middle. 'You've got to be strong,' he said, looking into her eyes. 'You knew this day would come and she would go back to Maeve.'

'I know. And it isn't as if we won't see her again. I mean she's only a few miles down the road. There'll be no stopping her coming over when Aimee gets back.'

'That's right.' Frank opened the door and stood to the side to allow Bess to leave first. 'We'll be in the dining room if anyone wants us,' Frank said, as they passed Jack. Bess's usual reminder to take messages and telephone numbers went unsaid. Today she had other things on her mind.

Bess had no appetite, but made the effort with a bowl of soup and a bread roll. When she had finished eating she remembered that, because Maeve was early, Jack hadn't had his lunch. 'I'll be on reception,' she said, leaving the table. 'With one thing and another, Jack hasn't had a break since this morning.' Frank stood up at the same time. 'You stay and finish your lunch, darling. Keep Maeve and Nancy company. See you before you go, sweetheart,' she said to Nancy. And, putting on a smile, Bess hurried out of the dining room before the sadness she felt in her heart manifested in tears.

Soon after taking over from Jack, Bess saw Frank, Maeve and Nancy coming out of the dining room. 'I'll go up and get little one's case,' Frank said, leaving them at reception and heading towards the staff stairs.

Bess watched as Maeve held Nancy's coat for her to put on. She then bent down and buttoned the coat up, straightened the left side of the collar so it was level with the right side. 'There,' she said, standing.

Frank was soon back with Nancy's case. He gave it to Maeve. 'Would you like me to drive you to Kirby Marlow?'

'No, thank you. I borrowed Reverend Sykes' car.' Maeve turned and looked at Bess, Bess looked at her, and they both looked at Nancy. 'Well, I suppose we'd better go and let Aunt Bess and Uncle Frank get back to work,' Maeve said. 'So, what do you say, Nancy?'

The little girl looked up at Bess. 'Thank you for having me.'

'It's been a pleasure.' Bess bent down and kissed Nancy's cheek. 'We've loved having you. Haven't we Frank?'

'We certainly have. Thank you for all the help you gave me, feeding the animals and collecting the eggs. I don't know what I'd have done without you.'

A bit of an exaggeration, but a lovely thing to say, Bess thought.

Nancy ran to Frank and stood on tiptoe with her arms outstretched. Frank crouched down until his face was level with hers and she threw her arms around his neck. 'Bye-bye, sweetheart.' Nancy leaned in closer to Frank and hung on to him. 'Come and see us anytime you like,' Frank whispered. 'We'll always be here.' He looked over the little girl's head and Bess saw tears in his eyes.

Still clinging to him, her head buried in his chest, Nancy mumbled, 'Look after the chickens, Uncle Frank.'

Frank laughed and cuffed away a tear, 'I will.'

As the small party walked to the door, the telephone on the reception desk began to ring.

276

Bess turned immediately. 'I'll get it,' she said, relieved that she didn't have to watch Nancy leave. 'See you soon, Nancy,' she called after the little girl, blowing her a kiss.

Bess clenched her fists, took a deep breath to stem her tears, and picked up the telephone. 'Foxden Hotel. May I help you?' It was a booking for two, arriving on Monday and staying for five days. When she replaced the receiver on its cradle, Bess gripped the edge of the desk and took another breath. She felt no calmer.

'Well!' Frank said, striding across the hall to her. 'Saying goodbye to little Nancy was harder than I thought it would be.'

'I was pleased when the telephone rang, to be honest.'

'That's why I didn't offer to answer it. Hey?' Frank said, putting his arms round Bess. 'Why don't you go into the office and make yourself a drink? Better still, make two, and add a drop of brandy to each of them.'

Wiping her eyes, Bess laughed. 'Any excuse,' she said. 'But yes, I could do with a drink. Coffee for you?'

Frank nodded. 'And then, why don't you go up and have a lie down? I'll finish your shift. I'm on tonight anyway.'

'But then you won't get a rest.'

'Not sure I want one. I'm better staying busy.'

'You liked having her here, didn't you? I knew you would,' Bess said.

'I did. But, she has gone home with her aunt, which we knew she would do. So, where's my coffee, woman?'

277

When Bess returned with Frank's coffee, Jack was back from lunch. 'Right, you stay here with Jack and cover the rest of my shift and,' she looked at the clock, 'I'll be back before Jack leaves.'

'We're both on reception tonight. It'll be like old times.'

'We haven't had the hotel a year and you're--' Bess laughed and waved her hand in the air. 'Forget it. I'll see you both at five.'

Bess usually allowed herself an hour to get washed and changed for the evening. Every day, since the hotel first opened, Bess and Frank had been on duty, either on reception, or in the dining room. Even if they were in the office the rule was, if a guest wanted to speak to them they were available. The same rule applied in the evenings. It added a personal touch, which Bess and Frank enjoyed and, after the first couple of nights, the guests expected.

In the bedroom, Bess drew the curtains, kicked off her shoes and fell onto the bed. She pulled up the eiderdown and closed her eyes, but she couldn't sleep. She tossed and turned for a while, then got up and went through to the sitting room. Perched on the end of Nancy's single bed she turned on the wireless. Alistair Cooke's *Letter from America* was on. Bess didn't want to be reminded that her sister was on the other side of the Atlantic; not in America, but in Canada, and rotated the tuning button until she heard the voice of broadcaster Jean Metcalf on Woman's Hour. The magazine programme was one that Bess particularly enjoyed, when she had time. She put her feet up and laid back on the small single bed to catch the last fifteen minutes of the show. The next thing she heard was the opening music to *Mrs Dale's Diary*. She had slept for two hours.

After a quick bath, she brushed her auburn curls into a loose bun in the nape of her neck, put on a grey-green dress, appropriate for the evening, and applied powder and rouge. With time to spare, she glanced through the photographs in the chest of drawers, eventually coming across the one Nancy had found of her mother, Goldie. The resemblance between mother and daughter was striking. It was a wonder Margot hadn't noticed it. But then, Bess thought, her sister had only seen Nancy a couple of times.

Putting the photographs back in the drawer, Bess wondered why Maeve hadn't told her Goldie was Nancy's mother. She told her that Nancy was the daughter of her cousin. She had even told her how Nancy's mother had died. Bess decided to ask Maeve about Goldie when she returned to work on Monday.

After checking her hair in the mirror and adding lipstick, Bess went downstairs. Jack had already left, so she took her place behind reception and Frank went up to change. When he returned, Bess looked in on Chef to see if he, or any of the kitchen staff, needed anything. They didn't, so she checked the dining room to make sure the tables had been laid correctly for dinner. They had.

When she got back to reception, Ena was there talking to Frank. She gave Bess a warm smile, 'Katherine obviously can't come down for dinner, so I'll take something up to her. I'll ask Chef to make up two trays - one for me and one for Henry. I'll say Henry's working and I'm keeping him company.'

'Have you heard from Henry? Do you know how things are going?' Frank asked.

'No, but I'm sure he'll check in tonight. I hope he does anyway.'

'We'll put him through straight away, if he rings,' Bess said, looking at Frank.

'Thanks. I might risk coming down later. Katherine insisted I locked her in the room before I left just now, so when she goes to bed, I'll come back. It sounds awful doesn't it, locking someone in their room?'

'When you put it like that, yes,' Bess said. 'How is she?'

'Terrified, poor kid. Petrified that one of her father's friends will come looking for her. If they do,' Ena said, 'they'll have to get past me first.'

Bess felt her stomach churn with worry and she bit on her bottom lip. 'If either of you need anything, ring me and I'll bring it up to your room.'

'Thanks. Fingers crossed, I'll see you later.'

The following morning, while the guests were in the dining room having Sunday breakfast, Bess took the hotel's appointments diary into the office. She hadn't had time to check who was leaving, in order to prepare their bills, when there was a tap on the door. It opened immediately. 'Sorry to disturb you, Mrs Donnelly,' Jack said, giving Bess an exaggerated wink. 'There are two gentlemen in reception looking for their niece. They believe she is staying here.' Bess's heart began to thump against her ribcage and she got to her feet. 'The young lady's father has had an accident and they'd like her to return home with them. Immediately.' Jack rolled his eyes.

'Have you booked any young women in recently?' Bess asked, as casually as she was able.

'No, Mrs Donnelly. I told the gentlemen that, but they're insisting on seeing the hotel's appointments book, to look for themselves.'

Bess raised her eyes. 'I haven't taken any single bookings either,' she said, picking up the appointments diary, 'but it won't hurt to check.' Bess followed Jack out into reception. 'Good morning, gentlemen,' she said, putting on a professional smile.' She laid the diary down on the top of the reception desk, so it was facing her. 'What is your niece's name?'

The two men looked at each other, then at Bess. 'Hawksley,' the taller of the two men said, 'Katherine Hawksley.'

Bess ran her finger down the short list of guests that had arrived that morning, repeating the name. 'I'm sorry, but no one has booked in today by the name of... Hawksley?' She turned the page and shook her head. 'Nor yesterday, or the day before.'

The taller man snatched the diary from the desk and, turning the pages roughly, scrutinised each name. When he was satisfied Bess was telling the truth, he let the book fall onto the desk with a thump. He stared at Bess through cold steel-grey eyes, then looked sideways at Jack. 'It's important we find her, understand?'

'Of course. And don't worry, if she arrives later today we'll tell her to get in touch with you, Mr--?'

'Smith!'

'Smith. Do you have a card, Mr Smith, with a telephone number where Miss Hawksley can reach you?'

Mr Smith made an exaggerated show of lifting his hand to the breast pocket of his suit jacket. 'Dearie me,' he said, his voice dripping with sarcasm. 'Wouldn't you know it. I'm all out of cards.'

Several guests bustled into the hall from the dining room and the shorter of the two men spun round. 'Don't say anymore,' he hissed. Turning back to Smith he indicated with a flick of his head that they should leave.

'We'll be back later!' Smith said.

'As you wish,' Bess chirped. The two men lumbered across the hall to the hotel's entrance foyer, flung open the door, and left without a backwards glance.

Bess looked at Jack. His face was ashen. 'My legs feel as if they've turned to jelly.'

'Did that really happen, or were we watching one of those American gangster films?'

'It happened, Jack, and if it was a film we were in it.'

'Henry!' Bess ran across the hall, excusing herself as she disrupted a group of guests mid-conversation, to get to her brother-in-law. 'Did you see those two men?' Henry looked bemused. 'They've only just left. You must have passed them.' Henry turned at the sound of a car revving

282

its engine. 'They were asking about Katherine. They said she was their niece.'

'Did you tell them anything?'

'Of course not!'

'So she's still safe?'

'Yes. She's with Ena in her room,' Bess whispered.

'Good. Telephone Lowarth police station. Tell Inspector Masters to put every man he's got on the streets,' Henry said, as a white saloon car roared round the side of the hotel from the car park. 'Tell him to ring Market Harborough and Rugby - and tell them to do the same. They're looking for two men in a white Jowett Javelin, number plate beginning with CF and ending with 3, or 8.'

Bess ran back to reception repeating the details over and over in her head.

'Tell Ena I'll see her later!' Henry shouted, before running down the steps to his car.

Bess didn't return to the office. After what she and Jack had just experienced, she didn't think either of them should be alone on reception. However, when it was time for her break, Jack insisted he would be fine on his own for twenty minutes - and Bess, refusing to let thugs like the two who were looking for Katherine intimidate her, went outside to get some fresh air.

Still tense from having stood her ground against two fascist thugs, Bess needed to calm down and regain her composure. A stroll across the peacock lawn to the lake, she decided, would help.

She lifted her face to the indifferent afternoon sun and breathed in the early autumn air. She watched the wildlife on the lake. The ducklings, bigger now, reminded her of Nancy. She wondered how the little girl was. She hadn't been gone twenty-four hours, but Bess missed her so much it felt like a week.

She inhaled deeply and blew out a long calming breath. All around her nature was changing. Flowers were budding less, reeds in the lake were beginning to turn yellow and some trees were already shedding their unwanted leaves. It was what Bess called the in-between time of year. It wasn't summer, nor was it quite autumn. For the hotel, it would soon be the quietest time of the year.

Henry and Inspector Masters arrived at six o'clock. Jack had finished his shift and gone for the day, Frank was on reception and Bess was in the office, about to join her husband out front. She offered them tea, which they both refused - Henry saying he needed to see Ena and Katherine, and the inspector saying he didn't have time.

'I've only popped in to say thank you for your help today, Bess. Miss Hawksley's bogus uncles will be enjoying the sludge they dish up in His Majesty's prison Leicester now.'

'Thank goodness you caught them. They were a scary pair.'

'Dangerous too. They've been doing Hawksley's dirty work for a decade or more. They'd think nothing of disposing of Katherine, or anyone else, to save their own scraggy necks.'

'So, will Katherine be safe now?'

The Inspector's brow furrowed. He didn't answer immediately. 'I think so,' he said, 'but I'd feel happier if she stayed out of sight for a few more days, in case any associates of Hawksley's that we haven't come across yet decide to crawl out of the woodwork. The major players in the Fascist Association have been arrested, and,' he said, smiling for the first time since he had arrived, 'we are ninety-nine percent sure that the escape route to South America has been scuppered. But,' he put his hands up, palms together, and bowed his head, 'until I'm certain that there aren't any other Nazi sympathisers out there that think Katherine Hawksley is a threat to them, I'm taking no chances.'

CHAPTER TWENTY-THREE

'Mrs Donnelly, could I speak to you, please?' Maeve asked, when Bess came down on Monday morning.

'Of course, what is it?'

'In private?'

Leaving Jack to look after reception, Maeve followed Bess into the office. 'Take a seat,' Bess said, motioning to a chair on the left of the hearth. Maeve sat down and Bess joined her, sitting on the chair opposite.

Bess looked enquiringly at Maeve. Was she going to explain why she hadn't told Bess before that she knew of David Sutherland, and that she had attended his funeral? Or was she going to explain why she hadn't told her that Goldie Trick was Nancy's mother? 'How can I help?'

Maeve began to tremble. Her face was white and her eyes, brimming with tears, looked too big for their sockets. 'I don't know where to start,' she said, looking down at her lap and wringing her hands.

'Perhaps I can start for you. Margot's friend, the young dancer at the Albert Theatre called Goldie Trick, was your cousin and Nancy's mother?'

Maeve shot Bess a look of hurt and surprise. 'How did you know?'

Bess's accusing tone became more sympathetic when she realised how difficult it must be for Maeve to talk about Goldie in the past tense. 'Nancy told me. She found an old photograph of

Margot and some of the dancers at the theatre - Goldie was in one of them. I checked the photograph against a programme from a show that I'd seen in 1939 and matched Goldie's picture to her name. I'm so sorry, Maeve. I know from Margot that Goldie was a very special young woman.'

'She was,' Maeve said. 'When she came home to Ireland, after Margot and her friends got her out of London because David Sutherland had beaten her up, I was working in England as a translator, listening to conversations between Luftwaffe pilots. I was based at Kirby Mansion and billeted at the Vicarage with Reverend and Mrs Sykes.

'My mother wrote and told me that Goldie had come home and was in a bad way. She didn't say more than that. She knew not to be specific in letters because all incoming and outgoing correspondence was censored. I immediately asked for leave and was given forty-eight hours. It wasn't long enough,' Maeve lifted her shoulders, 'but it was all my commanding officer would give me, so I took it.

'I spent a day with Doreen-- Goldie.' Maeve fell silent and closed her eyes. When she opened them, she said, 'According to my mother, by the time I got home, Goldie's physical injuries had begun to fade. The cuts on her face were healing and the bruises on her arms and legs had grown fainter - but the mental scars hadn't. To tell you the truth I don't think they ever did. She was terrified that David Sutherland would find her. She had terrible nightmares. She would wake up in the night screaming. I suggested she leave the light on when she went to bed, but it didn't help. She stopped getting undressed, and eventually she stopped getting into bed altogether. At first she laid on top of the bed fully dressed, then she sat in a chair facing the door, and dozed.'

Maeve fell silent again. She clenched her fists and closed her eyes. Then, as if she had somehow been fortified, she took a deep breath and started speaking. 'Goldie became paranoid. She looked for Sutherland everywhere, and she saw him everywhere she looked. She said she'd seen him in the grocery shop, and walking along the street. She even said she saw him in mum's garden.' Maeve began to cry. 'I'm sorry,' she said, wiping the flat of her hand across her face. She took a deep breath. 'Mother said she went out less and less until one day she announced that she was never going out again. And she didn't - until she became ill.'

'What was wrong with her?'

'She was being sick. She stopped eating because of it. My mother said her face became gaunt, and she was so thin she looked skeletal. Mother didn't know how to help her. She begged her to see our family doctor, but Goldie refused saying she was too frightened to leave the house. Eventually mum got the doctor to visit her at home. He did some tests and said Goldie was dehydrated because she hadn't been drinking liquids, and thin because she hadn't been eating - and she was three months pregnant.'

'Nancy?' Bess said.

Maeve's eyes lit up. 'Yes. Mother said from the moment the doctor told her she was having a baby,

Goldie changed. It was as if all the pain she had suffered, the beatings and mental torture she'd endured at the hands of Sutherland, just melted away. She had never known Goldie so happy.' A faint smile spread slowly across Maeve's face. 'From the minute she learned she was having a baby, Goldie started to look after herself. She began to eat properly, she went back to sleeping in her bed, and she swore the nightmares had stopped. Although Mum said she often heard Goldie crying in her sleep.

'For the most part, the old Goldie was back. She *lived* for the day she had the baby. Our next-door neighbour gave her a Moses basket and she lined it with pale pink cotton. She sewed sheets and a pillowcase to match it, and bought two pink blankets.'

'She wanted a girl then?' Bess said.

'Oh yes! She wrote to me and said she was praying for a girl. A boy, she said, might remind her of him, of Sutherland.'

Smiling, Maeve shook her head. 'My mother was happy because Goldie was happy. "Being sad is not good for the baby," Goldie would tell her. And she would caress her tummy and say, "Mummy loves you, Nancy."'

Maeve pressed her lips together tightly and looked up to the heavens. As if a black cloud was bearing down on her, Bess watched Maeve's expression change from one of joy and loving memories to heartbroken and vengeful. 'She didn't go full term. She wasn't much over seven months when she went into labour. Mother sent for me straight away and this time I was given two weeks' compassionate leave.

'From the moment I saw Goldie in the hospital, I didn't leave her side. She did her best to bring the baby naturally, but she wasn't able to push when they told her to, because she kept slipping in and out of consciousness.

'The doctor told us that Goldie was bleeding internally and they needed to operate. He said that if the worst came to the worst and it was a matter of saving the life of the mother, or the child, which should he save? Mother broke down. It was unfair to ask her to make such a decision, but she had no choice, she was Goldie's next of kin.'

'And she chose the child?'

'No. Mother chose Goldie. But Goldie rallied before the operation. She was conscious for an hour or more before they took her down to theatre. During that time she was talking and smiling. The day before she had looked exhausted, her skin had a grey pallor to it and her eyes were dull and watery - but suddenly all that was gone. Her eyes were bright and she no longer looked tired. She looked like Goldie again.

'She was fully aware of what was happening. She said she was contented and she told the surgeon if it came to it, and he had to make a choice between saving her or her baby, he was to save her child.' Maeve took a shuddering breath. 'It did come to it, and the surgeon saved the baby.'

Maeve lowered her eyes and silently cried. When she lifted her head, she said, 'Goldie told me on the day I arrived at the hospital, if the baby was a boy, she was going to call him Charles, after her father. But if it was a girl - and Goldie was sure it would be - she was going to call her, Nancy Margaret, after her two friends in the theatre where she worked who had saved her life by getting her away from David Sutherland and out of London.'

The two women sat in silence. Maeve, Bess thought, was reliving the pain she had felt eight years before, and Bess, wishing she hadn't brought the subject of Goldie up, was riddled with guilt because she was powerless to help her. 'Bess?' Maeve looked at Bess, her eyes filling with tears again.

'What is it?'

'I have to go back to Ireland. My mother is ill, as you know, and she needs me. My young brother, Callum, has been looking after her, but Mum is so embarrassed that her boy has to do private, personal things for her. It isn't fair on her, she feels she's losing her dignity. It isn't fair on Callum either. He says he doesn't mind, because she's his Ma, but it isn't right. A young man shouldn't have to do those things for his sick mother.'

Maeve smiled. 'He's engaged to the sweetest girl and had put a deposit down on a lovely little cottage before Mother had her stroke. He says as soon as Mother is better, or I go back to Ireland to live with her, they'll be married. My brother has done a lot for our mother. Now it is my turn.'

'I shall be sorry to lose you, Maeve, as a friend and as a work colleague, but I understand.'

'I'm not sure you do understand, Bess,' Maeve said. 'You see, I'd like Nancy to stay here and live with you and Mr Donnelly.'

Shocked by what Maeve had asked of her and

Frank, Bess was unable to speak.

'Seeing Nancy every day would break my mother's heart. You see, she blames herself for not being able to keep Goldie safe. And the school?' Maeve shook her head. 'It's fine, don't get me wrong, but it's a village school with children of all ages clumped together in two classrooms. Nancy is brighter than average for her age. She needs to go to a school where she'll grow, reach her full potential, and I believe she'll do that at the school in Kirby Marlow. There are few children of Nancy's age or her intelligence at home.

'Then there are the gossips. Some of them even said, when Goldie came home from London so badly beaten up, that she had got no more than she deserved. And when she was pregnant? Well, you can imagine. I don't think anyone from the village had ever visited London, let alone lived there and worked in a theatre as a dancer. Small village with small-minded people. When Nancy was little, she didn't understand what some of the children said about her mother - and to be fair it wasn't their fault, they were only repeating what they'd heard their parents say.'

'But she's older now and you don't want her hearing malicious gossip about her mother,' Bess said.

'That's right. So, will you at least consider taking Nancy?'

'I would love to look after her. She's an adorable child. Frank would too, I know he would.' Bess lowered her eyes. 'Because I can't have children, I've tried talking to Frank about adopting a child, but he has never warmed to the idea.' An involuntary smile brightened Bess's face. 'But, after spending time with Nancy, I think he might come round.'

'Then will you ask him?'

'I will, but--' Bess saw the relief in Maeve's eyes, but she had to ask, 'What about Nancy? It's all very well you and I talking about what's best for her, but what does she want? Have you asked her? She missed you so much when you were in Ireland, she literally counted off the days.'

Maeve looked across the room to where the wall calendar hung above Bess's desk, her eyes sparkling with tears. 'She told me.'

Bess reached out and took hold of Maeve's hands. 'I'll talk to Frank. I'm sure he'll agree to Nancy staying with us again, while you're in Ireland looking after your mother.'

Maeve looked questioningly into Bess eyes, as if she was searching for something. 'What is it?' Bess asked.

'There are reasons why I might not be able to come back to England.' Maeve took a deep breath, as if she was plucking up the courage to go on. 'I want Nancy to have a good life, a happy life. She needs a mother and father, not someone who is constantly looking over their shoulder. Bess, I want you to adopt Nancy.'

CHAPTER TWENTY-FOUR

It was less busy in the hotel, so Bess and Frank had started taking the occasional Monday evening off. After six o'clock or thereabouts, if they'd done everything that needed to be done, they would go into Rugby and see a film at the Granada. If they were too late to drive the seven or so miles, they'd go to the Ritz at Lowarth. And on one occasion, when there was nothing playing at either cinema that they fancied, they went to the Denbigh in Lowarth and had dinner. As much as they both loved the hotel, getting away from it for a couple of hours to recharge the batteries was necessary.

On the Monday Maeve asked Bess if she and Frank would adopt Nancy, Bess made sure she worked until it was too late to go out. After dinner, she and Frank retired to their private quarters. Bess went straight through to the bedroom and kicked off her shoes. After taking off her clothes and hanging them up, she went into the bathroom, had a wash and cleaned her teeth, before putting on her nightdress, dressing gown and slippers.

Returning to the sitting room Frank said, 'Wireless or gramophone?'

'Do you mind if we don't have either?' Bess dropped onto the settee, tucking her legs under her.

Frank sat next to her and took the newspaper from the occasional table at the side of the settee. He didn't open it. 'What is it, love, you've been preoccupied all day.'

Bess blew out her cheeks. There was no way of telling her husband what Maeve had asked of them, other than to come straight out with it. 'Maeve wants us to adopt Nancy.'

'Good God!' Frank said. Neither of them spoke for some time. Bess thought it best to let the idea percolate in Frank's mind. 'We enjoyed having Nancy here while Maeve was in Ireland,' he said at last, 'but adopt her? What did you say?'

Bess took her time to answer. Frank was the kindest, the most understanding man, but he could be stubborn. Bess knew him too well to think she could coerce him into anything. 'I said I'd ask you, of course,' she replied, her voice as steady and impartial as she could make it.

'She's asking us to adopt Nancy because she has to go back to Ireland to look after her dying mother. Apart from thinking we'd make good parents, Maeve said because Nancy is bright, the village school wouldn't be good for her. And if she took Nancy back there the gossips would stir up all the stuff about Goldie again. She said when she lived there before Nancy was too young to understand, but now she's eight, she'll understand every word.'

'Looking after a child for a week is one thing, but adopting?'

'You said you'd consider adoption after Nancy had stayed with us,' Bess said, impatience creeping into her voice which she hadn't intended.

'I said I would think about it! But that isn't the point.'

'Then what is the point?' Bess snapped.

'Nancy is David Sutherland's child!'

'She is also sweet, dead Goldie Trick's child,' Bess cried. 'But who her real parents are isn't important. She's a little girl who needs looking after and her aunt, her only relative other than her dying great-aunt, can't do it.'

'Can't do it?'

'All right, she doesn't think it would be fair on Nancy to take her back to Ireland.' Maeve had also said she couldn't look after Nancy because she would be looking over her shoulder all the time. What she meant by that Maeve didn't say and Bess didn't ask. She wished she had now.

Frank put his arms around Bess. 'You want this, don't you?'

'I want a child-- *We* want a child, and Nancy needs a mother and father.'

'I know, love. I just can't get past the idea of Nancy being David Sutherland's daughter.'

Bess pushed herself away from Frank, astonished by what he had said. 'I can't believe I'm hearing this. Do you think that innocent little girl will have any of Sutherland's wickedness in her?'

'No! What do you take me for?' Frank was angry, but Bess could see he was more hurt by what she had said. 'I was thinking of you. Worried that because Nancy is Sutherland's child, she would remind you of him, and what he did to you in London.'

Bess hauled herself off the settee. 'I'm going to bed.'

'Bess?' Frank leapt up. He checked the door was locked and switched off the light. By the time he got into the bedroom, Bess was in bed. 'Darling, don't be angry with me.' Frank sat on the bed and leaned into Bess. She turned over so her back was to him. 'I'm sorry. I'm just frightened for you. Frightened that seeing Nancy every day would be a constant reminder of what Sutherland did - and that you would never be free of him.'

Bess turned back to face Frank and sat up. 'If I had been pregnant after Sutherland raped me, I would not have gone to live with a distant relative in outer-Timbuctoo until the baby was born - like so many young unmarried women are made to do - and then give the baby away. I'd have kept her, as Goldie did. And if it came to it, if I had to decide between my life or my baby's, I would have made the same decision as Goldie.' Frank started to protest, but Bess put her forefinger to his lips.

'When we met again after James had been killed and you asked me to marry you, you said you had always loved me and no matter what had happened in my past you always would.' Bess searched Frank's face. 'Would you have taken me and my baby on, if you had known the circumstances in which she had been conceived?'

Frank held Bess's gaze. His brow creased in pain and thought. 'It might have taken me a little time, but yes. I would like to think that I too would have made the right decision.' Frank stood up and undressed. 'We'll talk more tomorrow,' he said, getting into bed. 'But before we make a decision that could change our lives for ever, we need to ask Nancy if living with us, being adopted by us, is what she wants.'

The following morning when the telephone rang, Bess turned over expecting Frank to be lying next to her, but he wasn't there. He must have got up, she thought and, as she couldn't hear any sound coming from either the bathroom or sitting room, assumed he'd gone down. Heaving herself out of bed, Bess draped her dressing gown round her shoulders and stumbled still half-asleep out of the bedroom. 'Morning,' she said, picking up the receiver and yawning.

'Bess, can you come down straight away?'

'I'm not dressed, where's the fire?'

'You're needed in the office. Detective Inspector Masters is here. He's talking to Katherine Hawksley.' Bess gasped. 'He needs a woman, a chaperone for Katherine, before he can begin an official interview.'

'Isn't Ena down there?'

'No, she's gone to collect...' Frank paused, '*someone* up north.'

Bess knew exactly who the someone was and took off her dressing gown. 'I'm on my way,' she said, dropping the receiver onto its cradle.

'Mrs Donnelly. Thank you for coming down so quickly,' DI Masters said, shaking Bess's hand.

'Inspector? Katherine, are you all right?' Bess said, going over to the girl who stood shaking by the window.

'I've told the inspector it was me who killed David Sutherland.' Bess groaned inwardly. 'I thought about what you said, Mrs Donnelly, but when I hit him I saw him stumble backwards. He was right on the edge of the lake. His body was found in the very same place, so it must have been my fault.' Katherine began to cry. 'I can't live with what I did any longer.'

298

'You know you didn't kill him, Katherine. We've talked about that night. You couldn't have killed him, you're not strong enough.'

The Inspector walked round the desk to Frank's chair, 'May I?'

'Yes.' Bess pulled out the chair in front of the desk for Katherine and fetched her own chair from under her desk.

When the three of them were seated, the inspector took a pen and a notebook from his briefcase. 'Why don't you start from when you and Sutherland left the hotel, Miss Hawksley?' Bess knew the policeman from London was a good man. He had shown Bess understanding and compassion, she hoped he would show the same to Katherine.

Katherine took a deep breath. 'We were waiting for my father to bring the car round to the front of the hotel. David was getting impatient. He wanted to start walking. He kept on about it, so I gave in to him. We started down the drive and just before the bend he began to laugh really loud. He said he wouldn't mind--' Katherine cast her eyes down and shook her head.

'It's all right Katherine,' the Inspector said, sympathetically. 'Take your time.'

Katherine cleared her throat. 'He said he wouldn't mind giving Bess Dudley *one*, again.' Katherine's cheeks flushed scarlet and she looked up at Bess. 'I'm sorry.' Bess shook her head and gave Katherine an encouraging smile. 'But it wouldn't be as much fun now she's married, he said. It's the first bite of the cherry that's the sweetest.

'I shouldn't have said anything, but I asked him if he had raped Miss Dudley - Mrs Donnelly - and he went crazy. I should have known better than to ask. He was so angry I thought he was going to explode. "She was begging for it, like you are!" he shouted in my face. "You're all the same. You're all stupid bitches." He grabbed my arm and dragged me across the field to a big clump of reeds. He jerked me to him. He was holding my bottom and rubbing up against me. I tried to get away. I tried to hit him, but he'd pinned my arms down at my side. He was kissing me so hard, so roughly, that my lips were hurting. Then he let go of me with one hand and started forcing it up my dress. I was so frightened, I pushed him as hard as I could, but he just laughed. "And when I've had you," he shouted in my face, "Daddy will pay me to keep quiet like Bess Donnelly's husband does."

'It was then that I saw my father's car pull up. I cried out, but David put his hand over my mouth. "Call out again and I'll kill you," he said, in a horrible scratchy voice. He would have done too, so I closed my mouth. I watched my father's car drive off and I thought, this is it, I'll never see him again.

'David's face looked like thunder. His eyes were narrow slits. He grabbed my wrist and dragged me to the edge of the lake, then he held my neck by the skin at the back, the way you hold a puppy or a kitten, but he held it really tight.

'I was terrified. I thought he was going to kill me. He forced me to look down at the frozen lake. I closed my eyes and he eased his grip on my neck. But instead of letting go of me, he pulled my hair until I lifted my head. I knew if I didn't do something, I'd end up dead in the woods, or drowned in the lake.'

Katherine put her hands up to her face and shook her head. 'I saw another car stop on the drive. I couldn't see it properly because it was snowing hard. I thought it was Dad come back for me, but it wasn't. Then I saw Mrs Donnelly and Mrs Burrell. I called out to them and he slapped my face. He went to hit me again, overreached, lost his balance and fell down. This is my chance to escape, I thought. So, while he was on all fours scrambling to get to his feet, I hit him as hard as I could with my handbag and I ran.

'I heard a crack. I thought it was a branch, because we were so near the wood, but now!' Tears fell from Katherine's eyes and she put her hand over her mouth. 'Now I know it was the ice giving way beneath his weight.'

Bess took hold of Katherine's hand. 'At the time, I didn't think about the lake,' she said, 'I didn't think about anything, I just ran crying.'

The inspector, his head tilted on one side, looked at Katherine quizzically 'And you're sure it was your handbag that you hit him with?'

Katherine looked from Bess to the inspector. 'Yes. Why?'

'No reason, I just need to be sure of the facts.' The inspector made a note on his pad and said, 'Carry on, Miss Hawksley.'

'Well, I saw Mrs Donnelly and Mrs Burrell. They were halfway across the field. They were calling my name, telling me to come to them because it wasn't safe on that side of the lake. I knew it wasn't, but it was snowing really heavily, and I couldn't see properly. I was confused. I didn't know which way to turn, so I turned back. It was then that I spotted the headlights of a car through the trees of the small wood that borders the lake and main road, so I made a run for it. The car was my father's and to my relief he was on his own. I opened the front passenger door and as soon as I sat down we sped away.'

'Did you see anyone else besides Mrs Donnelly and Mrs Burrell?'

'A man got out of a car, but he couldn't have been anything to do with David Sutherland, because the car was going to the hotel, not from it, and he didn't come anywhere near the lake or the woods.' Katherine paused. 'There was something. It was only for a second, but I thought-- well it was more of a feeling really - that someone was watching me from the woods, or from the other side of the lake.'

'The mind plays tricks on us when we're frightened, Miss Hawksley.'

'I suppose… What's going to happen to me? Will I go to prison? Will they hang me?'

Before the inspector could answer, there was a sharp knock at the door and Maeve burst into the room.

'Good Lord, Maeve,' Bess said, jumping up and going to her. 'You look as if you're going to faint.' Bess stuck her head out of the door, 'Find Frank, Jack, ask him to help you on reception.' Jack nodded that he would. 'Here,' Bess said, motioning to the chair at the side of the fire. 'Sit down.'

'I would rather stand.' Maeve looked at the inspector, and then at Bess.

'Maeve, what is it?'

'I telephoned Lowarth police station. I left a message for Sergeant McGann to come here, but I needed to speak to you first. I hope that's all right?'

Bess shot Inspector Masters a worried look. He picked up the telephone on Frank's desk and passed it to her. Bess asked Jack to get her Lowarth Police Station. He connected her without preamble.

'Constable Peg? Hello, this is Mrs Donnelly at the Foxden Hotel.'

'Hello, Mrs Donnelly.'

'Hello.' Bess looked to the heavens. There was no time for pleasantries. 'I believe our receptionist, Miss O'Leary, telephoned you a short while ago?'

'Yes. She sounded upset.'

'She was at the time, but she's fine now.' Bess's throat felt restricted, but she forced herself to laugh. 'I don't think we need to trouble the sergeant over a few broken dishes.'

Now it was Constable Peg's turn to laugh. 'She didn't say why she wanted to see him.'

'She found the kitchen window open and several plates smashed on the floor, and thought we'd had a burglary. I'm afraid she worried for nothing.' There was a long silence. 'Anyway, I'm sure you and the sergeant have more important things to do than traipse all the way out here for nothing.' There was another pause. Bess forced herself to laugh again. 'I suppose that's what you get for employing a receptionist who worries too much and a chef who is temperamental.' Bess waited for the police constable to respond.

'I'll take the note off the sergeant's desk.'

'Thank you. I'm sorry to have troubled you.'

'No trouble at all,' the constable said. 'You can't be too careful these days.'

Bess put down the telephone and looked up at the inspector. He nodded in Maeve's direction and Bess went back to her. 'Now, Maeve, tell me what this about?'

Maeve shook her head. 'First I need to be certain that if anything happens to me you'll take care of Nancy?'

'Nothing is going to happen to you, Maeve.' Bess put a comforting hand on Maeve's arm but she withdrew it.

'Will you look after Nancy?' she shouted. 'I need to know Nancy will be safe, loved. Please, Bess. Please!' Maeve begged.

'Yes. Yes, of course I will.' Bess searched Maeve's face. 'What's is it, Maeve? What are you frightened of?'

'Miss Hawksley didn't kill David Sutherland. I did!'

CHAPTER TWENTY-FIVE

'I can't let an innocent girl hang for something I did, something that I'm responsible for,' Maeve said.

'I don't understand,' Bess said. 'How are you responsible for David Sutherland's death?'

Maeve looked at Katherine Hawksley. 'I'm ashamed of myself for not coming forward sooner. I had my niece to consider you see, but now--' Maeve turned to Bess, her eyes moist with tears. 'Now I can tell the police the truth.'

Inspector Masters walked from the back of the desk to the front and took Maeve by the arm. 'Why don't you sit down, Miss O'Leary, and tell me what happened.'

Maeve let the inspector guide her to the chair by the fire. He sat opposite. 'Now,' he said, 'will you tell me why you think you are responsible for David Sutherland's death?'

'On New Year's Eve, I left the hotel just after Mrs Donnelly and Mrs Burrell. I was worried about the girl Sutherland was with, Miss Hawksley. She looked so frightened. She reminded me of my young cousin, Goldie, who... who Sutherland knew in London.'

Maeve inhaled deeply and, as if she was remembering the order of events, exhaled slowly before relating her movements. 'I left by the back door of the hotel. I spotted Sutherland and Katherine along the drive and, later, crossing the lawn to the small wood. Mrs Donnelly and Mrs Burrell were walking towards them, so I went around the east side of the lake. I saw Sutherland grab hold of Katherine and pull her to him. He was mauling her, trying to put his hands up her clothes. I saw her push him, but he just laughed a horrible, guttural--'

'Take your time,' the inspector said.

'Katherine hit him with something. It looked like a handbag, but I'm not sure. Anyway, he stumbled backwards. The terrain is rough on the south side of the lake, by the trees, and he lost his balance. I heard the ice crack.' Maeve put her hand to her mouth, caught her breath and began to choke.

Bess got up and went to the water jug. She poured a glass of water and took it over to Maeve. Trembling, she took a sip. She put the glass on the shelf at the side of the fire and resumed her story. 'I heard a car screech to a halt. Katherine turned at the sound, by which time Sutherland was crawling out of the water. He tried to shout. I think the water was so cold it had affected his vocal chords, because all I heard were hoarse curses. Katherine must have heard him too, because she turned back as he was heaving himself out of the water. He was clinging to the bank, but Katherine was unable to move. She just stared at him, as if she was paralysed with shock. Then she slowly walked towards him and when she was within a foot or so of him, he gave a hoarse groan, lunged at her, and she ran.

'A car stopped on the drive and a man jumped out of the passenger door. Mrs Donnelly and Mrs Burrell ran over to him. At first I thought it was someone with Katherine's father, then I remembered he would be driving away from the hotel, and this car was going to it. Anyway, Katherine ran towards the drive. It was snowing by then and I can only think that, as she neared it, she saw it wasn't her father's car, because she turned and ran back.

'She would have run into Sutherland, but a car screeched to a halt on Shaft Hill and she stopped. I saw its lights through the trees. Katherine must have too, because she turned and made a bolt for it through the wood by the lake.' Maeve looked at Katherine. 'You were right, Katherine, there was someone in the wood watching you. It was me. I wasn't going to let him hurt you the way he had hurt my cousin.'

Inspector Masters had listened carefully, first to Katherine and then to Maeve. When Maeve had finished speaking, he asked her the same question that he had asked Katherine Hawksley. 'Why do you think you're to blame for David Sutherland's death?'

Maeve took another sip of water. 'It happened so quickly, and it's been almost a year, not that what I did on that night has become any easier to live with.' She looked across the room at Katherine and smiled warmly. 'When Miss Hawksley ran away from Sutherland, and he lost his footing and fell--' Bess could see the pain etched on Maeve's face as she fought to make sense of what had happened that night.

Maeve looked away from Katherine and stared into mid-distance, as if she was recalling the horror of what had happened. Then she turned her gaze on the inspector. 'Sutherland had a knife in his

307

hand. When he lunged at Katherine he fell on it. As he slowly slipped down the bank into the lake, he saw me and he reached out to me with his other hand. He begged me to help him.' Maeve shook her head. 'His eyes... When I didn't move, he looked at me as if he knew I wasn't going to help him.

'I shall never forgive myself. I don't know whether it was shock, or because he was responsible for my cousin's death and leaving my niece without a mother. I suspect it was the latter. Whatever the reason, I stood and watched Sutherland slowly disappear beneath the ice.'

Maeve took a deep breath and exhaled loudly. 'Then I struggled through the snow as quickly as I could back to the hotel. I took off the fisherman's sou'wester and waterproof hat, which I had taken from the lost property cupboard, changed from my boots to my shoes and combed my hair.

'While Mrs Donnelly and Mrs Burrell were speaking to Sergeant McGann I went to the kitchen, made tea and coffee, and brought it to the office. By then I had calmed down and as far as everyone was concerned, except for a brief visit to the kitchen, I had been on reception all night.'

The inspector ran his hands through his hair, and leaned forward. 'You and Katherine both believe you killed Sutherland,' he said, after some time.

'Feel responsible for his death,' Bess interrupted. 'There's a difference - if you don't mind me saying?'

'Yes, there is a difference,' Inspector Masters said, smiling at Bess. He turned back to Maeve.

'You didn't kill David Sutherland, Miss O'Leary, nor did Miss Hawksley, so there is no need for either of you to hand yourself over to anyone, especially not to Sergeant McGann at Lowarth. Maeve looked up at the inspector, her forehead creased in a frown. 'The sergeant is on sick leave until he leaves the force officially at the end of the month.

'Myself and Henry Green have taken over the Sutherland case - and it's a great deal more complicated than a drowning. If it's all right with you, Mrs Donnelly, I would like to leave Miss Hawksley in your care until Mrs Green gets back from--?'

'Yes, of course. And Maeve?' Bess turned to the receptionist. 'If you would like to take the rest of the day off, Frank will cover your shift while I'm with Katherine.'

'I'd like to take a break and freshen up. Then, if it's all right with you, Mrs Donnelly, I would prefer to carry on as normal. Being busy stops me from dwelling on what happened that night.'

'Work is a great way of distracting yourself,' the inspector said, standing up. Crossing the room, he took his notebook and pen from the desk and dropped them into his briefcase. 'I don't think there's anything else,' he said, walking to the door. 'Ah, there is just one thing.' He looked at Katherine and then at Maeve. 'Do not discuss any part of the conversation that the four of us have had today with anyone. What has been said in this room must stay in this room. Is that understood?'

Both women nodded. 'Henry and Mrs Green are involved in the enquiry, so if you need to speak to anyone other than Bess, speak to them. And on *no account* must you say anything, even if you are asked, to Sergeant McGann. He has no jurisdiction where this or any other case is concerned.'

Bess gave Maeve the keys to her and Frank's rooms. If she insisted on working the rest of her shift, she needed to have a rest.

Bess then took Katherine to Ena's room. She asked for a sleeping draught. Ena had given her a sedative the day before, which Bess didn't feel qualified to administer. Katherine begged her saying she was exhausted. She said she wanted to sleep but daren't without the draught, because she would have nightmares, so Bess succumbed.

When Katherine had fallen asleep, Bess slipped out of the bedroom, locking the door behind her, and ran along the corridor to her and Frank's rooms. She turned the doorknob, but the door was locked. Thinking Maeve was still resting, she tapped gently and waited.

It was Frank who opened the door. Seeing him, Bess fell into his arms. 'Katherine's asleep. I gave her a sedative, but I don't know how those things work, so I can't stay long.'

'Did you lock her door?'

'Yes. I didn't like doing it, in case there's a fire, but I did it anyway.' Bess followed Frank into the sitting room. 'I saw you talking to Inspector Masters in the dining room when I was taking Katherine upstairs. Did he tell you Katherine and Maeve have both confessed?'

'Yes, he told me everything.' Frank looked more than sad, he looked worried. 'He said you'd agreed to have Nancy live with us.'

'I had to. Maeve was frantic. She was adamant Katherine wasn't going to be hung for a crime that she'd committed. She said before she confessed that she needed to be sure Nancy would be looked after. She begged me, so I said yes. She didn't actually kill Sutherland, neither woman did, but--' Bess struggled to keep her emotions in check, 'Katherine was the reason he fell into the lake, and Maeve, when she could have helped him, didn't. She watched him drown. So, if Maeve does go to jail for her part in Sutherland's death, Nancy will have to live somewhere.'

'She won't go to jail,' Frank said.

'You can't possibly know that, no-one can.'

'Inspector Masters can. He told me as far as he is concerned, both women acted in self-defence. He said the reason they hadn't helped Sutherland when he was drowning was because they were terrified, panicked, and froze. His findings are conclusive.'

'And they are?' Bess asked.

'Accidental death. Sutherland was drunk, fell onto the blade of his own knife - and it *was* his knife - stumbled into the lake and drowned.'

Bess lifted her head and laughed. 'And is the inspector coming back to put Katherine and Maeve's minds at rest?'

'Yes, but he has to wait until McGann has gone. He said he'll include Sutherland's *accidental* death report with the report on Gerald Hawksley, which he'll send to the Yard to coincide with Henry's findings for MI5 - and McGann's departure.'

Bess relaxed back into the soft fabric of the

settee and closed her eyes. 'It's over.'

'Or it's just beginning,' Frank said.

Bess's eyes shot open. 'There can't be anything else, can there?'

'Well, these rooms aren't big enough for three.' Bess held her breath. 'Nancy is eight. She won't want to sleep in here, she'll want her own bedroom. And we won't want her trotting though our bedroom if she gets up in the night to go to the toilet, will we?'

Bess threw her arms around Frank. 'No,' she said, laughing and crying at the same time, 'no we won't.'

'There's an adjoining door in this room somewhere.' Standing up, Frank pulled Bess to her feet and led her across the room to the far wall. 'It leads to what they called a nurse's wet-room in the old days.' He began to tap the wall.

Bess's mouth fell open. 'How do you know?'

'I went to see Lord Foxden's solicitor in Lowarth. He showed me Foxden Hall's original plans.'

'When?'

'After we'd talked about adopting. There are all sorts of hidden passageways and tunnels. Some are centuries old.'

'Never mind passageways and tunnels.' Bess kissed Frank full on the lips. 'Thank you.'

'I'm doing this for me too,' he said, kissing Bess back, hungrily.

'I don't want to go,' Bess whispered, responding to Frank's ardour, 'but I should get back to Katherine. If she wakes…' Frank lifted her hair and kissed her neck. 'I do love you,' Bess said, breathlessly. Easing herself out of Frank's arms, she stood back and searched his face for signs of doubt. 'You are sure adoption is what you want, Frank?'

'I've never been more sure about anything.'

Bess turned the key in the lock of Ena's room and slowly opened the door. Locking it behind her she crept across the room and looked at Katherine. She was still asleep. With a broad grin on her face and butterflies flying around in her stomach, Bess took off her shoes and laid on the adjacent bed. Too excited to sleep, she lay awake thinking about what being a mother would entail. When she did eventually drop off, she was woken by a gentle tapping.

Bess slipped quietly from the bed and opened the door. Ena was in the corridor with a woman who looked so like Katherine she could only have been her mother.

'Bess, this is Mrs Hawksley.'

'Dorothy, please.'

'You don't know how pleased I am to see you,' Bess said, pumping the woman's hand. 'But, would you mind if I had a quick word with my sister before she takes you in to see Katherine? I won't keep her a minute.' Opening the bathroom door opposite Ena's room, Bess ushered Ena in. 'You know Katherine blames herself for David Sutherland's death?' Ena nodded. 'Well she confessed today.'

'What?'

'So did Maeve, to Inspector Masters.' Ena's mouth fell open. 'But don't worry about either of them. They are both fine. I'll tell you all about it later. I just wanted you to know that the inspector is writing Sutherland's death up as an accident. The case is closed. The facts can't be made public yet.' Ena looked anxious. 'Again, don't worry, the reason is nothing to do with Katherine or Maeve, he has to wait until McGann has gone, at the end of the month.'

'Sorry about that, Dorothy,' Bess said, when she and Ena were back in the corridor.

'So,' Ena said, 'are you ready to see your daughter?' Katherine's mother put her hands together as if in prayer, and nodded. 'Right. I'll go in and wake her, get her dressed, and break the news to her that you're here.'

Dorothy picked up a leather holdall. 'For Katherine,' she said with a sad smile. 'When the policemen raided Gerald's house they found this bag. It contains the letters I wrote to Katherine after he took her away, including the note I left in the house when his people evicted me telling her how much I loved her.' She hugged the bag, holding it tightly as if she would never let it go again. 'All the letters I sent over the years… He didn't give my daughter one of them.'

CHAPTER TWENTY-SIX

Among the letters and cards wishing, Mr and Mrs Donnelly and family a Merry Christmas was a letter from Maeve.

"My dear friends, Bess and Frank.

I hope this letter finds you both well. Since my mother's passing, I have become a Friend of the Sisters of Mercy Convent. It's a grand old place on the outskirts of a small town called Killern in County Galway. I began working there as a volunteer, helping out in the office a couple of days a week. At first it was just keeping the books straight and doing the occasional stock-take. I'm now working pretty much full time. I teach the little ones in the orphanage two days a week, which I found heart-breaking at first. There are so many children in need of a family. I thank the Lord every day that my darling niece is loved and looked after by you.

This morning I was in the kitchen cooking, and later I was on lunch duty. We have forty guests for lunch and tea most days. Nearly all are men who haven't been able to settle down to civilian life after being demobbed. They come from far and wide. Some have taken to the drink, others feel they have been let down by the government and are angry. Some feel they have no purpose now they are not fighting in a war - and some are simply lost.

'I find the work fulfilling. I hope I am giving something back for the good life that I have had. And, yes, I am still paying penance; still trying to make amends for the mortal sin of ignoring David Sutherland's cries for help and watching him drown. I know as far as the law is concerned it was an accident, but in my heart I know it was the hate I felt for the man that stopped me from trying to save him. Working with the nuns is helping me to forgive him for what he did to Goldie. And you never know, one day I may even be able to forgive myself.

I have sent a letter and a Christmas gift to Nancy. I think of her often and I am counting the days until I see her, and both of you, next summer.

Wishing you and your family a happy and peaceful Christmas. God bless you.

Your grateful friend, Maeve."

Bess felt a lump in her throat and she put the letter back in its envelope. Laying it on Frank's desk for him to read later, she left the office and went out to see how her husband and daughter were getting on with dressing the Christmas tree.

The spruce that graced the marble hall was not as tall as the giant firs of Lord and Lady Foxden's time, before the war, but it was every bit as beautiful.

Trying to find decorations similar to those that had adorned the Foxden family's Christmas tree, Bess had scoured the shops in Rugby without success. She had almost given up when she spotted a bay window down a side street called Barrow Lane, off Market Street. Approaching the shop, Bess peered through its dusty window and almost cheered. Lined up in front of her, as if they were on parade, were rows of brightly painted Grenadier

Guards in red uniforms with black bearskins on their heads and tiny black boots on their wooden feet. They stood in front of two shallow oblong boxes. One was called 'The Changing of The Guard,' the other simply 'Victorian Characters.'

She had never noticed the shop before. A sign hung on rusty hinges above the door. 'The Old Curiosity Shop.' Bess laughed, went in, and was stopped in her tracks. The interior of the shop was packed to the rafters with every curio imaginable. Tarnished silver candle sticks, bone-handled sets of silver cutlery and dozens of cruet sets. One wall had been given over to fire guards, brass coal scuttles and copper oil lamps. Further along, tall plant stands, squat china flower pots and crockery of all colours, shapes and sizes was stacked precariously.

Looking behind her, Bess wrinkled her nose. Stuffed animals and birds eyed her. Among them a tiger baring long dagger-like yellow teeth and a brown bear with huge leathery paws and black claws. Bess turned quickly back to the window and asked for the box of soldiers and the Victorian Characters.

The elderly shop assistant leaned into the window and cautiously lifted the soldiers off the lid of the box, returning them carefully to their original homes in the raffia base, before replacing the lid. He did the same with the Victorian characters. 'These are not new,' he said, 'but they're as good as. They are all perfect, none are chipped.'

'They are exactly what I want,' Bess assured him and turning, caught her breath. 'I would also

317

like the gold angel in the corner of the window.'

The shop assistant put Bess's items in a delivery box and tied string around it, so it was easy for her to carry. Delighted with her purchases, Bess paid considerably less than she had expected for such a beautiful collection and left the shop.

From Market Street she walked to Church Street, where she had left the car, put her treasures safely on the back seat and drove home.

Bess got back to the hotel to find the Christmas tree, stable in a large bucket of soil, tied to the banister of the stairs. Seeing the decorations, Nancy squealed with joy. Frank blew out his cheeks and made a funny face. 'It'll be worth it when it's finished,' Bess assured him, taking the other bits and bobs she'd bought through to the office: stocking fillers, wrapping paper and ribbons.

Decorating the tree brought back wonderful memories of the Christmases Bess had spent with the Land Girls on Foxden Acres during the war. She giggled remembering how Polly and Laura had felled one of Lord Foxden's biggest fir trees. Bringing it back in a trailer on the back of the tractor, they had almost collided with Annabel Hadleigh - a family friend of the Foxdens, and an honorary Land Girl at every opportunity.

Annabel had come up from Kent with food and gifts for the growing number of evacuees staying at Foxden Hall. She helped to decorate the tree, and put prettily wrapped gifts under it, not once asking where the tree had come from.

That was a few days before Annabel and Bess's

brother Tom were secretly married. Bess looked up at the clock. Her brother, sister-in-law, and niece Charlotte would be at her mother's cottage now. She couldn't wait to see them.

Ena and Henry were driving up from London on Christmas Eve and staying until New Year. Margot, Bill, and baby Natalie, who was thriving after her premature birth, had to divide their time between the Dudley family and the Burrells, so were coming from Coventry on Christmas Day morning and going back on Boxing Day. And Claire... Claire, Mitch and Aimee would be in Canada this Christmas.

Deep in thought, Bess heard Jack calling her name. 'Mrs Donnelly? Mrs Donnelly?'

'Sorry, Jack, I--'

'Mrs Mitchell,' he said, shoving the telephone across the desk at Bess, and then letting go of it as if it was on fire, 'from Canada.'

'Claire? I was just thinking about you.'

'Hello, Bess. We're on our way home. Can't stop, we're about to board the aeroplane. I'll telephone again when we land.'

'I'm so pleased. How's Aimee? Is Mitch--?' The telephone started to crackle and Bess only heard the words see and Christmas. 'Claire? Claire?' The phone went dead. Bess handed the receiver back to Jack. 'Claire's coming home,' she said, laughing. And, hugging the receptionist she said, again, 'Claire is coming home.'

Bess ran across the marble hall to Frank and Nancy. 'Guess what?' She said, 'Claire has just telephoned. They're about to board a plane for England.' She crouched down in front of Nancy.

319

'Your friend Aimee will be here for Christmas.'

Nancy's face lit up. 'Then we had better get this fairy on top of the tree,' Frank said. Taking it out of the box, he followed Nancy to where, three-quarters of the way up, on the bend of the sweeping staircase, he had tied the tree to the banister.

Frank gave Nancy the gold fairy and, picking her up, leant over the banister. Bess held her breath. In Frank's strong arms Nancy reached out and placed the fairy on the topmost branch of the spruce.

Bess picked up the empty boxes that the decorations had come in and Frank and Nancy joined her to admire the tree.

'You made a good job of putting the fairy on top, Nancy,' Frank said.

'She's an angel,' Nancy replied, wearing her serious face. 'Her name is Goldie.'

Frank looked at Bess and winked. Bess returned the wink and bending down to Nancy said, 'I think Goldie is a perfect name for an angel.'

THE END

ABOUT THE AUTHOR

Madalyn Morgan has been an actress for more than thirty years working in Repertory theatre, the West End, film and television. She is a radio presenter and journalist, writing articles for newspapers and magazines.

Madalyn was brought up in Lutterworth, at the Fox Inn. The pub was a great place for an aspiring actress and writer to live, as there were so many different characters to study and accents to learn. At twenty-four Madalyn gave up a successful hairdressing salon and wig-hire business for a place at E15 Drama College, and a career as an actress.

In 2000, with fewer parts available for older actresses, Madalyn taught herself to touch type, completed a two-year correspondence course with The Writer's Bureau, and started writing. After living in London for thirty-six years, she has returned to her home town of Lutterworth, swapping two window boxes and a mortgage, for a garden and the freedom to write.

Proud to be an Indie Author, Madalyn has successfully published four novels in The Dudley Sisters Saga. Foxden Acres, Applause, China Blue, and The 9:45 To Bletchley. Set in WW2, the novels tell the wartime stories of Bess, Margot, Claire, and Ena Dudley. Foxden Hotel is the fifth book in the series, but not the last.

FUTURE BOOKS

Madalyn is currently making plot notes for the next novel. It doesn't have a working title yet because Foxden Hotel was going to be the last in the Dudley Sisters Saga. It was going to have a happy ending with every member of the Dudley family together at the Foxden Hotel celebrating Christmas. However, that was not to be. I wrote three endings, but not one of them rang true. They each felt contrived, forced, and unnatural.

Because you have reached the end of Foxden Hotel, you know that Bess is waiting for her sisters to come home for Christmas. Ena is coming up from London, Margot from Coventry - and Claire, after a distressing time with her husband Mitch who is suffering from shellshock, is flying home for Christmas from Canada. No spoilers, but there is much more for Claire and Mitch to go through. And, with the cold war round the corner, there is more to come from Ena and her husband Henry, who both work for MI5.

OUTLINE OF EARLIER BOOKS IN THE
DUDLEY SISTERS SAGA

FOXDEN ACRES:

http://www.amazon.co.uk/dp/B00BCX59LE/

Foxden Acres, the first book in the saga, begins on the eve of 1939 when twenty-year-old Bess Dudley, the daughter of a Foxden groom, bumps into James Foxden the heir to Foxden Estate. Bess, a scholarship girl, lodges at Mrs McAllister's boarding house in London while studying to be a teacher.

With offers of a teaching job in London and Foxden, Bess opts for Foxden, to be near James. However, when she is told that James is betrothed to the socially acceptable Annabel Hadleigh, Bess accepts the teaching post in London.

When war breaks out and London's schoolchildren are evacuated, Bess returns to Foxden to organise a team of Land Girls, and turn the Foxden Estate into arable land. James, having joined the RAF, is training to be a bomber pilot at nearby Bitteswell Aerodrome.

German bombs fall on London and Mrs McAllister's house is blitzed to rubble. South Leicestershire is scarred too, when an RAF plane carrying Polish airmen crash lands in a Foxden field. Traditional social barriers come crashing down when Flying Officer James Foxden, falls in love with Bess, but is it too late? During the time Bess has been back at Foxden she has grown to like and respect Annabel Hadleigh. How can Bess be with James knowing it would break her friend's heart? Besides, Bess has a shameful secret that she has vowed to keep from James at any cost.

APPLAUSE:
http://www.amazon.co.uk/dp/B00J7Y5LCW/
Applause is the second book in the saga. In the early years of World War Two, Margot (Margaret) Dudley works her way up from usherette to leading lady in a West End show. Driven by blind ambition Margot becomes immersed in the heady world of nightclubs, drink, drugs and fascist thugs – all set against a background of the London Blitz.

To achieve her dream, Margot risks losing everything she holds dear.

CHINA BLUE:
http://www.amazon.co.uk/dp/B00XD85NQW/
China Blue, the third book, is Claire Dudley's story. At the beginning of World War II Claire joins the WAAF. She excels in languages and is recruited by the Special Operations Executive to work in Occupied France. Against SOE rules, Claire falls in love. The affair has to be kept secret. Even after her lover falls into the hands of the Gestapo, Claire cannot tell anyone they are more than comrades.

As the war reaches its climax, Claire fears she will never again see the man she loves.

THE 9:45 TO BLETCHLEY:
https://www.amazon.co.uk/dp/B01GEVW3Z8/
The 9:45 To Bletchley is the fourth book in the Dudley Sisters Saga. In the midst of the Second World War, and charged with taking vital surveillance equipment via the 9:45 train, Ena Dudley makes regular trips to Bletchley Park, until on one occasion she is robbed. When those she cares about are accused of being involved, she investigates, not knowing whom she can trust.

While trying to clear her name, Ena falls in love.

Made in the USA
Columbia, SC
10 February 2018